THE PREY

SEQUEL TO THE KEEPER

"Will a lion roar in the forest, when he hath no prey?"

Kay Chandler

This is a work of fiction. Characters, places and incidents are the products of the author's imagination or are used fictitiously.

Scripture taken from the King James Version of the Holy Bible

Cover Design by Chase Chandler

Dedicated

To the precious memory of my sweet brother, Ronald McCall, who unwittingly fell prey to the charms of a pretty little Lioness from Cottondale, Alabama, and spent the remainder of his life, living happily ever after.

CHAPTER 1

What she'd give for a do-over. She should've let it go. Gone on to bed. Perhaps if she had, he'd still be alive.

Yesterday. So long ago. So very, very long ago. Jackie Gorham's husband had promised to come home early to go with her to place a wreath where their missing daughter, Camille, was last seen, thirty-five months, two weeks and three days ago. Some folks whispered their darling Cami ran away, but Jackie knew better. She knew because she knew her daughter.

Just when she thought she could take no more heartbreak, Jacob managed to prove her wrong. From four o'clock yesterday afternoon until well past midnight, Jackie waited for him to walk through the door. Why didn't he answer his phone? With each passing hour, her fears grew as her imagination conjured up all sorts of frightening scenarios. She checked every hospital in Crandle County, but there was no Jacob Elijah Gorham listed.

Sometime around one or one-thirty a.m., the front door

opened, and Jacob staggered into the house. Or was it closer to two? Regardless of the time, it was well past midnight—placing it a day *after* Camille's birthday.

Fear turned to anger. Jackie's muscles stiffened. She had every right to be furious, didn't she? Without waiting for an explanation, she screamed, "You do realize *yesterday* was Cami's birthday, don't you? Where've you been, Jacob?"

What if she hadn't asked? What if she'd gone to bed, instead of waiting up and infuriating him further with her questions? Somehow, the blame always fell back on her. Was it really her fault? The lump in her throat couldn't have ached more if she'd swallowed a bull frog.

His curt response sliced into an already fractured heart.

"None of your business where I've been, woman. Leave me alone. I'm tired." He fell stretched out on the sofa, turned his back toward her and shoved a throw pillow under his head.

"I'm your wife, Jacob. That makes it my business." If only she'd kept her mouth shut, instead of egging him on. Why? Why did she insist on pushing his button?

He rolled over, staring at her through blood-shot eyes. She noted a peculiar sounding sadness in his voice but assumed at the time it was his way of trying to make her the villain to excuse his own bizarre behavior. When his lip trembled and his voice broke, she contributed it to the liquor.

"My wife? Get real. You've never been a wife to me, Jackie. I don't even know why you married me."

She'd reached her boiling point, and the words she'd kept buried for so long, rushed out of her mouth like water gushing from a flowing well. There was no stopping them. "Jacob, you *know* why I married you," she screamed. "The same reason you married me. You raped me, Jacob. Raped me! When I discovered I was pregnant, our parents forced this on us. But I've never been unfaithful to you. Never. Yesterday was our daughter's birthday. You promised to go with me to lay the wreath on her memorial." What came next, she couldn't have possibly prepared for, even if she'd had an inkling of Jacob's absurd suspicions.

He pulled a flask from his coat pocket and took a swig. "You can stop the ruse, Jackie. I've known from the first day I laid eyes on Camille in the hospital nursery." He sat up and with his elbows resting on his knees, he buried his face in his hands. "I wasn't the only one who saw it. My mother brought it up first."

Jackie sucked in a lungful of air at the mention of her mother-in-law. What crazy notions did the meddlesome woman put in his head? Afraid to ask, she let it slide. "I'm going upstairs to bed."

She'd reached the second step on the stairs, when he yelled out, "Red! It was red!"

Jackie rolled her eyes. "Go to sleep, Jacob. You're drunk and have no idea what you're saying." Her first thought was that he'd received a ticket for running a red light, which would account for his anger. After all, he was Amos Gorham's son. He believed himself to be above the law. She was half-way up the stairs when he shouted. His words were slurred, but not so indistinguishable that she didn't understand.

"Camille . . . Camille had red hair."

She didn't know exactly why she stopped on the stairs, but the mention of her sweet daughter's name cemented her in place. Her heart softened. So, he was missing her, too? Of course. That could account for the drinking and the melancholy mood he was in. In the three years since Cami had been missing, Jacob had never brought up her name. Not once. Sometimes it almost appeared as if he didn't care, though Jackie knew the notion was ridiculous. People grieve in their own way. Right? Perhaps there was more pain inside him than she realized. After all, he'd lost his only child, also.

Was he ready to talk about their sweet Cami, or was it wishful thinking on her part? She walked back down and stood at the foot of the stairs. For years, every time she'd want to hate Jacob for what he did to her when she was only seventeen, she'd instinctively think of her darling Camille. How could she harbor regrets when the horrid experience presented her with such a beautiful gift? It would do them both good to talk, instead of bottling the pain.

His voice took on a somber tone. "Her hair changed later, but it was definitely red when she was born. Definitely, red."

All the hurt and anger she'd experienced earlier vanished now that they were reminiscing about their precious daughter. "Yes, it was. And remember those big, beautiful eyes? They were the color of the ocean. Wasn't she the most beautiful baby you'd ever seen,

Jacob?"

"No one in my family has red hair."

She smiled, remembering how she felt the first time she laid eyes on her baby girl. "I couldn't recall anyone in my family, either. It was quite a surprise—but a nice surprise. She was perfect."

"How stupid do you think I am, Jackie?"

His antagonistic words caught her by surprise. She let out a long sigh. "For Heaven's sake, Jacob, what are you talking about, now?"

"If I remember correctly, Bubba Knox's hair was almost carrot-colored when he was in elementary school."

"Bubba Knox?" Her pulse raced at the mention of an old flame's name. "Oh, Jacob. I know you don't really believe what you're inferring."

"Inferring? I'm saying it, Jackie. You think I didn't know all those years why you doted on her the way you did? You never loved me the way you loved that girl."

"Jacob! Why are you doing this? You know she's yours. My hair is dark, yours is light which often accounts for an offspring with red hair. Besides, it would've been impossible for her to be Bubba's, since Bubba and I were never intimate, but I'm sure you know that."

He picked up the flask and discovering it was empty, slung it across the room, and let out an expletive. His words slurred. "I thought after she ran away, things would be better, and you'd pay more attention to me. Can I tell you a secret, Jackie?" He staggered when he walked toward her and attempted to whisper in her ear. The rancid stench stole her breath as he stumbled closer. "I was glad when she left. Happy, happy, happy. But I soon learned she might as well still be here, because you've never let her go."

"Stop it, Jacob. That's the alcohol talking. You can't mean what you're saying?"

"I mean every word of it. The alcohol gives me the nerve to finally say it. I thought when she left, I'd have you to myself. But nothing changed. She's still coming between us. You have her pictures plastered on every wall. You might as well have *his* hanging over our bed. I see his face every time I look at her pictures."

Her stomach wrenched, and the taste of bile rose to her lips. "I can't believe you could be so heartless, even if you are drunk. She was your own flesh and blood, Jacob. Yours."

"Well, every lining has a silver cloud, they say. Or vice-versa. Whatever." He shrugged. "The good news is I won't be tormented by looking at your old boyfriend's kid's pictures much longer."

Her body stiffened. "I'm not taking them down, Jacob."

His bizarre laughter sent chills down her spine. "You won't have to, my dear wife. I'm the one going down. Down, down, down, down."

"Great idea. You need to lay down and sleep this drunken stupor off. You're talking out of your head."

"You think so? You won't, after you read the morning paper.

Embezzlement, I believe they call it." He wagged a finger in her face and yelled, "Don't look at me with that self-righteous glare. I had to do it. And you know why I did it? So, you could have all this." He made a sweeping motion with his arms. "You really think I made enough money to afford a 9,000 square foot house, a condominium at Dauphin Island, a chateau in the mountains and all the other luxuries you and your daughter have become accustomed to?"

Her heart pounded. "Jacob, I don't believe you. Embezzlement?"

"Don't act so naïve, sweetheart. Surely, you suspected as much."

"You know I didn't. How could I? You never discuss your business and don't even pretend you did it for me. This was the life you were accustomed to, Jacob. Not me. I know you must've made enough money to live comfortably without stealing. Why? Why would you do it?"

"Why? Don't you know? I wanted you to love me, Jackie. *Me!* The way you loved him. I thought if I brought home enough money, I could buy that love. But you only loved *her* and it was because she was a part of him."

"Oh, Jacob, that's not true. After we were married, I honestly *wanted* to love you. I tried, but you wouldn't let me. You kept shoving me away. Now, I know the reason why, but you were wrong. I've never been with any man but you, and you know it's the truth."

13

A sad, pitiful man fell on his knees at her feet and bawled like a baby. "Who cares? Doesn't matter anymore. I'm ruined. Ruined!"

She placed her hand on his shoulder. "I'm sorry, Jacob. I truly am. We'll pay the money back. I'll get a job. It's not the end of the world."

He lifted his head and glared through blood-shot eyes. "Don't you get it, dummy? It might as well be the end of the world. It's over. My goose is cooked. Done. I'd be better off dead."

Seeing him like this caused a lump the size of a tennis ball to form in her throat. "What's gonna happen?"

"I'll be going to prison, that's what's gonna happen. But I'm not sure I'll know a difference. It's been a prison for almost twenty-three years, living under the same roof with you, knowing you were thinking of him every time I tried to hold you in my arms."

Why respond to such absurd accusations? She couldn't remember the last time he held her. Jackie turned and went upstairs to bed, leaving Jacob sprawled on the floor.

At six o'clock a.m., she made the bed, opened the Plantation shutters and went downstairs to make a pot of coffee. Upon entering the parlor, she screamed, seeing her husband's lifeless body sprawled on the floor, with an empty bottle of sleeping pills still clutched in his hand.

Moments later, shrill sirens blared as the haunting flashing lights outside their home lit up the darkened sky. Where were the tears? Had she become so numb after twenty-two years and seven months of agony that there were no tears left? She crossed her shivering arms as the Emergency Medical Team placed her husband's corpse onto the stretcher.

The last painful conversation with Jacob flooded her mind, as if every thoughtless, cruel word had been recorded in full. *Did I do this to you, Jacob?*

Jacob's parents, Judge and Mrs. Amos Gorham, drove up as the body was being lifted into the back of the ambulance.

Mrs. Gorham ran toward Jackie, screaming. Shaking a finger in her face, she bellowed, "You're the cause of this, you little slut. I'll never forgive you. Never. Everything my Jacob did, he did for you, yet it was never enough, was it? Is this the thanks he gets for agreeing to marry you at the time you were carrying another man's baby? You murdered my son as sure as if you poured the pills down his throat."

Maybe his mother was right. Maybe it *was* her fault. If she'd stood up to her parents 'and refused to marry Jacob when she discovered she was pregnant, he'd still be alive. She gave in to the pressure because every baby deserves to have a daddy. But it didn't work. Though the same blood ran through Jacob and Camille's veins, he was never a daddy to their beautiful little girl.

Last night the truth came out. After over two decades of marriage, Jacob finally confessed the baseless demonic lies he'd believed from the moment of Cami's birth. Lies fed to him by his manipulative mother. Lies he chose to believe.

CHAPTER 2

At five-thirty a.m., Forty-two year-old Bubba Knox drove up to the establishment that bore his name, and parked. He took a long look at the outdated building. In the early years, before the interstate redirected traffic, Bubba's Diner was a bustling business, with a dozen employees working around the clock.

Now, he could often manage with one waitress, and he no longer stayed open twenty-four hours. He'd considered selling, but anytime he came close to making a deal, he backed down. Sure, he could make more money in another location, but the locals depended on him being there. His customers were like family. He'd watched their kids grow up and hosted their birthday parties. He couldn't deny the business had served him well in the past, but lately, he'd lost his zeal. He was tired of the same monotonous schedule, day after day after day. He opened at five-thirty in the morning and closed at nine at night. It had begun to take a toll on him. He hadn't had a vacation since finishing high school.

He ambled out of the car, picked up the morning paper, and trudged slowly toward the building. If only something would happen to break the monotony. Once inside, he turned on the lights, and made a pot of coffee. Keeping the routine, he sat down at a table to read the morning paper, and in exactly twenty-five minutes, Homer and Lorene Maitre would walk through the door. He never had to ask what they wanted for breakfast, since they ordered the same thing every morning.

Bubba pulled out the Sports Page, skimmed over the scores, then turned to the local news section. His heart stopped. He laid the newspaper on the table, thrust his hand across his chest and struggled to catch a breath. *Jackie? A widow!*

FORMER MOBILE RESIDENT, JACOB E. GORHAM SUCCOMBS

Jacob Elijah Gorham, age 44, of Cooksville, Virginia, passed away January 27th. Arrangements are incomplete at time of printing, but it is the understanding of this newspaper that Mr. Gorham's body will be shipped back to Mobile, the home of his youth, to be laid to rest in Travelers Rest Cemetery. Survivors include his distraught parents, the Honorable Judge Amos Gorham and Mrs. Agatha Hamilton Gorham. Other survivors include his wife, Jacquelyn, and a devoted brother, John Randall (Johnny) Gorham of Cooksville.

Bubba's stomach ached as if he'd swallowed a bag of marbles. He picked up the paper and read the article a second time. His initial thoughts shamed him. He couldn't deny he'd never stopped loving her, but for his mind to conjure up "what ifs" at such a time as this was reprehensible. UnChristian, even.

Hadn't he prayed for years for Jackie to be happy? Prayer was the only way he survived the traumatic heartbreak of losing the only girl he'd ever loved to such a vile—he swallowed hard. *Stop it, Bubba.*

Bubba tossed the newspaper in the trash can when he saw Mr. and Mrs. Maitre, the elderly couple he referred to as Uncle Homer and Aunt Lorene, entering the restaurant. He had no desire to discuss the subject. Not now. It was too soon. And especially not with Aunt Lorene.

Confused feelings see-sawed back and forth between compassion for Jackie's loss, and—and what? With a fake smile plastered on his face, he greeted the couple. "Well, if it's not my two favorite customers. Have a seat, and I'll have your breakfast in two shakes of a dog's tail. I assume you want your usual?"

Homer nodded, but from the expression on Aunt Lorene's face, Bubba didn't have to guess what was on her mind.

"Bubba, shug, I don't reckon you've heard the news."

"What news?" The moment the words left his lips, he recoiled. Now, she'd feel the need to enlighten him by quoting the article word-for-word.

"Oh, m'goodness, get hold of your hat, Bubba. Have I got news for you!"

The hairs on the back of his neck prickled. Why not admit the truth and hope she'd let it go? He shrugged. *Aunt Lorene? Let it go?* Not likely. He loved the old woman dearly, but no one could take a tad of gossip at daybreak and turn it into a full-length novel before sundown the way she could.

"Aunt Lorene, I suppose you're referring to the death notice in this morning's paper. I did see it. Sad. Now, if you'll excuse me, I'll go get your breakfast on the grill."

She reached out, grasped his hand and held tightly. "Law, I didn't know the obituary was in the paper already."

"Not in the obits, since the arrangements are incomplete. Just a short notice of Jacob's death on page four."

"Naturally, I thought of you, sugar, when Maudie Lee called last night to tell me the news. If what Maudie said is true—and I have no reason to think otherwise—it's a crying shame what Jackie's been through. But some might say she made her bed and now will have to lie in it. Can't deny there's a bit of truth in it. Maybe I shouldn't say it but—"

Homer lowered his newspaper. "But we know you will, Renie. Wild horses couldn't stop you from spreading *news*, as you call it." He rolled a menu to look like a megaphone. "This is Station R-E-N-I-E, Coming to you, folks, with the latest dirt, straight from the Maudie Wire."

"Homer Maitre, shame on you. You talk as if I'm some gossipy old lady. I might not can verify all that Maudie Lee told me, but I find it hard to feel sorry for Jackie, after the shameless way she broke Bubba's heart."

Bubba bit his lower lip—his voice, barely above a whisper.

"That's all in the past, Aunt Lorene. We've both moved on."

Homer threw up his hands. "For goodness sake, Renie, he's right. Why can't you let an old dog lie? It's none of our business. Besides, you know what a gossip Maudie Lee Lundy is. How in tarnation would she be privy to details about Jackie's private life? Likely she dreamed up half that garbage she told you."

"Well, maybe Maudie does talk more'n she ought, but talk didn't get Jackie pregnant, and neither did Bubba. It makes me furious when people whisper behind his back, claiming he's the father of her illegitimate child. I wish she would've stayed in Virginia. Coming back is just stirring up a hornet's nest."

Homer looked up from his Crossword Puzzle. "Here's one for you. It has five letters and means People Devourers. My first thought was Maudie, but there are six letters in her name." He put his pencil to the paper. "Hmm. . . Ogres? I believe that's a synonym for Gossips."

Lorene lifted a shoulder in a shrug. "Well, the Bible says, 'Be sure your sins will find you out.' It's a fact nine months later, Jackie's sin was certainly revealed, and poor, innocent Bubba was left to suffer the blame for her and that Gorham boy's shameful fornication."

Bubba looked down at the dishrag in his hand, and the thought of stuffing it in the old woman's mouth crossed his mind, though he'd never do such. He loved Aunt Lorene, but sometimes she didn't know when to shut up. He could tell her the truth—that in high school, Jackie loved him as much as he loved her, but she was

21

raped by Jacob. Then, when she discovered she was pregnant, her parents, insisted Jacob and Jackie marry. But what good would it do to rehash the past? Wouldn't change a thing. No, as much as it hurt, it was best to swallow hard and keep his mouth shut. He put it all behind him years ago. Or had he?

She turned her attention to Homer. "Land sakes, Daddy, you can do that ol' puzzle later. Bubba says there's a notice about the Gorham boy's death in the paper. Read me what it says."

Bubba made a quick exit into the kitchen. Why were his knees weak, his head swimming and his breath coming out in such quick spurts he felt he might hyperventilate? Was Aunt Lorene responsible for this anxiety attack? Or was it the thought of seeing Jackie again?

CHAPTER 3

Lexie Garrison tilted her head back and sucked in fresh air, allowing her lungs to fill with the invigorating smell of freedom. Bitter-sweet tears welled in her eyes at the clanging sound of the prison doors slamming behind her.

The sky seemed bluer than she ever remembered. The grass greener. The pines taller. She reached up and blotted the corner of her eye with her finger. It wasn't as if this was the first time she'd been outdoors—but it was the first time in two years she'd been outside the walls of Tutwiler, a prison for women in Alabama.

Free at last. Or was she? With no forethought, the song that hummed inside her for twenty-four months, now made its way from her diaphragm to her lips. She stopped short after the first few bars and apologized.

River Braxton, the Prison Chaplain who escorted her outside the walls of Tutwiler Prison, smiled. "No, please don't stop. I suppose it's a religious song, since I think I heard the word 'angel' in there somewhere."

She glanced at her feet and mumbled, "It's an old Johnny Cash song. *If I had the Wings of an Angel.*"

His head tilted. "Oh, yeah, I vaguely remember that one. Something about flying over prison walls, I believe. So, I suppose you're ready to try out your wings."

Lexie blinked, then blinked again. Where were the birds that sang only seconds ago? And the clouds . . . where did they come from? The grass appeared withered and a pine cone fell at her feet, as if the trees were throwing things at her. Her pulse raced. Now that the time had come, she was more frightened than the day she arrived. There was so much she wanted to say to River but the words stuck in her throat.

With the back of his hand, he caressed her cheek, then glanced around, and drew back. Lexie was aware of his need to be discreet. He'd never laid a hand on her before now, even though she'd seen the longing in his eyes. For months, she'd ached to feel his arms around her, pulling her close, but he'd never know. She loved him too much to ruin his life.

He shifted on his feet and took a quick glance over his shoulder. His expression verified they were alone "Lexie," he whispered, "you know how I feel. I only wish—"

"Don't go there, River. We've had this conversation before. It leads nowhere. Never will. Forget me."

His brow furrowed. "Forget you? Do you know what you're asking? Can I forget how to breathe? Lexie, the mere thought of you is in every breath I draw."

"You're engaged, River. Remember?"

He didn't answer. He didn't have to. When an old red pickup truck drove down the long road and parked on the far side of the fence, River sighed. "Your sister, I presume."

Lexie felt a dull ache inside her stomach. "Step-sister." The thought of staying with Molly and her deadbeat husband, Chet caused shivers to crawl up her spine. She should be grateful they agreed to sponsor her. As much as she loved her father, she'd rather spend the remainder of her life at Tutwiler Prison than live in the house with the malicious step-mother responsible for her confinement.

Lexie's apprehension lessened when Molly jumped out of the truck and made the long trek toward the prison. Short and on the pudgy side, Molly favored her mother. Upon spying Lexie, she squealed and ran the remainder of the way with open arms.

Not accustomed to being hugged, Lexie instinctively pulled away. "Good to see you, Molly . . . and thanks for doing this."

"Land sakes, shug, what are sisters good for if we can't be there for one another."

Lexie made a thin smile. "But we aren't sisters. Not really. You didn't have to agree, but it was sweet of you to come for me."

"Of course, we're sisters. Your daddy married my mother. That makes us kin, right?"

"But we don't share the same—" She stopped. If it made no difference to Molly, why should it matter to her? The important thing was someone cared enough to come forth as a sponsor, though Molly would've been the last on earth Lexie would've expected to come to her rescue.

Molly turned and motioned for her husband, who lagged several steps behind, "Lexie's gonna love Foley, won't she hon? We've only lived there a couple of years, but it's close to the beach, and oh m'goodness, Mobile is just a skip and a hop away and Mardi Gras there is a blast. You ever been to Mobile?"

As they walked the long path toward the truck, Lexie glanced back to see River still standing in the same spot. What was it about him that caused her heart to flutter? For a fact, his looks would never win him a spot on a magazine cover. Not that he was ugly— but certainly no one would ever describe him as handsome. There was something about his long, lean, bearded face that reminded her of pictures she'd seen of Abraham Lincoln. She recalled the first time he visited her cell, she was drawn to him. She didn't want him to leave, and it had nothing to do with his physical features. It was the slow drawl in his gentle voice and those piercing blue eyes that made her feel secure, as if nothing could touch her if he was near. If it hadn't been for his kindness, Lexie was convinced she couldn't have lasted those two long years in prison.

River caught her looking and threw up his hand, then turned and lumbered back through the heavy double doors. Would she ever see him again? She blinked to keep the moisture from escaping. "I'm sorry, Molly. What were you saying?"

Chet said, "Like you really care? Did you and that preacher boy have a little hanky-panky going on while you were in there?"

"Of course not."

"You sure about that? I saw how he was ogling you, and you haven't taken your eyes off him. Do they allow . . . you know what I'm talking about . . . men slipping in to visit the women folk for a little old-fashioned companionship?"

Molly playfully slapped at her husband's arm. "Be ashamed, Chet. You're embarrassing her. Don't pay him no mind, hon. He's just funnin' with you. I was asking if you've ever been to Mobile?"

"Uh, I'm not sure."

"Oh, I'm sure you'd remember if you had. It's a beautiful city. There's a tunnel that runs right smack under the Mobile River. It can be a mite scary at first. But then there's the big, gorgeous old oak trees lining both sides of Government Boulevard. It's something to behold, alright. Yep, I think you'd remember if you'd ever been there. Don't you agree, Chet?"

Chet leaned to the side and spat out a wad of chewing tobacco. "I reckon."

Lexie said, "My mother lived in Mobile when she and Daddy met, so we may have lived there before Mama died, but I was too young to remember."

"Is that a fact? Your mama was from Mobile? Got any relatives still living there?"

"I doubt it, but I wouldn't know how to locate them, even if I did. Daddy didn't keep in touch."

"Hey, I'll be glad to help. I done the research on my family, and you won't believe the stuff I uncovered. Chet says I'd make a great PI. Ain't it so, hon?"

"She's good alright. Traced her folks back to the 1800's and found she's related to Jack the Ripper."

Lexie bristled. "You're kidding, right?"

Molly's eyes lit up with enthusiasm. "No, it's a fact. My mama was a Pearcy, and my great-great-great grandmother's last name was Pearcy. There's evidence to prove she was Jack the Ripper."

"But I thought Jack—"

"Was a man, right? I know. Who'd a guessed it was a woman, huh? Her first name was Mary. Far as I can tell, she's the most famous relative in our family. Before she turned serial killer, she killed her boyfriend's wife with a butcher knife." Her forehead wrinkled. "Chet, hon, was it a butcher knife or an ax? I forget."

"Knife."

"Thought so. I'll be happy to help you research your kinfolk, Lexie."

"No thanks. I doubt my grandparents are still living, but even if they are, for personal reasons, I'd rather not pursue it."

"I don't mean to sound nosey, but why not? Who knows, maybe they're rich and famous, and what if you're the only living heir? It's worth checking out, and it's a lot of fun. I can't tell you how exciting it was to find out about my family history."

"Thanks, but no thanks. I don't want anything they have. They accused Daddy of murdering my mother."

"Yeah, Mama told me about that, but I didn't know they were

from Mobile. Mama said if your daddy done it, he probably had good reason. You think he killed her?"

Lexie held her tongue, realizing she needed Molly, and was quite certain her step-sister was several ounces short of a pint, and meant no harm. "I know he didn't do it, Molly. Daddy went to trial and was acquitted, but after that, he decided to change our names."

"So you're saying you aren't really Lexie Garrison?"

She giggled. "Yes, I'm Lexie Garrison. That's been my name for as long as I can remember. It was difficult for Daddy to get a gig after the trial, so he changed his name, hoping for a new start."

"Gig? What kind of gig?"

"He was a musician. You didn't know?"

"No. He's never mentioned it. What did he play?"

"Guitar."

"Is that where you got your talent?"

"I suppose."

"I understand why he changed *his* name, but why would he change yours?"

"There were times when he was struggling financially, and he didn't want my grandparents to use it against him to take me away. So, he changed my name to keep them from locating me."

"Do you know what your name was before he changed it?"

"Laurie. Daddy would often forget and call me Laurie when I was younger."

"Pretty name, but so is Lexie. Chet and I are looking forward to having you stay with us, ain't that so, honey?"

"Tickled pink."

Lexie twisted a shank of hair around her finger. Was he being sarcastic? Maybe he was no more thrilled about it than she was. "Thanks. I appreciate it."

Tall, lanky Chet lumbered slowly toward the old red pickup on the other side of the fence. He looked like a wannabe cowboy with his tight jeans, fringe shirt, big belt buckle and fake reptile skin boots. He threw his cigarette down and put it out with his foot. He opened the passenger door and Molly slid in.

Chet stood, holding the door for Lexie. "If you really want to thank me, come 'ere and give your brother-in-law a big ol' hug. That's all the thanks I want."

Molly said, "Chet had to pull strings, but he got you a job working at the same nursing home where he works."

Chet lit up a cigarette. "Yep. We'll be working side by side. Took some doing, but I managed to pull it off. Wadn't easy convincing 'em to give a former jailbird a job. No offense, just tellin' it like it is."

Molly grabbed her husband's hand and gushed. "I reckon I'm about the luckiest girl alive to have such a thoughtful husband. He'd do anything for me, and you being my sister and all, you might say he did it as much for me as he did for you. He came home a couple of weeks ago and surprised me with the good news about the job. Ain't he a keeper, though?"

Chet leaned down and pecked his wife on the forehead. "Aw, honey bun, I'm sure Lexie ain't interested in hearing you go on and on. You ain't stopped talking since we left the house." He turned toward Lexie and winked. "Sometimes my wife don't know how to turn off that motor mouth of hers."

Molly's lip split into a wide smile, as if he'd just paid her a fine compliment. "It worked out great since one of the attendants is taking maternity leave. You'll be working the midnight shift with Chet, so you two can ride together every night. How cool is that?"

Lexie forced a smile. "I don't know what to say."

His wicked smile and roving eyes brought Lexie's anxieties back ten-fold. If only she could turn around and run back into the safety of her cell. She blinked away the tears as she thought of never seeing River again. He was a minister. She was an ex-con. Nothing good could come from such a union. It was over. Lexie loved him too much to destroy him.

If only . . .

Lexie's life was one long book of melancholy chapters that began with "If only." A book full of tears with not one happy ending.

CHAPTER 4

Keely Cunningham, Bubba's niece, sprinted into the diner in her usual cheerful mood, but her smile quickly faded. "Sheesh! Who died?"

His pulse raced. "I don't know what you mean."

"It's like a tomb in here. Cold and dark. Why haven't you opened the blinds?"

Bubba leaned down, when she raised on tip-toes to peck him on the cheek. He recalled the many years the family spent wondering if Keely was alive or dead, after she was kidnapped. She was his heart. Having her back was nothing short of a miracle.

She wrapped her arms around her midsection and shivered. "Geez, it's cold in here, Bubba." She walked over to the thermostat and frowned. "Sixty-five degrees? Is the heater broken?"

"Sorry. Guess I forgot to turn it up when I came in."

She grabbed an apron from off the nail near the kitchen door, the way she'd done so many times, before she married Trey Cunningham. "What's on the menu for lunch?"

Bubba's forehead scrunched into a frown. "Hon, hang that apron back where you found it. You're a customer, now. Have a seat I can handle this."

"Sure, you can. That's why two tables haven't been cleaned and the coffee pot's empty."

"If you recall, priss, I've worked alone, many times."

"Yes, and don't pretend it was easy, because I know better. But I'm back, and there's lots to be done." She slipped the apron bib over her head and tied the sash in the back.

He patted her on the shoulder. "You're looking mighty thin. I suppose that means there's no little grand-nephew on the way?"

Keely rolled her eyes. "Trust me, when that happens, you'll be the first to know." She ignored Bubba's urging to sit down, and proceeded to stack dishes from an empty table.

"You know you don't have to do this."

"I know. But Trey's out of town, and I'd much rather be around folks I know and love, than sitting in a big house, all by myself. Besides, why is it so hard for you to admit you need me?"

She was right, he did need her. The customers loved her, and Bubba couldn't love her more if she were his own daughter.

His heart swelled, watching her traipse over to Uncle Homer and Aunt Lorene's table. The way she could make the elderly couples' eyes light up when she called them Maw-Maw and Paw-Paw was a sight to behold. Bubba rubbed his hand across his mouth, hiding his smile. He wasn't sure if the Maitres really believed Keely was their long-lost granddaughter, Laurie, or if they wanted to believe it so desperately, they continued to pretend—the way a kid continues to pretend in Santa Claus, long after knowing the truth.

Bubba headed back to the kitchen when he felt moisture backing up in his eyes. *If Jackie and I had married, we might have a daughter almost the age of Keely.* The bitter taste of bile filled his throats. *Jackie does have a daughter, almost Keely's age. Just not my daughter. Forget it, pal.* Twenty-three years was a long time. What would a beautiful woman who'd been married to a handsome, wealthy attorney for two decades plus, want with a nobody running a roadside diner?

Wednesdays were typically slow days, and this one was no different. "Keely, please go on home. Business has been slow all afternoon, and you must have a thousand things you'd rather be doing than baby-sitting me."

"No way. It's Wednesday, and I plan to stay and help with the Singles Group. They do still come here after church, don't they?"

"They do, and I'm sure the gang would love seeing you. I don't have as many showing up as we had before you and Trey married. A couple of the regulars have since married and others have finished college and moved on."

"Does Jamal, Haley, Cherie and Brock still come by?"

"Cherie got a job in Atlanta and moved the beginning of the year. Haley and Brock will both graduate in the Spring, and we've added a few new ones to the group."

"What about Jamal? I suppose he graduated, also?"

"Ah, I'm afraid Jamal is enjoying college life too much to want to graduate. He's one-of-a-kind, but they don't come any finer than that boy."

"I'm looking forward to seeing him again." Keely jumped up and grabbed a menu. "Oops. Here comes a customer."

A tall, well-dressed fellow, slightly gray at the temples and extremely handsome, came strolling through the door with his shoulders back and his chest stuck out. Bubba blinked twice but before he could say anything, the man thrust out his hand.

"Bubba Knox! It's been a long time. When I saw the sign, 'Bubba's Diner,' out front, I figured it had to be you, since I knew of only one other Bubba in Mobile, and he was my dentist, growing up." He let out a funny little chuckle that sounded more like a gurgle. "Doc was an humble man, but I couldn't conceive of him giving up a lucrative profession to run a little off-the-beaten-path eating joint."

Bubba turned to Keely. "Sweetheart, suppose you tidy up in the next room? I'll call you if I need you." He reluctantly extended his hand. "How ya' doing, Johnny?"

"Doing great. Thank you for asking, Bubba. Business is booming. I own Gorham Realty with offices all over Florida, but you probably know that. I'm sure you've seen our ads plastered all over the newspapers."

"Can't say that I have."

"Well, I don't imagine you have much time to read the paper.

I'm sure it takes a lot of man hours to make ends meet, trying to eke out a living in a little place like this." His head turned slowly as his eyes seemed to be taking in every inch of the dining room. "I imagine it was a blow when the interstate cut you off from the flow of traffic. What a bummer, huh?"

"I do okay."

"Okay?" He swept his hand through the air. "You call this okay? Look around, Bubba. It's not as if this place is packed."

"Your concern is touching, Johnny. What is it you want?"

"Why so defensive? If I offended you, I'm sorry. I just remember how smart you were in school, and I happen to know you can do better than this. Say, why don't you consider taking the Real Estate Exam? I'm seriously considering opening a Gorham's Realty across the bay. Real Estate is booming around here, and I'd be happy to consider hiring you if you had a license."

"Thanks, but I'm happy doing what I do."

Johnny's face twisted. "Fine. Just thought I'd offer."

Bubba lowered his head and silently counted. He had to get hold of his emotions. Perhaps he was taking everything Johnny said, much too personal. Was Johnny responsible for his brother's actions? "Sorry if I sounded unappreciative. It's true, the diner will never make me a rich man, but my needs are met. Truth is, I look forward to coming here every day. The people who walk through these doors are like family. In fact, they're the only family I have and they're very special to me."

Johnny reached over and gave him a patronizing pat on the

back. "Hey, I understand. Family means a lot. I don't know if you've heard the news, but I just lost my brother."

Bubba felt his face burning. He glanced down at the floor. "Yes, I heard. I'm sorry."

Johnny's lip curled on one end. "Sorry? Really?"

"What's that supposed to mean?"

"Aww, don't get all riled up. I happen to remember you had a giant crush on my beautiful sister-in-law in high school. I could certainly understand if you might not be too upset that she's now single. Have you seen her in the last few years? Man, she's still a looker. As soon as they lay poor Jacob in the ground, I imagine she'll have a line of suitors following her, panting like a pack of dogs, Who knows? I might even be first in line. She's quite a woman."

Bubba's jaw flexed. "Don't judge everyone by your own moral standards, Johnny." He called out to Keely who was sweeping the floor in the adjoining dining room. "Keely, you can come take the man's order, now." And with that, he stomped into the kitchen.

Johnny pulled out a chair and took a seat.

Keely walked over, handed him a menu. "It's too late for lunch and dinner isn't served until after 4:30, but Bubba baked fresh Coconut Cakes and made lemon pies today. They're really good."

"Thanks, I'll bet they are. You a local?"

"I am now."

"Where did you grow up?"

She bit her lip, not wanting to share her story of spending her childhood being drug from pillar to post by the homeless man who kidnapped her. "My parents have lived in Pascagoula all my life." It was the truth, and she hoped her answer would eliminate further questions.

"So what's a pretty young girl like you doing in a place like this?"

"A place like this?"

"You know what I mean. This isn't exactly a five-star restaurant. My name's Johnny. What's yours?"

"Keely. Keely Cunningham."

"Cunningham? You aren't Carlos Cunningham's daughter, by any chance?"

"Carlos, Sr. is my father-in-law."

"No kidding? You married little Carlos?"

"Little Carlos?" She giggled. "Six-four and 195 pounds. How do you know the Cunninghams?"

"I grew up here. Now, I *am* perplexed. Carlos Cunningham's daughter-in-law is a waitress in a diner? There's got to be a story behind this. How did you wind up in a diner?"

"It's a long story. But Bubba is my uncle."

"Is that a fact? Bubba and I were friends in high school."

"Oh, that's awesome. Everyone loves Bubba. I'll bet he was popular in school. What brings you back to Mobile?"

"My older brother died, and Mom and Dad wanted him

brought back to be buried in the family plot. I gather the news of my brother's sudden passing has thrown your boss for a loop."

"I'm sorry to hear about your brother." She couldn't deny something caused Bubba to act strangely. "So, was your brother and Bubba close?"

He laughed. "Why don't you ask Bubba that question?"

Keely didn't like the smirk on his face. "I'll do that. Now, what can I bring you sir?"

"A cup of coffee will be fine." He glanced down at his watch. "Oh, never mind. It's later than I thought. I need to run. I'll come back when I have more time. Nice meeting you Miss Keely Cunningham."

"That's Mrs."

"Yeah. That's what I meant to say."

Keely walked into the kitchen where Bubba was hacking stalks of celery in rapid motion. "Whoa! What do you have against that celery?"

"Don't know what you mean."

"You aren't just chopping, you're killing it. Why don't we sit down and talk about what's bothering you?"

"No time. Got things to do."

"Bubba, I've never seen you like this. What is it about that guy that has you upset?"

He laid the knife down and placed both hands on the counter. His head dropped. "It's all in the past, Keely. Forget it."

"I can if you can."

"Fine."

"Does that mean you can forget it?"

Bubba's chest protruded when he heaved in a lungful of air. "I wish I could truthfully say yes. Truth is, if I haven't forgotten in twenty-some-odd years, I'm not sure I'll be able to, anytime soon."

"Can you tell me about it?"

"Not now, sweetheart. Maybe a little later when I've cooled down."

CHAPTER 5

When the Singles Class from the church rushed through the door, Wednesday night, Jamal spotted her first and yelled, "Keely, baby! Long time, no see. Where's that ol' man of yours? Run him off, didja? I knew he wasn't good enough for you, and you'd be coming back for me."

"Jamal, you never change. Trey's out of town on business. How've you been?"

"Super. And I can see your ol' man is taking good care of you." He gave her a hug. "We've missed you, doll face."

"I've missed you guys, too."

Others gathered around, all talking at once. Haley threw her arms around her and squealed. "You look fantastic. I've missed you so much, since you and Trey moved away to that swanky neighborhood. Will you be working with Bubba again?"

"If he'll have me."

"Of course, he will. Why wouldn't he?"

"He says it's too far for me to drive across town, but he has the idea I'd be doing it for his benefit. He doesn't understand that there's nowhere I'd rather be than here at the diner, when Trey's out of town."

Dani stepped up and thrust out her hand. "I'm surprised to see you donning an apron again. Why in the world would you be waiting tables, now that you're married to Mr. Moneybags?"

Keely forced a smile. The sudden chill in the air wasn't caused from the low thermostat setting. So, Dani was still upset that she didn't wind up with Trey. Keely glanced sideways and saw Bubba gently shaking his head. It was her cue to consider the source.

Bubba said, "Welcome kids. I see a couple of new ones with us tonight. In case the old-timers haven't told you the drill, have a seat, and the only thing on the menu this late at night is coffee and dessert. All I ask is that you clear out by 9:30. This ol' fellow needs his beauty sleep."

After Keely served the dessert, she took a seat next to Jamal. "So, Jamal, who are you dating now?"

"I wish I had an answer for you."

The sudden change in his demeanor caused Keely to wish she hadn't asked, yet now that she had, she attempted to lighten the mood. "I get it. You're too much man for just one woman." The old Jamal would've gleefully affirmed her response. Something wasn't right. She slid her chair closer. "What's going on, Jamal?"

"I don't know what you mean."

"I think you do."

"It's complicated, Keely."

"If you need to talk, I'm a good listener."

"Hey, I'm fine. Don't worry about me. It's all good." He jumped up and grabbed the coffee pot. "Ok, everyone, hold your cup in the air if you need a refill."

A wide smile spread across his face, but Keely had a peculiar feeling he was clowning on the outside while aching on the inside. How could she help, if he refused to confide in her?

****

Thursday morning, Bubba arrived at the diner earlier than usual. He grabbed the newspaper, sat down at a table and quickly turned to the obits. Just as he figured—Jacob Gorham's obituary covered almost half a page. He glanced over the first several paragraphs, outlining the deceased's many achievements and searched down until he came to the survivors. Listed first was Jacob's mother, father, and brother. Then came his wife, Jacquelyn, as if it were an afterthought. Peculiar, there was no mention of a daughter. No doubt an oversight but the newspaper would most assuredly be held accountable by the prestigious Gorham family.

He groaned when the Maitres walked through the door, even earlier than usual. Aunt Lorene's eyes focused on the open newspaper on the table. "Bubba, I see you've already seen today's obituaries."

"Yes'm. Y'all excuse me while I get breakfast started."

"We're in no hurry, son. Tell me, what did you think about that preposterous, flowery write-up? I Suwannee, if that didn't beat all."

"I don't know what you mean, Aunt Lorene."

"I'm talking about how it went on and on, outlining the family's accomplishments. Who cares? The only details needed was name of the deceased, date of death, and his survivors. If you ask me, the basic information was sufficiently covered in yesterday's paper, but I've known Amos and Agatha Gorham since they were kids. I'm sorry about their son's death—but it's a crying shame they'd take this opportunity to brag about their holdings."

Bubba lifted a shoulder in a slight shrug. "People grieve differently and handle things their own way, Aunt Lorene. I suppose that's their way." He hoped he sounded as nonchalant as intended, though Lorene Maitre was no one's fool.

"Well, it was long enough to fit in the category of a short novel. I wouldn't be surprised if ninety-percent of it isn't fiction, anyway."

The front door opened, and Keely came bouncing in, in her usual happy mood. "Morning, everybody." Glancing from one sullen face to another, her smile quickly faded. "What's going on? I've never seen such a sad looking bunch?"

Mrs. Maitre appeared to take a cue from Bubba. "Hon, you wouldn't understand. It happened a long time ago, before you were born."

Changing the subject, Keely said, "You look awfully pretty this morning, Maw-Maw." She bent down and gave the old woman a hug. "And Paw-Paw, you're always dapper looking." She giggled and kissed the top of his bald head.

Bubba grabbed the paper, threw it in the trash, then made a quick exit into the kitchen.

Keely's brow furrowed. "Y'all excuse me. I'll be right back." She pushed open the swinging door, walked into the kitchen and saw Bubba leaning against a counter, head bowed and eyes closed.

She grabbed a ham slice from the refrigerator and threw it on the grill.

He looked up. "I'll do that."

"I've got it. What's going on, Bubba."

"Nothing." He poured flour into a bowl and nodded toward the refrigerator. "Mind handing me the buttermilk?"

"Sure." Why pry? If he wanted her to know, he'd tell her. Right? Maybe. But what if he needed to talk but didn't want to worry her? She knew too well how secrets fester when kept under wraps. Hadn't Bubba always been there for her? Keely was confident if Trey were here, Bubba would confide in him. But Trey wasn't here. It was up to her to encourage him to talk. Maybe it'd be best to wait until after lunch at the three-o'clock lull, when they'd be less busy.

The phone rang, and Keely grabbed it. "Bubba's Diner. . . I'm sorry, I didn't catch your name? Oh. . . Sure. I'll tell him." She hung up. *But not now.*

Keely trekked back into the dining room, with two breakfast platters, sat them down and winked, "Y'all enjoy. I slaved over a hot stove to cook this ham just the way you like it, Paw-Paw."

"Well, sugar, if you cooked it, it's gonna be good. Mama and I were just saying how good it is to see you here, again."

Maw-Maw said, "Hazel was a good waitress, but she didn't stay long. Sad it was. Her daughter went through a nasty divorce, and Hazel wound up taking in those three little grand-youngun's. I declare if Bubba doesn't have the hardest time keeping good help. Folks just don't seem to wanna work anymore."

Her husband frowned. "Renie, I don't think we oughta judge folks. After all, it wasn't Hazel's fault her daughter's marriage failed." He abruptly changed the subject. "Keely, shug, are you here for the day only, or will we be seeing more of your pretty face in the future?"

"We'll have to convince Bubba to let me stay, Paw-Paw. He said this morning he hired a new girl, but that was her on the phone. Appears she's quit before she even started."

Mrs. Maitre's jaw dropped. "Well, if that don't beat the band. Poor Bubba. He'll have to let you stay, now. Why wouldn't he?"

"He thinks I'm doing it as a favor to him because he needs me, and you know Bubba wants no favors."

Mrs. Maitre said, "Well, I know you don't need the money, honey, but it makes our day to see your smiling face in the mornings. I just wish your mama could've lived to see what a beautiful young woman you are. I declare if you don't look more like her every day. Your mama was a real beauty. Miss Murphy High. Did I ever tell you that?"

Keely grinned. "Yes'm. Several times." Sometimes Keely

questioned her decision to allow the Maitres to continue believing she was their deceased daughter's child. In the beginning, it seemed the compassionate thing to do, but was it really? What if it hindered them from locating the real Laurie?

Mrs. Maitre cupped her hand around her mouth and whispered, "Well, dear, you couldn't have come at a better time, for Bubba's sake. If anyone can get his mind off all this mess, it'd be you. You're good for him."

"Mess?"

Maw-Maw glanced toward the kitchen, then bent forward and said, "I understand he's lonely, but I declare, I'll die if he lets her worm her way back into his life."

Keely's brow crinkled. "Her? Maw-Maw, I have no idea who or what you're talking about."

Homer Maitre reached over and laid his palm on top of his wife's arm. "Sugarfoot, I don't think it's our place . . ."

"Fiddlesticks. It's not as if it's a secret."

Keely didn't ask. She didn't have to. It would only be a matter of seconds before Maw-Maw would blurt it out.

Mrs. Maitre leaned forward in her chair. "Hon, the Gorhams are back in town."

"The Gorhams?" Where had she heard that name? "Is that supposed to mean something to me?"

She turned at the sound of Bubba's gruff voice. "No, Pretty Girl. And it means nothing to me, either."

Mrs. Maitre rolled her eyes. "I'm sorry. I didn't see you

standing there, Bubba, but I hope to goodness you're right. However, you watch what I say. That girl nearly ruined your good name back in high school, and I wouldn't be surprised if she doesn't try to worm her way back into your life."

"Ain't gonna happen, Aunt Lorene, so stop worrying. We were kids." He turned and stomped back into the kitchen.

CHAPTER 6

When the last customer finally walked out the door of the diner, Keely grabbed a slice of pie, and sat down at Bubba's table. He gave a dismissive shrug when she broke the news his latest hire wouldn't be coming in.

"Not surprised. I didn't really think she wanted to work." He looked at her plate. "Is that all you're gonna eat?"

"Yep. If I ate lunch, I might not have room for this pie, and I've been eyeing it since you took them out of the oven."

They sat in silence for what seemed like thirty minutes, though it was barely five. "Bubba, I know it's really none of my business, but I can't help wondering what Maw-Maw was talking about. She says everyone in town knows. Do you mind telling me what's going on?"

"Trey hasn't told you?"

She shook her head. "Apparently not. Nothing Maw-Maw said made sense to me."

His lip curled up. "Not surprised. My faithful accountability partner." Bubba reached for the sugar and put four packets in his coffee.

Keely watched quietly, knowing he never used more than two. For sure, something had him addled.

He stirred his coffee, took a sip, then made an awful frown. "Too sweet." He shoved his cup aside.

"Bubba, your hands are trembling. What's going on? Maw-Maw seems to think there's a woman in your life? Is there?"

He smiled. "You look surprised. Didn't think a woman would look at your ol' unc, did you?"

"Don't be silly. Any woman who could land you would be getting a prize. Who is she?"

"Keely, there is no woman in my life. Not anymore." He sucked in a lungful of air and slowly let it back out. "It was a long, long time ago."

"Can you talk about it?"

"Sure, kid, but it's history."

"I love history."

"Her name was Jackie, and she was beautiful. We were just kids—our last year of high school. I've never loved anyone so deeply, and there was never a doubt but that she loved me with equal passion. Then one day, she didn't show up at school. I tried to call her, but her Mother wouldn't let me talk to her. Long story short, the first time I knew where she was, I received a letter postmarked from Virginia."

"From Jackie?"

"Yes, but it didn't sound like the Jackie I knew. Said she'd transferred to a girl's school. It was short and blunt, as if she were writing to the landlord, cancelling the lease."

"You're saying she never mentioned she'd be leaving? But why would she hide it from you?"

"Frankly, I don't think she knew she'd be leaving, until she got home from school and found her Mother had made arrangements to ship her off." He glanced away. "She was pregnant, Keely."

"Oh, no. I'm so sorry, Bubba." She hoped she managed to veil her shock. "So . . . so you have a child? Boy or girl?"

"Whoa! You're jumping ahead. The baby wasn't mine."

Keely swallowed hard. "I'm sorry. I just assumed . . ."

"So did half the town."

"Did you know she was seeing someone else?"

"No, because she wasn't."

"I don't get it."

"She was raped, Keely."

Keely clinched her eyes shut. "Oh, Bubba. I don't know what to say. That must have been so hard on you both."

"You can't imagine,"

"Did she contact you after that?"

"No. Word got out she was pregnant, and because everyone in town knew we'd been an item since Middle School, they wrongly assumed I was the father. Not only that, they accused Jackie of being promiscuous, which was another lie."

"I'm sorry I asked. It was none of my business. You don't have to go on. I can tell this is hard for you."

"I'd rather you hear it from me, Pretty Girl. Jackie is back in town, so you'll likely hear all sorts of rumors. I want you to know the truth."

"Do you know if she ever married?"

"Yes. At first, I believed the father was Johnny Gorham."

Her eyes widened. "Gorham? . . . Gorham! The guy who was in here earlier."

"That's the one."

"*He's* the father?"

"No, but when I first heard she was pregnant, I thought he was. People were saying she married 'that Gorham boy,' so I assumed it was Johnny. He'd always had eyes for her, and Johnny was accustomed to getting what he wanted. Turns out it was his older brother, Jacob. I didn't learn the truth until two years later when Jackie returned for her grandfather's funeral, with Jacob and a baby girl."

"You mean she married the rapist? How odd."

"Not really. I'm sure Jackie's parents insisted Jacob marry her and naturally, old man Gorham couldn't afford a scandal, since he was up for reelection. I figure Jackie was not given a choice. If only she'd told me, I would've married her in a minute . . . but I *didn't* know, and even if I had, her parents would've objected. I always knew I wasn't what they wanted for their daughter."

"How horrible to be forced into a marriage with a man you

don't love—especially a monster who raped you. I can't begin to imagine what a miserable life she must have."

"She looked happy enough when I saw her at her grandfather's funeral twenty-years ago. I assume she forgave him."

"Are they still together?"

"Jacob Gorham died Tuesday, and they've shipped the body back here. His funeral is Saturday."

"Oh, my. So that's what's stirring up the talk. Have you seen her?"

"No. Don't want to."

"I suppose their daughter would be about my age. Right?"

"That's right. Strange though, there was a brief notice in the paper Wednesday morning, and there were no children listed among the survivors."

"You think the child may have died?"

"I suppose. Still, I think it odd that there was no mention of her at all. I also found it weird that Jacob's mother, father and brother were listed as survivors first, and his wife was listed last."

"Sounds like a peculiar obit."

"Peculiar, for sure. If Jacob Gorham was as wonderful as the paper made him sound, he would've been a candidate for Sainthood." He glanced at his watch. "Goodness, look what time it is. I need to finish up in the kitchen. Thanks for listening. Perhaps I needed to talk more than I realized."

After dinner, Keely left, and Bubba was counting the receipts when a woman cracked open the door. "Sir, I see you close at nine o'clock. I realize it's almost nine now, but if there's still coffee left in the pot, I'd be mighty grateful for a cup, and then I'll be out the door. Promise!"

Bubba glanced over at the empty pot. "Come on in. I'm in no hurry. Have a seat."

It was impossible not to notice how attractive she was. Five feet six or seven, slender, big brown eyes and thick black hair that she had a habit of slinging over her shoulder. He guessed her to be in her mid to late thirties, but there was no ring on her left hand. Strange, he should notice.

He finished counting the day's receipts, then carried her coffee to the table.

She reached up and touched his sleeve. "Have a minute to relax? I'd love the company. I've been on the road for hours and would welcome a voice besides my own." Her eyes lit up when she smiled. "I realized I was about to go to sleep and saw your lights on. Thank you for letting me in." She sipped her coffee, then blotted her ruby red lips with a napkin. "The coffee is wonderful. I'd love it if you'd grab a cup and join me."

"Sounds good. I could use a cup." He walked over and poured himself a cup of coffee, then sat down across the table. "Where are you from?"

"Everywhere and anywhere, you might say. I owned a small trucking business, but it's a lonely life for a woman."

"I wouldn't think it'd be very lonely for a woman as lovely as

54

you." His face heated up. What made him say such a thing? Sure, she was attractive, but he was out of line. "I'm sorry, I shouldn't have said that."

She grinned. "Why? You didn't mean it?"

"No, I meant it, but I suppose you have truckers hitting on you all the time, and it must've sounded like that was my intention. It wasn't."

"You seem nervous. Relax, I wasn't offended. I thought it was sweet. Trust me, I've learned to tell the difference between a compliment and a hit."

Bubba wiped beads of sweat from his upper lip. "I'm glad."

"This is a little embarrassing, but could you point me to your Rest Room?"

"Back corner, you'll see the sign. Can't miss it."

He watched as she walked away and wondered how she managed to get into such skin-tight slacks. Her long slender legs and trim body reminded him of the runway models he'd seen on television, only prettier than any he could remember.

She returned minutes later, and Bubba noticed she'd tied the tail of her long shirt into a knot at her waist, drawing attention to her fine figure. She picked up the coffee pot and refilled their cups, before sitting down. "Bubba, I have a favor to ask, and I'll understand if it's against your rules, but would you mind if I left my truck parked on your lot, just for tonight?"

"Mind? Not at all. So, you're leaving out tomorrow?"

"I wish. Truth is, I've hit on some hard times, so I've sold my truck to a guy who plans to pick it up here in Mobile, tomorrow. I'm not ashamed to tell you it's a little frightening."

"Frightening? How so?"

"It's my only truck, and with no way to make a living, I've got to come up with a plan."

"I'm sure a rig like the one you parked out front will pad a nice nest egg, until you find what you're looking for."

"That would be awesome if it worked that way, but I didn't get half what I paid for it, and the money I'll get goes to pay off debts." She smiled. "Listen to me, telling my troubles to a stranger. I'm normally not so vocal, but you have such a nice face . . .like someone I can trust."

"Thank you. If you don't mind my asking, how did you get into the trucking business?"

"I'm asked that a lot, and it was quite by accident. I've always been the adventurous sort, and it seemed like a good way to see states I might never see, otherwise. I had a friend who owned a trucking business and I started out driving for him and loved it. However, when things became complicated in the relationship, I took my savings, bought that fine truck parked out front, and opened my own business, called Best Trucking Company. As it turns out, it wasn't the best after all. My goal was to operate the office, hire a driver and eventually buy additional trucks. It didn't work that way. Now, I'm trading my truck for a used car and hope I can find a job. Things don't always go as we plan, but I'm not a quitter. I'll get by, somehow."

"If I'm not being too inquisitive, what do you plan to do?"

"Pray a lot?" She giggled. "Just joking. I have no idea, but I'll dig ditches if I must. I need a job and I'll need one soon. I don't mind telling you, I'm desperate. Bookkeeping was my best subject in high school, and my goal was to become an accountant, but life got in the way and college was out of the question. Now, I have no idea what I'll do."

Bubba pursed his lips. "Frankly, I think the prayer idea is a great one."

"Oh, please forgive me. I didn't mean to make light of it. Did I offend you?"

"Not offended. Just stating a fact. I don't suppose you'd be interested in waiting tables in a diner while you search for something better?"

Her face lit up. "Here? Is that an offer?"

"I need a waitress. You need a job." He glanced away, when he realized his eyes were roaming. How long had it been since he'd looked at a woman and felt his heart thumping erratically against his chest wall. With his gaze positioned on the floor, he said, "To have a waitress with bookkeeping skills would be a plus. What d'ya say?"

Their gaze locked. "Oh, Bubba Knox, I could hug your neck." She snickered. "I won't, though. Not unless you want me to, that is." She grabbed both his hands with hers, then rubbed her fingers over his third finger, left hand. "What? A hunk like you, and there's no ring?"

Bubba licked his dry lips, then let go of his grasp. "Nope!" He stuttered, then cleared his throat and said, "What hours would work best for you?"

"Since you're asking . . . what about ten until two, then I'll come back and work five until closing?"

"Fantastic! You're hired."

"Really? Are you sure that's acceptable?"

"Acceptable? It's perfect. You'll be working lunch and dinner, and I'll hire someone to cover breakfast in the mornings."

"Bubba, perhaps I should've mentioned that I have fibromyalgia, but I keep it managed with meds. However, occasionally, I do have a flare-up . . . just thought you should know."

"I don't see it as a problem, if you don't."

That night he lay in bed, with the image of a beautiful woman floating around in his head. What was it about her he found so captivating? She was a looker, for sure, but he'd met a lot of beautiful women, yet not one caused him to take a second look. Not since Jackie. Greta Pugh was different, for sure.

Was God intervening to keep his mind off the one who'd occupied his every thought for twenty plus years? Surely, it was no coincidence this woman showed up when she did. He turned over in bed and stuffed a pillow under his head. He lay there for hours, eyes closed, but sleep wouldn't come.

A shimmery pink blouse and khaki slacks. So feminine. So clingy. So alluring. He swallowed hard. So unlike him to notice a woman's wardrobe.

CHAPTER 7

Saturday morning Keely showed up at the diner at nine o'clock, disappointed that Maw-Maw and Paw-Paw Maitre had already left. She greeted a young couple sitting near the window, cleared plates from two tables, then walked into the kitchen to find Bubba peeling potatoes.

"Need some help?"

Without looking up, he mumbled. "No, I got this."

"Well aren't you the grumpy one this morning. What's wrong?"

"I don't know what you mean."

"I think you do. Something has you tied in knots. But it's understandable why you'd be stressed. You're trying to do too much. You need help, Bubba."

"That's why I've hired a waitress."

She made an obvious point to search the place with her eyes. "Did you now? An invisible woman?"

"Nope, she's very real and will start Monday morning." An

image of the beautiful woman who waltzed into his life Friday evening, invaded his thoughts. He handed Keely his potato peeler. "Sorry for being short with you. I was up all night. Mind finishing these potatoes?"

"Not a problem." She picked up a potato. "Were you sick?"

"No, just had a lot on my mind." Bubba washed the lettuce, diced the tomatoes and floured the cubed steak. He glanced in Keely's bowl. "That's more than enough potatoes. Go sit down, Keeper, and let's have a cup of coffee, while things have slowed down."

Keely loved it when he referred to her as a Keeper. Growing up, Wylie Gafford, the homeless kidnapper she grew up believing to be her father, kept her beaten down with a fishing analogy, insisting she was a trash-fish and not a keeper. How many times did she hear him say, "When that ol' boy gets ready to pick him a wife, he won't pick the likes of you. No sirree. He'll choose him a keeper to take home to mama. You ain't no keeper, girlie."

But that was all in the past. A past she tried to forget. "What time's the funeral?"

"Doesn't matter. I'm not going."

"Bubba, you have to go."

"No way."

"Why not?"

"You wouldn't understand."

"Try me."

"Keely, you can't imagine the stares I'd get. Everyone in town who'll be attending the funeral is aware of the history between Jackie and me. I'll guarantee you my every move would be scrutinized by those looking for something."

"Bubba, do you not realize by not showing up, it gives them more to speculate? Why wouldn't an old beau of the widow be present to offer his condolences—unless of course, it's too painful for him to see her again?"

He placed both hands on the counter, leaned forward, and with his head lowered, sucked in a lungful of air. "I hadn't thought of it that way. You really think that's how it would look?"

"Absolutely! Now, let me ask you again. What time's the funeral?"

"Two."

"What time will the new girl be in?"

"Her hours will be ten until two, then five until closing."

"Gotcha! I need to run an errand, but I'll be back in time to help with lunch, since she's new. What's her name?"

"Greta. Greta Pugh."

"Is she related to the Pugh's from Citronelle?"

"Not likely. I take it she's alone. Doesn't seem to have family living."

"Where did you say she worked before you hired her?"

"I didn't say." When it appeared Keely was waiting for an answer, he rolled his eyes and groaned. "She drove a truck."

Keely giggled. "Who knew being a truck driver was good training for waiting tables?"

"She needed a job, okay? And I hired her. It works for me."

"Sorry. I didn't mean to offend you."

"It's not you, Keely. I have a lot on my mind." He pulled off his apron and hung it by the door. "I'll be back as soon as the funeral's over . . . if not sooner."

****

Bubba slung another necktie across the bed, before settling on the first one he tried on. Why was he trying so hard? Who was he wanting to impress? Certainly not Jackie. She wouldn't even know he was there. Who else mattered? It wasn't his answer that sucked the air out of him, but the fact that he'd even ask, 'Who else,' as if she still mattered. Well, of course, she mattered. Just not in the way she once did.

Taking a last look in the mirror, he groaned, then jerked off the tie and unbuttoned his shirt collar. Was it appropriate to attend a funeral tie-less? Perhaps he should call Keely and ask her. She knew about these things.

He picked up the phone, hung up, grabbed the tie and walked out the door.

The funeral was held at a large church on Government Street and the parking lot in back was packed. Not that Bubba was surprised. After all, it was a Gorham funeral—the social event of the season. There were as many tags from out-of-town as there were from Mobile County, which caused a sigh of relief. Not everyone would be scrutinizing his reactions. He took a seat on the

63

back pew, only minutes before time for the service to begin.

The man next to him introduced himself and extended his hand. "Joe Daniels."

Bubba reached out, then grimaced, realizing his palms were sweaty. He whispered, "Bubba Knox." The minister approached the pulpit as the organist began to play. An eerie hush came over the crowd as they stood in honor of the grieving family. Bubba's knees locked, as a tearful Jackie walked down the aisle, escorted by her deceased husband's younger brother, Johnny. Seeing her tears broke his heart.

She was even more beautiful than Bubba remembered. Her chestnut hair was neatly pulled up in a twist. Was it still long, the way she wore it in high school? He fantasized reaching up, pulling out the tortoise shell comb that held it in place, and watching the locks fall in curls around her shoulders. He swiped his sweaty palms across his pants legs. The stylish black jersey dress embraced her femininity, as it clung to her upper torso and flowed freely at the bottom. She didn't appear an ounce heavier or an ounce lighter than the last time he saw her. His throat tightened as he recalled the day of the school picnic at the lake when he reached around her tiny waist with both hands. He was certain if given the chance, he still could.

When the service ended, he attempted to disappear into the crowd, but was stopped by someone pulling on the tail of his jacket. "Wait for us, Bubba. Homer and I would like to ride to the cemetery with you."

"Aunt Lorene!" He groaned, disgusted with himself for not getting away faster. "To tell the truth, I hadn't planned to go to the cemetery. I have a new waitress, and I'd rather not leave her by herself on her first day."

"But she won't be alone, sugar. Homer and I went to the diner before coming here to see if we could catch a ride with you, since Homer don't like to drive in crowds, don't you know. Keely was there and said she'll be staying to help the new girl, so there's no reason for you to rush off. Where's your car parked, sugar? We'll ride with you over there. I hope I don't bog down in the mud at the cemetery. These are my best shoes."

To argue with Aunt Lorene would be an exercise in futility. He'd never won in his forty-two years. He pointed ahead. "I'm parked underneath the big oak. But now, Aunt Lorene, I don't plan to stay long, so don't wander off once we get there."

"I Suwannee, you worry too much, Bubba. I'm not a child. Why would I wander off?"

Bubba and Uncle Homer exchanged knowing glances. "Just sayin'."

Standing around the gravesite, waiting for the service to begin, Bubba said, "This wind is bitter. You sure you want to wait here in the cold, Aunt Lorene? I don't think it's a good idea for you and Uncle Homer to be standing outside in this kind of weather."

"Would you stop worrying about us? I checked the weather report before coming, and it's sixty-one degrees. Chilly, I'll grant you, but when I was young I walked five miles to school every morning in weather a lot colder than this."

He wanted to remind her she was no longer young but trying to convince Aunt Lorene to listen to reason would be a waste of both time and energy.

He groaned when she grabbed his arm. "Come on. Let's see if we can't get a little closer to the front. I can't hear the preacher from way back here."

Bubba rammed his hands in his pockets and kept his feet planted firmly in place. "I'm fine where I am."

"Well, I'm going to where I can hear. Come on Homer. Now, you stay put, Bubba so when it's over we'll know where to find you."

"Go straight to the car after the service, Aunt Lorene, because that's where I'll be."

"Shug, you know we'd never find your car in this crowd. There must be two-hundred black automobiles out there. We'll come back to this same spot as soon as the last prayer is uttered."

"Yes ma'am." He groaned. Why did he let that woman lead him around as if a noose was fastened around his neck?

CHAPTER 8

The graveside service ended, and Bubba waited. And waited. Where were they? No less than two dozen people stopped to shake his hand and comment on what a lovely service it was. It was a funeral, for crying out loud, not a theatrical production. But where was Aunt Lorene and Uncle Homer?

"Bubba Knox. I feel I owe you an apology."

Bubba didn't have to turn around to recognize the voice of Johnny Gorham.

Johnny threw his arm around Bubba's shoulder. "I meant no harm when I encouraged you to take the Realtor's test. I just thought . . ."

"I know what you thought, Johnny." He glanced away to keep from looking at Jackie Gorham, who was linked to her brother-in-law's arm.

She spoke first. "Thanks for coming, Bubba."

He muttered something that even he wasn't sure what he said. Then added, "I'm sorry for your loss."

"Thank you."

Johnny put his arm around her waist, pulling her close. "Didn't I tell you she was still a looker? Have you ever seen anything as beautiful?"

Bubba didn't fail to notice how quickly Jackie jerked from his grasp. He had a sudden urge to sock him in the nose. Ignoring Johnny's question, he gave a nod in Jackie's direction. "I'll be praying for you, Jackie." He felt a deep blush rising from underneath his collar and landing on his cheeks, when their gaze locked.

Johnny's wry grin caused Bubba's face to burn. He knew Johnny misunderstood his comment, but why should he worry what the nincompoop thought? Jackie understood. She knew he didn't mean he was praying for *her*, the way he once prayed . . . for her. God, in His wisdom had chosen to allow Jacob to have her. Bubba didn't pretend to understand the ways of God, but it wasn't for him to question. He waved when he saw the Maitres. "Over here, Uncle Homer."

Aunt Lorene's jaws had to be tired by the time he returned them to the church to get their car. Bubba was glad she had too much to say to slow down long enough to ask questions.

He had plenty of questions of his own to ponder. Apparently, Jackie not only lost her husband but her only child as well. With no family left, would she be returning to her home in Virginia? He gnawed on his left thumbnail, pondering the absurd thoughts flitting through his head. Of course, she would. Why wouldn't she?

She'd lived there over half her life. Her friends would be there. With her parents gone, what reason would she have for moving back to Mobile?

He couldn't think of a single one.

****

Jackie Gorham went straight from the funeral to the airport, and from there, she took a taxi to the offices of Collier, Gorham and Collier. The sign would soon be changed to Collier and Collier.

Her late husband's former business partner greeted her with a warm hug, then pulled a handkerchief from his vest pocket and wiped away her tears.

She said, "Silas, if I'd had any idea that Jacob was . . ." She found it difficult to even say the word. "Embezzling." She cringed. "I want to pay it back. Every penny that he took, even if it takes a lifetime, and I suppose it will."

"Jackie, I've told you that no one holds you responsible for what Jacob did. Even if you'd known, there's no way you could've prevented it. I don't mean to speak ill of the dead, but the truth is, Jacob Gorham answered to no one. What's done is done. I just hate that you've lost your home and all your earthly belongings because of something that you had no part in. If it'd been up to me, you wouldn't have lost your home. I feel bad about that."

"Please don't. I didn't want the house, the money or anything it bought, once I found out he stole to get it, Si. I would've given it up, even if the courts hadn't seized it. It was never my house, anyway. It was Jacob's. He bought it before I ever saw it and had a decorator to furnish it. I merely occupied it."

He reached for his wallet. "Jackie, I'd like to give you a little money to help until you land on your feet."

"Thanks, but I don't want your money."

"I wish you didn't feel that way. Surely, you know I don't blame you for any of this. Will you be staying in Virginia?"

"No. I'm going back home."

"Home? To Alabama?"

"Yes. Mom and Dad left me the house I grew up in, so it's not as if I don't have a place to stay. It's been vacant for several years, but with a coat of paint and a little TLC, it'll be fine. I only came back to apologize to you and to put flowers on Cami's memorial. I feel close to her when I'm standing at the last place she was seen. I'll miss that. If she should come back looking for us, you'll tell her where I am, won't you?"

"Of course."

It was evident from his forlorn expression he didn't expect Cami to come back. Like everyone else, Silas believed she was dead.

He gave her a hug. "I'm glad you have somewhere to go, Jackie. It'll be good for you to get away from all the allegations. Please, keep in touch. Delia and I will miss you and will want to know how you're doing."

****

Keely drove past the local hardware on her way to the diner. The weather was unusually warm for February and the Garden

Section had pallets of spring flowers sitting out front. As usual, eager gardeners were filling carts, wanting to believe the cold was over and spring was just around the corner. If the past was an indicator of what was to come, another cold blast would soon kill the new plants and the scene would be repeated around mid-March.

Keely pulled up at the diner at ten after eleven. Bubba appeared to be both waiter and cook as he plopped two lunch platters on a table along with a breathless apology for taking so long in the kitchen.

Keely said, "Where's Greta?"

He shrugged. "Don't know. She's running a little late."

"A little? She should've been here over an hour ago." Keely had kept her thoughts to herself concerning the girl Bubba recently hired, but after numerous times of showing up late, it was obvious the woman was taking advantage of his good nature. He hadn't been himself lately and appeared oblivious to what was going on. She seethed at the notion of someone taking advantage of such a sweet guy. "Bubba, don't you see what she's doing? Don't let her do you this way."

"Keely, I don't have time to discuss Greta. Can't you see I'm swamped? She'll show up soon." He grabbed the coffee pot and stomped across the room.

Her throat ached. He had never talked to her in such a curt manner. But he was right. The dining room was crowded and from the looks on the faces, even the most patient regulars were becoming irritated. With wounded feelings, Keely weighed her choices. She could run into the stock room and bawl—or she could grab a couple of menus, take the orders and allow Bubba to do his job in the kitchen. She turned on her heels, trudged across the room with the menus and decided to cry later. At the moment, Bubba needed her.

By eleven-thirty, everything was running smoothly.

Ten minutes later, Greta rushed through the door. "Hi, Keely. Good to see you, again. I had a monstrous migraine last night, but I'm feeling much better now. Looks as if everything is under control. Thanks, I owe you one." She tied an apron around her waist. "You been here long?"

"Yes, Greta, I have. It's almost noon, and you didn't bother to call and let Bubba know you'd be late. If you can't be on time, you should turn in your resignation. Bubba needs someone he can depend on. Someone reliable. Now that you're here, would it be too much to ask you to wait on Table 12 and refill coffee for Table 26?"

"Not a problem." Greta put her hand on Keely's shoulder and winked. Then, in a patronizing-sounding voice, she said, "Sounds like someone got up on the wrong side of the bed this morning." Without waiting for a response, she waltzed off, waited on the tables, and after turning in the order, strolled back into the dining room where Keely was filling ketchup bottles. She swept her long black hair back of her shoulders and whispered, "Keely, are you angry with me?"

Keely bit her trembling lip. "Sheesh! You really have to ask?"

Greta puckered her lips. "No, and you have every right to be upset. You were right when you said I should've called, but unless you have migraines, you can't possibly understand what I was going through. I'll do better next time, I promise."

Keely bit the inside of her cheek. "I'm sorry about the headaches, and I shouldn't have snapped at you. I won't deny I'm overly protective when it comes to Bubba. He's so trusting, I can't stand the thought of someone taking advantage of him." She picked up dirty dishes from a nearby table.

"Oh, dear, is that what you think? That I would purposely take advantage of Bubba? Keely, I'd never do anything to hurt that sweet guy. I didn't know such men existed in today's world. In case you haven't noticed, I'm crazy about him."

Bubba came into the dining room from the kitchen. Glancing from Keely to Greta, his forehead creased. "What's going on?"

Greta laid her hand on his shoulder. "Don't look so worried, big guy. Keely and I were having a friendly discussion about someone very dear to both of us." She giggled. "Bonding, you might say."

His face lit up like a full moon. "Awesome. I'd hoped you two would get along."

Greta reached up and with her thumb and forefinger, straightened his collar, then brushed the back of her hand across his jaw. "Are you kidding? Why wouldn't we get along? Keely's great. I had a terrific migraine when I awoke this morning, and it was so sweet the way she stepped in and took over when we needed her."

Bubba winked at Keely and smiled, as if to say, "Didn't I tell you she was an angel straight from Heaven?"

Greta twisted a lock of hair around her finger. "Just one more thing. Keely, I hope what I'm about to say next doesn't come out wrong. . . but if Bubba can trust me to handle things, I'd like to go solo to prove I'm capable of doing a good job."

Keely rolled her eyes. "You could've gone solo today, if you'd been here on time." Without looking at Bubba, she felt the daggers shooting from his eyes. He'd always been so perceptive. What did this girl have that caused him to toss common sense out the window?

Greta said, "You sound hurt. Maybe I should explain. I'm not inferring it's your fault, Keely, but your proficiency tends to intimidate me to the point I fail to perform as well as I might, with you looking over my shoulder. I hope that doesn't sound ungrateful, because I've learned so much from you. You're the best."

Bubba's eyes twinkled like stars. "I understand what you're saying, and I'm sure Keely does also. But you certainly have no reason to feel intimidated. You're a natural. The customers love you, Greta. It's true, Keely was a Godsend this morning, and I'm afraid I was an ogre. Thank you for your help, Pretty Girl, I couldn't have managed without you, but if Greta feels ready to try her wings, I think it's time to let her fly."

Greta brushed her hand across Bubba's chin and grinned. "Flour on your chin, sweetheart."

Sweetheart? Keely wanted to throw up.

Bubba put one arm around Keely and the other around Greta. "I feel blessed to have two such wonderful women in my life to keep me straight."

Greta reached out to give Keely a hug. "Thanks again for all your help, and don't forget to pick up your umbrella by the door, on your way out."

CHAPTER 9

Lexie Garrison cringed at the sound of her crude brother-in-law's voice. She thought she'd heard everything at Tutwiler, but Chet managed to use a few obnoxious words that even the most hardened criminal at the prison had failed to utter. Her mind constantly translated his every sentence, deleting the constant vulgarity, for fear such obscene talk would find its way into her vocabulary.

Prison had been a treat, compared to living under a roof where she was afraid to close her eyes at night. Her step-sister's husband gave her the creeps the way he ogled her.

"Come on sugar, it's time to go," he yelled. "We can't be late for work. I stuck my neck out for you to get this job, ya know." He grabbed keys from the kitchen counter and trekked across the oak floor, the taps on his cowboy boots clicking as he stomped toward the front door.

Lexie ran to catch up. Molly held out a small brown paper bag. "Wait, Lexie. Here's a little something to eat on your break."

"No need to prepare anything for me, Molly. I don't get very hungry at work."

"Shucks, it ain't no trouble—not really. Just a bologna sandwich and a bag of chips. I pack Chet a lunch, and it's just as easy to make two. Take it and enjoy." She shoved the bag in Lexie's hands.

"Thanks. You're super. I wish we could've spent more time together growing up, so we could have become better acquainted."

"Yeah, me too. But I was a little brat. I'm ashamed to admit it, but when Mama married your daddy, I was furious with you and your dad for invading our home and taking over." Her brows arched. "Oh, I know you didn't really take over—you were only four at the time, but I was nine and that's how I perceived it as a child." She snickered. "Oh, my! I was so jealous of you and the way your daddy treated you—like you wuz a little Princess."

"Molly, I'm sorry. I didn't know."

Her shoulders lifted. "Water under the bridge, sweetie. Water under the bridge. T'weren't your fault."

"Is that why you left and went to live with your grandparents? Because of me?"

Molly's shoulders fell. "Not really. I left because Mama didn't want me. Though I didn't like the situation at home, I didn't choose to leave. She shipped me off. To tell the truth, I'm sure I was better off with Grandma than you were, living in the house with Mama."

Lexie shrugged. "Well, if it makes you feel any better, she

didn't want me either—but daddy wouldn't let her send me away. Not until she figured out a way where he couldn't stop her. But I didn't mean to bring that up."

"It's okay. Believe me, I can understand why you'd hate her."

Chet blew the horn.

Molly's eyes widened. "Oh, he's getting impatient. You'd better run. That husband of mine is a sweetheart, but he *does* have a temper. We don't want to get him riled."

Lexie held on to the sandwich bag and ran out the door. She crawled into the truck and panted, "I'm sorry you had to wait on me. Molly and I got to talking."

His jaw jutted forward. "Aw, forget it. We ain't late, yet. But allow me to give you a word of advice, sugar. You're gonna have to learn not to let Lady Blimp start flapping her jaws or we'll be late every night. That bag o'wind don't know when to shut-up."

Lexie bristled that someone of his low character would dare stoop to name-calling. The smoke-filled cab caused her to choke. "Mind if I roll down the window?"

"Suit yourself."

She cringed when his eyes played up and down her body. The smoke stung her eyes and caused them to water.

"What's wrong? My cigarette bothering you?"

She nodded.

He rolled down his window and tossed it out.

They rode several miles in silence. Had she made him angry? Shouldn't they be there by now? What if— "Weren't we supposed to turn back there at the gas station?"

"I like to take a different route sometimes."

"How much further?"

"Exactly seven and four-tenths miles from my front yard to the parking garage."

She heaved a sigh when she spotted the big brick building.

Chet pulled into the parking garage. "I've been meaning to ask—why didn't you want to talk to the guy who called you on the phone today?"

She lifted her shoulders. "Just didn't."

"Who is he?"

"No one important."

"He must think you're important. He called back three times and Molly had to keep making excuses for you. You oughta tell him yourself. It ain't right for Molly to have to do your dirty work."

"She didn't have to. She could've told him the truth. I didn't want to talk to him."

"Is he someone you knew back before you stole my mother-in-law's car, or did you meet him wherever it was you went before you got caught?"

Lexie gritted her teeth. "I didn't steal the car. She told me it was . . . never mind what she told me. It doesn't matter now. The judge didn't believe me. Why should you?"

"Hey, frankly I don't care whether you done it or didn't. I ain't got no use for the ol' bag. She ain't never done nothing for me."

Lexie's heart pounded as she and Chet entered the garage elevator and the door shut. Maybe she was making too much of it all—perhaps her fears were unfounded. But founded or not, Chet Allums gave her the creeps.

Lexie enjoyed her job at the nursing home, and was especially fond of her supervisor, Brenda, who she presumed to be in her mid-sixties. Neatly cropped salt and pepper hair framed her pretty face and her green eyes lit up when she smiled. Brenda's funny sense of humor made Lexie comfortable from her first day. The duties were simple enough and the time ticked off fast.

All went well until around three-fifteen a.m., when Brenda sent Lexie to get an extra pillow for the patient in 314. Lexie loved Mrs. Higgins, and the poor lady had difficulty falling asleep. Lexie raced down the hall and opened the door to the linen closet, then jerked back, stunned.

A young nurse blushed and ran out the door, straightening her blouse.

Chet threw up his hands and chuckled, as he strode out. "Okay, so you caught me, little sister. Now, whatcha gonna do about it?"

. "I'm going to take a pillow to 314. That's what I'm gonna do."

"Good answer, sugar."

"My name's Lexie, Chet. I'm not your sister nor am I your

sugar and don't ever forget it." She snatched the pillow from the shelf and he followed her down the hall.

He leaned down and whispered near her neck, his tobacco breath causing chills to run down her spine. "Cool it, chick. Must I remind you? I'm the one who got you this job, and I'm the one who can take it from you?"

CHAPTER 10

Trey held his wife tightly, then reached up with his finger and caught a tear sliding down her cheek. "Honey, Bubba's a big boy. He doesn't need our protection."

"Trey. You weren't there. I'm telling you, Bubba's falling in love with that woman, and I don't trust her. She's evil."

"Okay, sweetheart. If it'll ease your mind, I'll run by the diner and chat with him before I catch the plane, but don't be upset if you're right, and Bubba has feelings for her. After all, he's had forty-two years to figure out what he's looking for, and frankly, I'm surprised you wouldn't be proud for him."

"And I'm surprised, Trey Cunningham, that you wouldn't be concerned that some strange woman could show up and have him wrapped around her little finger in such a short time."

"Keely, do you think you might be a bit jealous?"

"That's ridiculous. He's my uncle."

"Not in a romantic sense. But you've been the apple of his eye from the first moment you walked into the diner eighteen months ago, and he discovered you were his niece. I'm wondering if subconsciously you can't bear the thought of another woman occupying a place in his heart."

"Absolutely not. I'm telling you, I have a bad feeling about this relationship. Talk to him, Trey."

"I will, but I don't know what you expect me to do. Should I go in there, and say, 'Bubba, Keely is afraid you might be falling in love, so I've come to rid you of any such feelings."

"You're being facetious. I think when you meet her, you'll see I have cause to worry."

He glanced at his watch. "It's two-thirty. If I leave now, he shouldn't be too busy and maybe we'll have a chance to talk. Now, stop worrying. What's that verse you've quoted to me so often? 'Be anxious for nothing, but . . .'"

She smiled through her tears and finished it for him. "With prayer and supplication make your requests known unto God."

"My flight to Fort Lauderdale departs at six, so I'll go straight to the airport from the diner. If things go as I hope, I should be back home Thursday." His arms draped around her, pulling her close. "I'm so blessed to have you in my life, Keely Cunningham." He leaned down, planting his lips on hers. "I wish I didn't have to leave you, darling."

"I wish you didn't have to go, too." Keely's thoughts carried her back to her horrid childhood, being raised by a homeless kidnapper. Trey's strong arms enveloping her gave her a sense of belonging—a feeling of being truly loved—a feeling she only dreamed about, growing up. Only God could've pulled off such a miracle. Was she being selfish to want to deny Bubba that same sense of belonging?

Just as Trey hoped, the diner was empty when he arrived. Bubba sat at a table, wrapping silverware.

"Hi, Trey. Good to see you. Have a seat."

Trey turned a chair backward and straddled it. He looked around. "Keely tells me you have a new waitress."

"Yep."

"Where is she?"

"She goes home at two and comes back to work from five 'til closing. She left early today. Greta has some health issues."

"Nothing serious, I hope."

"Not sure. I think she's afraid to tell me the whole story, concerned I'll worry, but I worry more, not knowing what's going on in that pretty little head of hers."

"Well, I can't do much to help take the load off you, but I can at least help wrap the silver. Shove some my way."

"No need. I've wrapped more than enough."

Trey cocked his head. "What can you tell me about her?"

"Who?"

"The new girl."

His face turned red. "Not sure what you mean. She's fine."

"Fine? Is that all you can say about her?"

"What d'ya want me to say, Trey?"

"I don't know, but you blushed when I asked, so I'm guessing there's more that you aren't telling."

Suddenly, the air filled with tension. Bubba's eyes darkened. "Why do I feel like I'm being grilled. Do you know Greta?"

"Nope." He let out a hollow chuckle. "To be truthful, Bubba, Keely sent me here."

"I figured as much. To spy on Greta, right?"

"No, she already has her mind made up about Greta." He chuckled. "It's you I was sent to spy on. "

"Me?"

"Bubba, you know when Keely gets a bee in her bonnet, she has a hard time letting go, but she's got this crazy notion you're falling in love with your new waitress, and . . . well, she's worried about you."

Bubba's jaw flexed. "Is she saying falling in love is a bad thing? I had the impression it was working great for you two."

"It is. Honestly, I'm not sure any woman will ever be good enough for you in Keely's eyes, but she'll come around. You'll see." He raked his hands through his hair. "Okay, now that I've done what I was sent here to do. . . between you and your accountability partner, tell me the truth, bro, is this Greta chick fine? Or is she *FINE?*" He reared back in his chair and chuckled.

Bubba's lip parted in a smile. "You go back and report to Keely that I said she's fine. But if you're asking man to man? The woman is *FINE.*"

"You ol' codger. Keely's right. You're falling in love, aren't you?"

"Why wouldn't I? She's sweet, compassionate, funny, with a heart of gold—and not bad to look at, either. I know it's hard to understand, Trey, because Greta is truly all that and more. She could get any available man she wants, but I really believe she's fallen in love with me."

Trey rubbed the back of his neck. "Seems fast, doesn't it?"

"I suppose, but Trey, at our age, we've had plenty of time to rule out what we don't want in a relationship, and to know what we're looking for."

"You're saying you've found what you were looking for?"

"I wouldn't say that, since I haven't been looking. She just waltzed into my life one night as I was about to close. Ten minutes later, and I would never have met her."

"You love her?"

Bubba's gaze locked with Trey's. "You asking for Keely or for yourself?"

"This is strictly between us."

"Trey, do you remember years ago when you were in the Youth Department and you asked if the words in the song were true, that says, 'For every boy and girl, there's just one love in this whole world?"

Trey laughed. "I do remember. And I'm still not sure if it's true, since Keely has been the only woman for me. I can tell you, Bubba, when it comes to loving a woman, there's nothing to compare it with."

"Trust me, Trey, I know exactly what it feels like to love a woman, and it's the highest high and the lowest low—both the most exhilarating and the most painful feeling in the world."

"Wow. Yep, you're in love alright. Greta's a lucky woman. I'm happy for you."

The gruesome expression on Bubba's face gave Trey reason to suspect there was something missing. "What is it you aren't telling me, Bubba?"

"Trey, I lay awake at night and dream of what it'd be like to be married to Greta, but then I break out in a cold sweat, because I know I shouldn't think that way. I don't know what to do about this fix I'm in."

"I'm not following you. Start at the beginning."

"The beginning? I suppose that would be the night Greta walked into the diner. She was a truck driver and stopped in, just as I was placing the Closed sign on the door. She said she was too sleepy to drive and asked if she could come in for a short cup of coffee. She looked beat, so I let her inside and made a fresh pot. We got into a conversation, so when she told me she was selling her truck and would be needing a job—"

Trey nodded and smiled. "You of course, offered her one."

"I was smitten by her beauty, Trey. She needed work and I needed a waitress. I had no thoughts of suggesting she work here, until the words came out of my mouth. Even then, I had no idea she'd accept." Bubba glanced up at the clock on the wall. "I know you have a plane to catch. We can talk later."

"I still have plenty of time to catch my flight. Continue."

"Well, it seems I wasn't the only one smitten. I'm almost embarrassed to tell this, since it's too incredible to believe—but Greta started hitting on me from the first day she came to work. Not being accustomed to a good-looking woman paying attention to me, I couldn't believe what was going on, at first. When it became obvious she was coming on to me, I'll admit, I was flattered. I'm no woman's dream man, so when she flirted and . . . well, I won't go into the intimate details, but suffice it to say, I've never had a woman be so brazen in making her intentions known. She was relentless, Trey, and I'm ashamed to admit, the temptation has become a stronghold that I'm constantly struggling with."

"What was it you used to tell us guys in Sunday School? 'You can't help it if a bird flies over your head, but you don't have to let it make a nest in your hair?' If I remember correctly, you said the temptation isn't the sin, but the sin occurs when you act upon the temptation."

"Trust me, back then, I had no idea how many times I'd one day need to remind myself of that, but since meeting Greta, it's crossed my mind more times than I want to admit."

"Sounds like she knows what she wants, Bubba, and has figured out a way to get your attention."

"Maybe I've made her sound like a woman with no morals, but she's not like that."

Trey stuck his tongue in his cheek. "Really, because to be honest, that's the impression I was getting. But what do I know? If

Greta loves you and she's what you want, then I hope it works out for you, brother."

Bubba rubbed sweaty palms across the top of his jeans. "That's the thing, Trey. She's beautiful and I can't deny my heart beats so fast I can't breathe, when she walks up behind me and wraps her arms around me—but she's not what I want. She's what I want to want."

Trey's brow furrowed. "I'm listening."

"I've got myself into something I don't know how to get out of." Bubba leaned forward with his elbows planted on the table and his head buried in his hands. "It all started when Johnny came into the diner, bragging to me about how he planned to give Jackie a few months to get settled, before asking her to marry him."

"Wait! Jackie? Johnny? You aren't talking about Johnny Gorham, are you?"

"The one and only."

"Geez, it's a bit sudden to be making those kinds of plans with his brother's widow. I'm sure it means nothing. He was probably just running his mouth—a known family trait passed down through the generations, from what I've heard." Trey scratched his head. "But what does that have to do with you and Greta?"

His head lowered until his chin almost touched his broad chest. "I'm embarrassed to admit the truth, Trey."

"Hey, it's me you're talking to. We've been friends too long to hold anything back. What's bothering you?"

Bubba jumped up when the front door opened. "Can I help

you?"

A bedraggled looking fellow reached in his pocket and pulled out change. "I'm hungry. What will this get me?"

"Excuse me, Trey, this won't take long."

CHAPTER 11

Lexie liked her job at the nursing home, but living in the household of Molly and Chet, proved to be more of a prison than Tutwiler. She had to get out.

At eleven forty, she glanced down the hall of the nursing home to make sure Chet was not in sight, then made an excuse to Brenda about being sick. It wasn't a lie, was it? She *was* sick. Sick of Chet. Sick of the way he looked at her. Sick of the way he managed to slip his arm around her waist at every chance. She shivered at the thought of him touching her. *No more. I can't take it any longer.*

Brenda said, "I'm sorry you aren't feeling well. I'll page Chet to take you home."

"No! Please, Brenda, don't mention it to him. No need for him to worry. I don't need a ride." Lexie was glad she didn't ask further questions. She went out the back door of the nursing home, then ran three miles to the nearest RightSmart, went inside and pulled out the cheap cell phone she purchased two weeks earlier.

River Braxton rolled over in bed and grabbed the phone.

"River?"

He rubbed his eyes and glanced at the bedside clock. "Lexie? Lexie, is it really you?"

"Yeah . . . It's . . . it's me."

"Hey, it's great to hear from you. I've thought about you every day since you left. How are ya?" The thrill of hearing her voice waned at the sound of crying. His muscles tightened. "What's wrong? It's after midnight. Where are you? You in trouble?"

"I'm sorry to awaken you. I know it's late, but I . . . I . . . oh, River," she sobbed.

"Hey, no problem. You don't know how I've longed to hear your . . ."

The phone buzzed. "Lexie? Lexie?" But she was gone. He reached over and switched on the lamp beside his bed and sent a call to the last number on his cell phone. No answer. "Pick up, Lexie. Please pick up."

After numerous tries, his pulse raced when the ringing stopped, and he was aware she was on the other end. "Lexie, why did you hang up?"

"I never should have called you. It was wrong. Apologize to your wife for me. I suppose she must tire of having prisoners you've counseled calling you at all hours of the night, but I didn't know who else to call."

He swallowed. "You did the right thing. I'm not married. Not sure I'll ever be."

"But I thought the wedding was . . ."

"Postponed. Celeste is now planning a Spring wedding, but there are deep wrinkles that need ironing out before we walk down the aisle. But enough about me. Suck in and tell me what's going on with you. I've been so worried, Lex."

"It's Chet." Silence followed. "River, are you still there?"

"Yeah, I'm here." He closed his eyes, wanting to ask, yet not sure if he wanted to hear the answer. "What about Chet?" The long pause caused his heart to pump faster. "I had a bad feeling about that guy when he came to pick you up. Has . . . has he hurt you?"

River pounded his fist to his head and groaned when the phone went dead. "No, no, Lexie, don't do this to me." He dialed the number again.

Lexie's hand trembled as she put the cell phone to her ear. "I'm sorry, River. I don't know why I hung up. I . . . I just—" Her throat tightened. Did she dare tell him the truth? What if he should think she encouraged the jerk?

"Lexie, talk to me. Are you calling from your sister's house?"

"No. . . I walked to the RightSmart. It's the only store in town that stays open all night. I'm supposed to be at work, but I can't go. I just can't. Chet . . . he . . . he . . ." She burst into tears.

"Okay, try to calm down. Honey, you don't have to stay in the house with that creep another minute. You're free to leave."

Free to leave? Easy to say, but where could she go? Except for eight dollars a week, all the money she made went into Chet's pockets. He'd picked up her check with his, had her endorse the checks, then deposited them both to his account and gave her eight dollars in cash. According to him, she owed him for room and board. With nowhere to go, coupled with the fear he could have her sent back, did she have a choice?

"Lexie? Are you there? Listen to me. I don't want you going back into that house."

"Sure, River. That's it. I'll leave. Just walk away." Sarcasm dripped from her words. "Thanks for listening. I'll let you get back to sleep."

"Wait!"

"Why? There's nothing you can do. There's nothing anyone can do."

"You're wrong. I'll help figure this out. What about your father? I know how much you love him, and you've talked about how close you two were. Call him, Lexie."

"Never. I'll always love him, but he thinks I'm a thief. Forget it, River I don't even know why I called. I'm sorry . . ."

"Don't hang up, Lex. I have an idea. My college roommate's father is Pastor of Oak Hill Church in Mobile. You stay put, and I'll give him a call. I know he'll help you."

"No, River. I'm not his responsibility . . . or yours."

"But Lexie—"

"No way. I'm sorry I bothered you. Bye, River."

"Wait!"

She slammed the phone down, sat down in the women's restroom and squalled.

Forty-five minutes later while pushing a cart down the toy aisle, trying to look like a serious shopper as she mulled over a situation with no solution, a portly man with gray hair and a kind face, wearing khaki slacks and a striped pajama top said, "Hello, Lexie."

Her eyes squinted. "Are you . . . you must be—" She paused, embarrassed that she'd forgotten the name.

"I'm Pastor Bob Blocker. You weren't hard to find. You look exactly as River described you. My car is parked outside, and my wife and I are looking forward to having you come stay with us."

Lexie bit her lip. Had River failed to mention she was an ex-con? "You're kind but I can't impose."

"Nonsense. It's no imposition. River is wiring you money and I promised to go with you to find a good used automobile as soon as the doors open. The owner of the Ford Dealership is a member of my church. He'll give you a good deal."

Her heart pounded against her chest. "But I can't—"

"Oh, but my child, you must. Don't you get it? God is sending help your way. To not accept would be to deny the Lord's provisions. Come now, the sun will soon be coming up and I have a feeling you could use a little shut-eye."

"You don't know me. Why would you be willing to take a stranger into your home? Did River tell you—about me, I mean?"

His calm, sweet tone had a melodic sound. "Ah, yes, River

told me about you. But it was the words from his heart, which his lips didn't utter that spoke the loudest."

Lexie felt her face flush. "He's engaged, you know."

Pastor Bob's nose crinkled. "So he is."

"He's a good man. I've never met anyone like him. But I can't understand why either of you would want to get mixed up with someone like me."

"My dear child, God has a wonderful plan for your life, and River and I feel blessed that the Lord has given us the awesome privilege to be a part of His plan."

She swallowed hard. *Seriously? God has a plan for my life? Some plan!*

Celeste McDill sat in the hospital cafeteria and took a long look at her designer wristwatch and fumed. What was taking him so long? She twisted in her chair, causing her tight skirt to hike halfway to her thigh. She gave it a quick jerk. Her crossed leg swung back and forth at a fast, steady pace, as her impatience accelerated.

River stood across the cafeteria holding a breakfast tray and searching the room with his eyes. Within seconds, his attention—along with the attention of several other males—was drawn to the swinging motion of the slender, tan limb and the hard-to-miss six-inch red stilettos. He waved, then hurried over and bent down to kiss his fiancé.

Holding her wrist level with her eyes, she tapped on the face of her watch with her forefinger, making a point of the time.

"River, I've waited over an hour. You said the inmate's surgery was at seven. It's almost nine-thirty. What took you so long? One would think you had to personally perform the surgery."

"Sorry, Celeste, but I warned you I'd be busy today and told you it wasn't a good time to come to the hospital. There was a delay, and they've just now taken him back. He's terrified. I couldn't leave him alone."

"Well, you don't seem to have a problem leaving me alone. Sweetheart, I don't mean to nag, but the wedding is only weeks away and I refuse to postpone again. Seems to me you could make time to help with a few of the details. After all, it's your wedding too, you know."

Even as far back as sixth grade, he and Celeste had talked of one day getting married. People had come to expect it of them. But they'd both changed since graduating college. Couldn't she see it, too? How many ways did he have to say it? Yet, his words fell on deaf ears. "Celeste, we need to talk."

"I agree, darling." She pulled a bridal magazine from her tote bag. "Now, I want to show you what the wedding cake will look like."

He ran his fingers through his hair. "When I said we need to talk, I didn't mean now. I have to get back to the surgical waiting room. I'll call you when I get off work at five."

"Good grief, River. All I'm asking is thirty minutes of your time. You've just given that little two-bit knife-wielding hothead two hours."

He bit his lip. "Sorry, Celeste. I really am." He gulped down his orange juice, stood and threw his jacket over his shoulder. "I'll call you."

"Don't bother. Mom and I are driving to Birmingham after lunch to pick up my wedding gown. I'm having it altered. We'll be staying overnight to do a little last-minute shopping."

River turned and walked away. What a fine predicament. He wiped sweat from his upper lip. The wedding invitations had been sent. The caterer and photographer had been paid, the church reserved. Did he honestly think he could cancel a wedding at such a late date?

Six days after Lexie arrived in their home, Pastor Blocker and his wife, Joanie left for a week-long trip to attend a Convention in Birmingham, Alabama.

Lexie glanced around at all the family heirlooms. Antiques passed down through the generations. She found it hard to understand how anyone could be so trusting as to walk off and leave all their belongings in the hands of an ex-con. How wonderful it must be to possess such faith. The only person in her life she'd ever trusted was her father. Lexie loved him with all her heart, but no longer could she trust him. The letters he sent while she was incarcerated were packed neatly into a boot box and sealed with packing tape. Maybe one day, she'd read them. Not yet. The wounds were still too fresh.

As much as she'd learned to love the Blockers, she had to find a way to support herself. Lexie left a note, thanking them for all they'd done, then locked the house and walked outside, holding a set of keys to a car, which had her name on the title. A gift from River. Her pulse raced as she slid into the driver's seat and placed her hands on the steering wheel. *My car. He loves me. This proves it. He'll leave Celeste as soon as he finds a way to break it off.*

He'd be gentle when he ended it. River Braxton was the most compassionate man she'd ever known. It was the one thing that attracted her to him in the beginning.

CHAPTER 12

Trey gave a slight nod to the homeless man, while waiting for Bubba to return with a handout. Poor Bubba was an easy target for the down-and-out and it didn't take long for word to get around.

The soles on the ol' fellow's shoes flapped when he walked, which could account for his limp—or perhaps it was due to a bad knee. Trey noted the rope threaded through the belt loops in his oversized trousers and wondered if the pants had fit properly at one time. How does one wind up in such a sad state? Were there no relatives to come to his rescue, or had he abused the generosity and trust of others, until there was no one left to turn to? Had he, through no fault of his own, fallen on hard times and was truly hungry, or was he a professional panhandler?

Trey realized he'd become a bit callous, after having been bilked more than a few times.

Bubba walked out holding a tall iced tea and a bulging paper sack, which he handed to the old fellow.

"Thank you, Mister Bubba," he said, reaching into his pocket.

"What do I owe ya?"

Bubba looked at the change in the twisted, arthritic hand. "Got a quarter, Ralph?"

He grinned, nodded and handed a coin to Bubba.

After he left, Trey said, "I don't know what was in that sack, but this must be the cheapest place in town. A quarter? Really?"

"I know I can't save the world, Trey, but I can afford to feed the hungry that show up at my door."

"You softy, you. How do you know he doesn't have a wad of bills in his wallet?"

"I don't, but I didn't give it to Ralph, I gave it to the Lord. Now, what were we saying before I was interrupted."

"You mentioned being in a fix?"

"Right." He rubbed the back of his neck. "Trey, Greta is everything a man could want in a mate, and certainly too good for someone like me. I realize I should be overcome with deep gratitude that she'd give me a second look." He stalled and glared out the window.

"And you call that being in a fix? What's the problem?"

"The problem? After all these years, I'm still in love with Jackie." Bubba waited for a response. When there was none, he mumbled, "Shock you?"

"Should it?"

"Yeah. It shocked me, hearing it come out of my mouth. And it shocks me because it means I was a hypocrite when I taught you guys in high school and constantly warned you about the pitfalls of sexual sins."

"So, you're saying, you and Jackie . . .?"

"No. No, no, no. Of course not. I never touched her . . .neither before she married or afterward."

"Then I don't get why you'd say you're a hypocrite?"

"I told you. I still love her. Trey, I didn't suddenly fall in love with her the moment she became a widow. I realize now, I never *stopped* loving her. Don't you understand? All these years, I've been in love with another man's wife. I'm pretty sure that goes under the heading of adultery."

"Seriously? Did you act on those feelings? Ever send her letters, let her know how you felt, or try to sneak off with her?"

"Of course not. I would never have done anything to break up her marriage. I prayed for her every night and convinced myself it was concern. Maybe it wasn't concern at all. Maybe it was an excuse to keep her on my mind. When I saw her at the funeral, I knew, Trey. I knew that even after twenty-three years, I had never stopped loving her and now I know I never will. My heart ached for her." He looked down at his hands and popped his knuckles. "I wish I could erase her from my thoughts, because Greta and I are getting married."

"Whoa! Slow down, my head is spinning. I know it's none of my business, but why would you propose to Greta, if you're in love with another woman."

"I don't think I did."

Trey bit his lip. "I'm getting more confused by the minute. I thought you just said . . . "

"I said we're getting married, but I didn't say I proposed. She did, and I went along with it at the time. I was so upset thinking about Johnny claiming he was gonna marry Jackie, that I thought if I agreed to marry Greta, it would . . ." He stopped and lifted his shoulders in a shrug.

"Continue. It would do what, Bubba?"

He flung his arms in the air. "I don't know, Trey. I suppose I thought being married would help blot Jackie from my mind, but it won't work. I know that now. This is what I meant when I said I've got myself in a fix. Since seeing Jackie at the funeral, there's not been a single second she hasn't occupied my thoughts. I'm losing it. I wish I could lock the diner, disappear and never come back."

"Bubba, stop it! You're scaring me. This isn't you talking."

He let out a rueful sounding chuckle. "No? And who do you think it is."

"I think it's depression. Maybe you should go for a check-up."

"I don't need a doctor to tell me what's wrong with me, Trey. I know exactly what my problem is, and the guilt is killing me. I should've been the one to die, instead of her husband. Jacob had so much to live for."

"That's crazy talk. I'm serious, man. You need to see a doctor."

"If I thought a doctor could remove her from my thoughts, I'd gladly go, because heaven knows, I've tried, and I can't stop thinking about her. Night and day, she's on my mind. Jackie apparently loved Jacob very much to have stayed with him twenty-three years, and yet I keep pining over her. How crazy is that? You want to hear something else silly? I keep reliving a kiss that happened twenty-four years ago. We were just kids." He threw up his hands. "Maybe you're right. Maybe I *am* sick in the head."

"Bubba, you've got to call it off with Greta."

"It's too late, Trey. To go back on my promise would rip her heart out. She's a very special woman and I should fall on my knees thanking God that someone like Greta Pugh has found it in her heart to love me. If only I could find it in my heart to love her the way she deserves to be loved. I really want to love her."

"How do you think she'll feel when she learns you're in love with another woman?"

"She won't, and neither will anyone else. Greta is a sweetheart and I'd never do anything to hurt her."

"Except maybe lie to her? Bubba, don't you see, you aren't being truthful to her?"

"Trey, of all people, you should understand. Remember when I taught you guys, I stressed the importance of being true to your word? You listened well. You made a promise to Keely back then and never wavered, even when you had no idea if you'd ever see her again. You waited. And waited. For years, you continued to wait because of a promise. I was so proud of you for being faithful to your word. Remember?"

"Of course, I remember. But that was different. I loved her."

Bubba's brows meshed together, forming a vee. "Trey, I made a covenant with Greta when I agreed to marry her—I'll admit, it was a mistake—nevertheless, I entered into that agreement with a sound mind. Now, it's all she talks about, and I'm bound to my word. I'll make it work."

"I don't see it that way, brother, especially the part about a sound mind. I understand she wants to get married, Bubba, but what about your wants?"

"Trey, I don't know if you'll understand, but if this was about my wants, it would've been me, lying in that coffin."

"No, I don't understand. What are you saying?"

"I'm saying I would've gladly given up my life at forty-two, to have been Jacob, and to have had the privilege of being married to Jackie for over twenty years. But we don't always get what we want."

Trey reached across the table and placed his hand on top of his friend's. "I wish I could stay until I know you're okay, Bubba, but I need to get to the airport. I'll be praying for you, friend. Hang in there."

****

Keely arrived at the diner the following morning, only minutes after Bubba opened. She wished she could've talked to Trey before he left, although she was certain she wouldn't have learned a thing. He and Bubba had been accountability partners for years and both took confidentiality very seriously.

She cringed, recalling how she allowed Greta to practically

push her out of the diner, yesterday. Today, she'd go back, and she'd be strong. She wouldn't allow that woman to send her home. For Bubba's sake, she'd stick around to find out what Greta Pugh was up to. It wasn't that Bubba wouldn't be a fine catch for a good, decent woman, but it was disgraceful the way Greta couldn't keep her hands off him, and he didn't seem to be doing anything to discourage her inappropriate behavior.

Bubba cut her off. "Am I ever glad to see you here, Pretty Girl, and as for yesterday, it's . . . well, it's *yesterday*. I need to get to the warehouse, pronto. Think you can handle things until I get back?"

Her throat closed. "You know I don't mind, Bubba. I love being here. It keeps me from being so lonely while Trey's gone."

"Well, your timing is perfect. Today's menu is on the board. If I'm not back shortly, please brown the beef for the spaghetti."

"No problem."

"I asked Greta to come in at seven, and hopefully she'll be here, but her health is not good and sometimes the pain makes it difficult for her to get here on time."

Keely held her tongue. There was so much she wanted to say, but better to let him find out on his own. If she stirred the pot, it could upset him and propel him right into Greta's waiting arms. She shivered at the thought.

Greta walked into the diner at eight forty-five. "Hi, Keely. Wow, the place is packed. I can see you've been a busy bee."

"It's a good thing I came when I did, Greta."

"I agree, and I know Bubba appreciates it. You were sweet to come help. Have you taken the order for Table 14?"

Keely's stomach tied into knots. "Yes." Why did she let this woman get under her skin?

Greta patted her on the back. "Bless your heart, you probably haven't had time to sit down for a minute. Can I pour you a cup of coffee to take with you when you leave? You take cream and sugar, right?"

Keely's knees wobbled. "Greta, I'm not going anywhere. You are."

"Aww, thanks, you're sweet, but my medication is kicking in, and I'm feeling much better."

"Maybe I failed to make myself clear, Greta. You're fired."

Greta's mouth flew open. "Keely, please tell me your teasing."

"Do I look as if I'm teasing?"

"But why? What have I done?"

"Seriously? You don't know? Bubba expected you to be here at seven, so he could go to the warehouse. You didn't show up nor did you bother to call."

"I know, and I'm so sorry, but you don't understand what I went through last night, Keely. I was in serious pain and didn't fall asleep until around four o'clock. That's why I overslept this morning. I'm sure Bubba will understand."

"Greta, he needs someone he can count on, and obviously that's not you. We'll send your check to your box number. You're free to go." Perhaps she should've swallowed her pride and left it up to Bubba to handle Greta when he returned. But she didn't and what was done was done. Keely had no idea she possessed such a temper, until the harsh words spewed from her mouth.

Keely's stomach wrenched when Greta ran out the door, sobbing. Would Bubba be proud of her for firing his only waitress? Or would he say it was none of her business? Exactly what was it about the woman that rubbed her wrong? Keely couldn't deny Greta had always been exceptionally kind to her. Coming in late wasn't the real issue, so what was it? The notion of Bubba being duped by a woman with a nefarious agenda? Yes, that was it. Keely chewed her nails. But what if she was wrong?

What if Greta really was in love with Bubba and what if . . . what if he was in love with her? Bubba had always been a good judge of character. She cringed. Too late now to question her actions.

.

CHAPTER 13

After checking out every possible want-ad in the Classifieds, Lexie's hopes dimmed. She drove past a diner, then turned around and pulled into the parking lot. Her head pounded.

A beautiful young woman with a smile that lit up the room approached Lexie's table and handed her a glass of water and a menu.

Rubbing her temples, Lexie moaned, "Don't need a menu. Just need a cup of black coffee. I don't suppose I could buy a box of aspirin here? My head's splitting."

"We don't sell aspirin, but I have a bottle of acetaminophen." She reached in her apron pocket and uncapped the bottle. "One or two?"

"Two. Bless you. Thanks."

"I haven't seen you around. You new here?"

"Yeah. You wouldn't happen to know anyone who is hiring would you?"

"What kind of job do you have in mind?"

"Can't afford to be choosy. Just got out of the Pen." Her brow raised. "You hid your shock very well. Most people aren't as adept at it as you."

The server held out her hand. "I'm Keely Cunningham. You?"

"Lexie. Lexie Garrison."

"Pleasure to meet you, Lexie. Let me get you that cup of coffee, and we'll talk."

Keely came back with a tall mug of coffee and a slice of coconut pie, topped with a two-inch meringue. "Pie is on the house. Bubba makes the best." She pulled out a chair and took a seat. "Now, when can you start?"

Lexie's eyes widened. "You serious? You . . . you're saying I can work here?"

"Let's call it Providence. Bubba needs a waitress and you need a job. He should be back soon, and you can meet your new boss."

Lexie's shoulders drooped. "So, you're saying he has to approve? I might as well leave now. As soon as he asks where I've been for the past two years it'll be 'See you later, alligator.' I'll never find a job."

"Why do you need a job when you already have one? You'll find an apron in the drawer of the Hoosier cabinet in the kitchen."

Tears rained down her cheeks. "But I don't understand. You haven't asked . . ."

"I've asked all I need to know. You need a job. Bubba needs a waitress."

"Are you his wife?"

"His wife?" Keely laughed. "No, Bubba Knox is my uncle. He's at the warehouse but I expect him back shortly. He should be delighted to have a waitress he can depend on."

Lexie's lip trembled. "You can't imagine how much this means to me. How can I ever repay you?"

"Just take some of the load off Bubba, and that'll be all the pay I want."

"I promise. I'll work hard. I'm so grateful, Keely."

"So where do you live?"

"At the moment, I've been staying with a preacher and his wife, over on Old Shell Road, but I'm looking for a room or an efficiency apartment. Something cheap. I passed by a house on the way here with a Room for Rent sign out front, but it was senseless to stop until I had a promise of a job. I'll check it out when I leave."

Keely said, "Here comes Bubba, now. He'll be so surprised."

"Yeah, that's what scares me."

Keely grinned. "Me too."

"Are you saying he may not approve?"

"No, I'm saying he may be shocked when I tell him I fired his lazy waitress while he was gone. Bless his heart, he's so kindhearted, he can't bring himself to fire anyone." She shrugged. "So, I saved him the trouble."

"What did she do? Perhaps it's none of my business, but I wouldn't want to make the same mistake. I really need this job."

"Oh, I don't see you doing the same thing. She was all over

him, regardless of customers in the room. I know it embarrassed him, but again, he's too kind for his own good, sometimes."

"Was she in love with him?"

"Not a chance."

Lexie giggled. "I take it my new boss is not one to turn a lady's head."

Keely's brow creased. "I didn't mean it the way it sounded. He's no young stud, even though any woman would be lucky to be married to him. But I'm not gonna stand by and let someone like Greta Pugh make a fool of him—so, I did him a favor." She wrung her hands together. Was it true? Had she really done him a favor, or was she attempting to justify her actions?

Bubba walked in the door and squinted as he stared at the young woman wearing a Bubba's Diner apron.

He grinned. "Well, well, who do we have here?"

Keely said, "Bubba Knox, meet Lexie Garrison, your new waitress."

Lexie glanced down at the floor.

Bubba smiled. "You came along at a fine time, young lady. I was getting ready to fire my current waitress."

Keely looked at Lexie and winked. "You don't know how relieved I am to hear you say that, Bubba. I was afraid you'd think it was none of my business, when I tell you what I've done, even though I did it for your own good."

"Hold that thought, sweetheart, while I get a cup of coffee. You ladies care for a refill?"

Lexie jumped up. "Have a seat and let me get it for you."

"That's not necessary . . . uh, Leslie, is it?"

"Lexie, sir." She headed toward the coffee pot. "I'd be pleased to get it for you, Mr. Knox."

"We aren't formal around here. Bubba is fine."

Lexie handed him the coffee and he took a sip. "Now, that I've had my coffee, Keely, I've got a feeling you need to break it to me slowly. Just what is it you did, while I was gone, that you seem to think was for my own good?" Before she could answer, he flailed his hand in the air. "Wait. Don't tell me. You rearranged the kitchen, right? Lexie, I never know where to look for anything whenever I leave this girl alone for any length of time."

Keely's brows lifted. "No. It was more fun than organizing the kitchen."

He glanced around. "Hold on a sec. Have you heard from Greta? I suppose she's still not feeling well?"

"I heard, alright."

"What's that supposed to mean?"

"Greta didn't call nor bother to show up until almost nine, and then unleashed a litany of excuses. If I hadn't happened to drop by today, you would've been stuck here, acting as both cook and server, and couldn't have gone to the warehouse."

"Well, things usually work out, and it certainly did today. Your timing was perfect. You say Greta came in around nine?"

"Yes. Can you believe it?"

"How was she feeling? Did she have to go back home?"

"I guess she went home." She glanced at Lexie and lifted a shoulder in a slight shrug.

Bubba said, "Thanks, Keely. I'll call and check on her after I put the potatoes on to boil."

Keely fumbled with her apron sash. "Bubba, that might not be a good idea."

"Why?"

"There's more. You have a big heart—the biggest—and it burned me up the way Greta took advantage of your good nature. When she came dragging in here late again this morning, I told her to skedaddle—not to bother coming back."

"Slow down, I'm not following you. Sounded like you said—"

"I fired her, Bubba."

His reddened face resembled a giant tomato. He pounded his hand on the table, causing coffee to slosh from his cup. "You did WHAT?"

Keely's heart sank. She'd never seen this side of her sweet, mild-mannered uncle. Her eyes squinted. "But, Bubba . . . you said . . .you said you planned to fire her yourself."

"I never said any such thing."

"Of course, you did. When you walked in and I told you I hired Lexie, you immediately said she came along at the right time, since you were thinking of firing your current waitress."

"For heaven's sake, Keely, I was jokingly referring to you, as being my current waitress, since you were the only one here at the time. Now, I know why you were the only one here. You *fired* her?

Without even consulting me?"

Lexie stood and picked up her bag. "I knew it was too good to be true."

Bubba said, "No, Lexie, this has nothing to do with you. I need you. Greta has health problems and it's difficult for her to work at times, but when she is here, she tries very hard, despite her pain. She has fibromyalgia, but she let me know the night I hired her. So please don't go. This is between Keely and me."

Keely's lip trembled. "I can't believe what I'm hearing. Bubba, you haven't been yourself since the first day that woman came in here and put her fangs in you. She's been sucking the very life out of you." She grabbed a napkin and dried her tears. "Who are you? I don't know you anymore."

"Maybe I'm not the one who's changed. Keely, admit it . . . for some unknown reason, you had it in for Greta from the first day she came to work for me."

"That's not true." She swallowed hard. Suddenly, she knew exactly why she had it out for the woman. "Okay, so maybe I did, but it was only because I saw through her little scheme to make you her sugar daddy, and it turned my stomach every time I saw her pawing you. You couldn't sit down to eat without her standing over you to massage your shoulders, and the way she'd run her fingers through your hair was disgusting. She was a waitress, for crying out loud—not your mistress. I knew what she was after."

"Oh? Would you mind enlightening me?"

"The diner, of course."

"I see. So, you find it incredible to believe she could be romantically interested in *me*? Sheesh, I can't believe this. I should've listened to Greta. She was in tears last night and said she'd tried desperately to win your approval, but you wouldn't give her a chance. She was right, wasn't she?"

"Is that what you believe, Bubba?"

"It certainly looks that way, doesn't it? Let's be clear, Keely. I do the firing around here, and if I wanted Greta fired, I would've fired her myself. I was hiring and firing employees long before you came along."

"Fine. I'm sure you'll have no trouble hiring her back. What woman wouldn't want to put in a few hours of work a week, yet be paid generously for forty hours?" She jerked off her apron and threw it on the floor. "Fibromyalgia, my foot!" She held back the tears until she reached her car.

That evening Keely called her husband. "Trey, honey, can you come home? Please? I wouldn't ask you, but it's an emergency."

"What's going on, Keely? Are you okay?"

"Okay? I've never been so upset in my life, Trey. Please, honey? I need you here." After explaining what transpired at the diner, she heard a loud sigh.

"Sweetheart, this doesn't constitute an emergency. It'll all work out in time. You'll see."

Choking back the tears, she said, "So you aren't coming home?"

"I can't drop everything and leave, Keely. I'm in the middle of trying to close this account, but I should be home in a couple of days. Bubba's going through a tough time right now. I'm sure he didn't mean to sound so gruff. We might need to give him a little slack until he figures things out."

"But you didn't hear him, Trey. He doesn't want to figure things out. I think he's in love with her. If you'd been there, you'd know how serious it is."

"Honey, slow down and stop crying. I talked with Bubba before I left, so I know a little of what's going on. Trust me, there's more to it than you know, so be patient with him."

"Did he tell you he's in love with her?"

"Keely, you know I don't discuss what we talk about, but I can tell you that he loves *you* very much and he needs you more than ever, now, even if he doesn't realize it."

CHAPTER 14

Lexie breathed a sigh of relief, seeing the Room for Rent sign still in place. She parked in front of the small clapboard house, leaned back on the headrest in the car and lifted her eyes toward heaven. "Lord, I know I have no right to ask any further favors, but if I could impose on you to grant me one more answered prayer, I'd be obliged if I could use it now."

She swallowed hard, then opened the car door, straightened her skirt and walked slowly up the cracked cement walk. The house was small and could use a coat of paint. The shrubbery was overgrown and one of the dark green shutters was missing from a window. Lexie supposed to most women, these would be red flags, but to her it offered hope that the rent would be affordable.

She walked up the block steps and knocked on the door. A well-dressed woman with a kind face and sweet voice said, "Please tell me you're inquiring about the room!"

"Uh . . . yes. Yes, as a matter of fact, I am." She caught hold of the door facing when her knees wobbled. "Am I too late?"

The woman's eyes flickered, as she ushered Lexie into the house. "You're just on time. I have a feeling you're the answer to my prayer. Come on in and have a seat."

Just in time? Answer to her prayer? The woman was either an angel or a nut-case. Lexie sat on the edge of the couch and clasped her hands together to stop the shaking. "My name's Lexie. Lexie Garrison, and I'm looking for a place I can afford, so I don't know if . . ."

"I'm sure we can work something out. How soon will you need a place to stay?"

Lexie glanced around the small living room. Everything was clean and there was something about the modest furnishings that made the place feel like home. Home? What would she know about a home? She grew up in a house. It was never a home. But there was a warmth about this place that she couldn't put into words, yet her heart understood "Is immediately too soon?"

"Not too soon at all. I have hot tea brewing. Could I pour you a cup?"

Lexie nodded. "Thanks. Sounds good."

"Great. But first, I'd like to show you to your room."

Angel or nut, did it really matter? Lexie felt drawn to her. "But . . . you haven't told me . . . I mean, how much is the rent?"

"To be honest, I need a renter, yet I've been extremely nervous about sharing my home with a stranger. I had a good feeling about you, Lexie Garrison, the minute I opened the door. I know we'll get along just fine, so I'll take whatever you feel is fair that you can afford to pay."

Would she change her mind if she knew Lexie's history? She hadn't asked. Perhaps it was best not to mention it. They walked down the hall and entered a small bedroom that had tiny pink rosebuds on the wallpaper. From the white Priscilla curtains on the window, to the pink chenille spread on the mahogany poster bed, Lexie felt she'd been transported back into time—an era she wished she could've been a part of. "It's lovely." She picked up a white Teddy Bear from atop the bureau. "Yours?"

She nodded. "Yes. The house belonged to my parents, and I've recently moved back home. The room's just as I left it, many years ago."

Lexie walked over and picked up a 5x7 picture from off the dresser. "The guy in this photo looks vaguely familiar. He's handsome."

The woman's face flushed. "Yes, he was." She reached for the picture and stuck it in a drawer. "Feel free to change the furniture around or decorate any way you choose."

"I love it. I wouldn't change a thing. Was the guy in the photo your husband?"

Tears welled in the woman's eyes. "Goodness, no. He was nothing at all like my husband."

Lexie cringed. "Please forgive me. You must've loved your husband very much. I didn't mean to make you cry. I'm such a klutz sometimes."

"Oh, honey, it's not your fault. You'll soon discover my tears have no on or off switch. They come and go in their own time, not mine, so please don't feel you're responsible, when for no reason, I suddenly boo-hoo like a baby."

Lexie nodded as if she understood. Perhaps she did. A nutty angel?

Several times in the next few minutes, Lexie felt the urge to bring up her past. She hated deceiving such a nice person. But was it deceptive? Why take a chance on blowing a good thing when the woman hadn't asked for the information? It would come out soon enough. She glanced at her watch. "Goodness, I've stayed much longer than I intended. I'm supposed to be at work in fifteen minutes. I've just started this new job as a waitress, and I'd hate to lose it on my first day. I can pay you $100 today to hold the room for me, if that's agreeable. I'll be getting a check Friday."

"Works perfect. Will you be moving your things in tomorrow?"

"All I own is in my car. Would tonight after nine be too late to come over?"

The woman stood and embraced Lexie in a warm hug. "I'll leave the porch light on. If I've already gone to bed when you come in, you know where your room is."

Lexie laid her head on the steering wheel and sat in her car for several minutes, soaking in the events of the day. "I don't know why you're being so good to me, God, but I sure thank you.

You've given me a job and a place to stay, in less than twelve hours. I know it was you, because I couldn't have pulled it off by myself. I'll try not to bug you for anything else."

CHAPTER 15

Jackie Gorham rummaged through boxes in the attic. Opening a box of Christmas decorations, she smiled, seeing an ornament she made for her mother when she was in fourth grade. Christmas had always been her favorite season. Next Christmas, she'd pull out all these wonderful collectibles and decorate the house, just as she remembered it.

Jackie loved the bright lights, the tinsel, the beautiful colored balls, the whole nine yards, although Jacob had never shared her love for the special holiday.

He considered decorations gaudy and refused to allow her to put a Nativity scene in the front yard—but then he never really understood the reason for the season. She closed the box and shoved it against the wall. Would a few balls and glittery tinsel make her forget there was no one to share the season with? No one to put gifts under the tree for? *Cami, my sweet Cami. I miss you so much, baby.*

A knock at the door sent her scrambling down the ladder.

"The key—I forgot to give her a key!" She glanced at the clock as she ran through the living room. Eight-thirty. Too early for Lexie.

She flung open the door and gasped. "Johnny! What are you doing here?"

"Is that any way to greet your favorite brother-in-law?"

"You mean my only brother-in-law. I wasn't expecting you. Is something wrong?"

"Nothing's wrong. Isn't it okay if I want to pay my beautiful sister-in-law a visit?"

Jackie stiffened. "If you have something to say, Johnny, perhaps you should say it and leave. I have a ton of things to do. I'm still trying to settle in."

"Sheesh. You don't have to be so snarky."

"What do you want?"

His voice cracked. "I just lost my only brother, Jackie and although I try to hide the pain, it hurts. Jacob and I were only two years apart. We did everything together growing up. I've never felt so lost in my life . . . like a part of me is missing. I thought if anyone would understand, it'd be you."

Jackie bit the corner of her lip. "I'm sorry, Johnny, for being so short. I don't mean to make excuses for being rude, but everything I've believed for years has turned out to be a lie. I'm afraid it's made me skeptical of everyone's motives."

"Hey, I understand where you're coming from. You've been hurt. But I know Jacob didn't mean for things to turn out the way they did."

She rolled her eyes. "I'm sure you're right. He didn't intend to get caught." She chewed her lip. "Sorry, I shouldn't have said that. He was your brother and I know you loved him."

"I did, although I didn't approve of his actions. Jackie, I honestly believe he wanted to give you the world . . . even the part of it that belonged to someone else."

Though his words stung, it was best to keep her mouth shut. What good would it do to destroy Johnny's image of his deceased brother?

He said, "I have to be strong for Mother and Father. The grief is killing them. Jacob was always the favorite son, but I understood. He was a much better man than I'll ever be." His eyes welled with tears.

Jackie's heart softened. "Johnny, I'm sure that's not true. They worshipped both their sons, but I don't think it's advisable for you to be coming to my house, knowing how your folks feel about me. They blame me for Jacob's death, you know."

"They flew back to Virginia today, so that won't be a problem."

"Can I get you something to drink? Sweet iced tea? Coffee?"

"No thanks. To tell the truth, nothing sounds good. Haven't been able to eat or drink since the funeral."

"Johnny, you need to eat."

"Can't. I think if I tried to swallow anything, it'd make me throw up. Nothing has thrown me for a loop like losing my only brother."

"I'm really sorry. I didn't realize you two were that close, but then Jacob seldom confided in me about anything."

"That's because of the type family we grew up in. We were taught to hide our feelings and became quite adept at it, but I know Jacob loved me, and I'm sure he knew I felt the same about him. I was lying on the bed in my motel room tonight, staring at the ceiling and thinking of all the things I wish I'd said to him. Then, the idea struck me that it might help you and I both to heal if we could be together to share our deep loss. I see I was wrong." He stood and walked toward the door. "Sorry to have bothered you."

"Johnny, I assumed you knew."

"Knew? Knew what?"

"Jacob and I never had a real marriage, other than on paper. I tried to love him. For Cami's sake as well as for my own, I wanted to have a loving home. But he never loved me."

"Oh, you only have to look in the mirror to know that's not true, Jackie. You're a knockout. What man wouldn't want to come home to someone like you every night. I know I'd give the world to have that opportunity." He chuckled, as if recalling a humorous memory. "I was so jealous when you married Jacob. He had all the luck. I've always wished it was me."

She pushed her palm in the air. "Please! Don't go there, Jacob. That kind of talk makes me uncomfortable."

"I apologize. That wasn't my intention. But you seem to have such a low image of yourself, I wanted to let you know you're a very special woman that any man would be blessed to have on his arm."

"Apology accepted."

"I remember you and Bubba Knox had a real thing going before you married Jacob." His lip curled upward. "Any of those old feelings keep you awake at night?"

"I was never unfaithful to your brother, if that's what you're asking. Bubba had nothing to do with mine and Jacob's troubles."

"Never crossed my mind."

"Then why did you bring up his name?"

"I was in the diner earlier, and his animosity toward me was chilling. It didn't take long to discern the man is still in love with you. Naturally, I wondered if you might be having a little nostalgic heart burn, also."

She shook her head. "That was long ago. We were kids, and anything that was between us then, was over the day I left for Virginia."

"For you, maybe, but I don't think he feels the same way Would you like me to find out?"

Her jaw dropped. "You can't be serious. Drop it, Johnny. I'd be so humiliated if you said anything to Bubba. Please, promise you won't."

"No need to panic. Just asking. Maybe I wanted to find out what my chances are with you."

A knock at the door was a welcomed sound. Jackie jumped up. "That would be Lexie."

"You're expecting company?"

"She's not company. She lives here."

"Oh, I didn't know. A relative?"

"She's just a kid, Johnny, and she has no idea the chaos that Jacob created, so please don't bring it up."

Jackie unlocked the door. "Lexie, come in. I'm sorry I forgot to give you a key." She pulled a key from her skirt pocket. "This opens both the front and back doors."

Johnny stood. "I don't believe I've met this young lady."

Jackie felt her face flush. "Uh . . . Lexie . . . Johnny."

Johnny smiled. "Pleased to make your acquaintance." He walked over and planted a kiss on Jackie's forehead, causing her face to heat up. She wanted to reprimand him but thought it best to let it go.

He took a long look at Lexie, then whispered to Jackie. "She looks a bit like Cami, don't you think?"

"Not really. Bye, Johnny. I don't suppose I'll see you again. When will you be leaving for Virginia?"

"Didn't I tell you? I'm not going back. I've been looking at property across the bay. I've applied for an Alabama Broker's License, so we'll be seeing plenty of each other. Good night, sweetheart." He glanced over her shoulder and threw up his hand. "Hope to see more of you in the future, Lexie."

After he left, Lexie said, "He seems nice."

"Remember, dear, things aren't always as they seem. Alligators appear slow and harmless, but they move quite fast. Never allow one to get too close, less you become swallowed up."

128

Lexie laughed. "Not sure how alligators got into this conversation, but you warned me they were fast. I suppose I didn't see them coming."

Jackie winked. "I pray, for your sake, you never have to make the connection."

CHAPTER 16

Lexie's eyes widened when she drove up on the oyster-shell driveway in front of Bubba's Diner. The old red and blue sign was leaning against the building and a crew was hoisting another sign in its place. "B&G's Restaurant." She swallowed the lump in her throat.

She walked in, and approached a strange woman wearing a crisp new apron with the B&G logo. "Uh, excuse me, are you the new owner?"

The woman eyed her suspiciously. "Could be. And who are you?"

"Uh . . . I was hired as a waitress yesterday, but if this is no longer Bubba's Diner, I suppose I have no business here."

"New waitress, you say?" Her eyes rolled to the top of her head. "Well, Bubba should've discussed it with me, first, but I'll have to say, you look very capable. I'm sure I would've hired you, if I'd been here. My name's Miss Pugh. I'm Bubba's fiancé."

Strange, Keely never mentioned a fiancé. "Nice to meet you,

Miss Pugh. I'm Lexie."

"I'm sure we'll get along fine, Lexie. Bubba's in the kitchen, but would you mind grabbing a broom and sweeping the dining room? The workers putting up our new sign have tracked sand everywhere. You'll find a broom in the stock room."

"Yes ma'am." Lexie had questions, but her gut told her now was not the time to ask them.

She walked into the kitchen, looking for the stock room, and found Bubba stirring a pot of grits. "Good morning, Bubba."

He mumbled something she assumed was "Good morning," although she couldn't be sure. She could only hope his foul mood from yesterday had calmed. "Excuse me, but could you please tell me where I'll find the stock room? Miss Pugh asked me to sweep the dining room."

Bubba pointed, and Lexie went in and came out with the broom. Walking back through the kitchen, she said, "I really like your niece. What hours does she work?"

Without bothering to look up, he grumbled, "Keely won't be back."

"Oh. I'm sorry. So, have you sold the diner, or just changing the name?"

At this, he lifted his head, and glared. "Neither. What makes you ask?"

"The sign out front."

Bubba's face paled. He dropped the spoon into the grits. "Sign? What sign?"

"The new B&G Diner sign being installed on the roof."

Bubba stomped through the dining room, out the door, and onto the parking lot, with Miss Pugh following close behind. Lexie heard him yell to the men. "Stop!"

A few minutes later, she looked out the plate glass window and saw the crew hoisting the original sign back up. Lexie swept close to the front door and heard Miss Pugh say, "But darling, I wanted to surprise you. I thought you'd be happy. After we're married . . ."

Bubba said, "But we aren't married, Greta, and you were out of line. As sole owner, I reserve the right to make decisions concerning the diner."

The woman threw her arms around his neck and squalled. "I'm sorry, love. I made a terrible mistake. Forgive me?"

He nodded. "Forget it. I overreacted. My nerves have been on edge lately."

"Then can we keep the sign?"

He leaned down and kissed her on the forehead. "No, sweetheart. It's been Bubba's Diner for years, and I have no plans to change it."

****

Jackie scrolled through the classifieds, searching for a job. What could she possibly do? She had no skills. All she'd ever done was volunteer work, yet no longer could she afford to work for free. An ad jumped out at her. A public library?

She walked up the steps to the beautiful historical building and sucked in the pleasing aroma as she entered. An avid reader, she'd always loved the smell of books, though her books all came from bookstores. After stumbling over the answers to the first three questions, Jackie thanked the nice woman for her time, and left.

Hoping the many hours spent volunteering at the Junior League Dress Shop would help her land a job in Retail, she applied at every store in the Mall, only to hear the same disheartening refrain, "Sorry, we aren't hiring at this time." Discouraged, she went home and waited for Lexie's return.

Strange how Jackie had been immediately drawn to this young woman, since she knew so little about her. Maybe it was her sweet spirit. Or the childlike innocence she projected. Or maybe it was because Lexie reminded her of her darling Cami.

She paced the floor, waiting. The clock struck ten. Still, no Lexie. At ten-fifteen, she heard the door unlock, and Lexie tip-toed in, holding her shoes.

"You're still up. I was hoping I wouldn't wake you, ma'am."

"I'm usually in bed before now, but I was eager to hear about your first day on the new job."

"Really? You waited up for me?"

"I did." Jackie patted the cushion on the sofa, beside her. "Sit down and tell me all about it."

"Only after you tell me about your day. Did you find work?"

Jackie heaved a sigh. "Unfortunately, no. But tomorrow's a new day. Enough about me. Tell me how things went with you."

"There's a lot to tell. Are you sure?"

"Of course, I'm sure. Do you like it?"

"Ugh. That's a hard one to answer."

"Oh, dear. I gather it's not so good."

"The pay is decent, but it's too soon to tell whether I'll like the people I'm working for. They're a strange crew, which reminds me, I have a question for you. Is your name Jackie?"

Her mouth flew open. "For crying out loud, I didn't even introduce myself yesterday, did I?"

"No, ma'am."

"I'm sorry, honey. When you came to the door, asking about the room, I was so excited, I must've forgotten my manners. Yes, my name's Jackie. Jackie Gorham." Her face scrunched into a frown. "But if I didn't tell you my name, how would you have known it was Jackie?"

"I put pieces together after my boss said, 'Lexie, I know your mom.'"

"Really? What a small world. So, how does he know your mother?"

"He just thinks he does. I knew he had me mixed up with someone else, since I don't even know my mother. She died when I was very young. Here's the funny part—my boss knows you, but he thinks you're my Mom."

"Impossible. He *does* have you confused with someone else. I left Mobile many years ago. I'm positive he doesn't know me."

"Actually, I think he does. I had to fill out a form for his records, and when I handed it back to him, he stared at the paper, as if there was a big problem. Then he said, '104 Bay Street,' and frowned, as if he thought I lied about the address. I was too nervous to say anything, so I just nodded, and that's when he said, 'So you're Jackie's daughter.' Just like that. Not a question, but a statement—'you're Jackie's daughter.' Then he said, 'Lexie, your mother and I went to school together. I heard you were moving back into your grandparents' home.' I realized then, it was the address he recognized, since you said you've just moved back into your parents' home. I didn't have a chance to tell him differently."

Jackie thrust her hand over her heart, as if doing so could slow the pounding inside her chest. "Lexie, where is this place you work?"

"It's a diner on Highway 90. The boss's niece, Keely hired me, yesterday, while the boss was out running an errand. When he came in, she told him she'd hired me and fired his other waitress. Oh m'goodness, he blew his top."

Jackie popped her hand over her mouth. "Oh, dear. He was upset because she hired you?"

"Fortunately, no. It was all about a waitress named, Greta. He told Keely if he'd wanted Greta fired, he would've done it himself. I don't know what happened, but, when I went in today, Keely was gone and Greta's back. Turns out Greta is his girlfriend. Lucky for me Keely was there yesterday, since she's the reason I got the job."

"I don't think it was luck, Lexie. God has his hand on you, sweetie."

"You sound like Pastor Blocker."

"I take that as a compliment."

"Jackie, do you recall someone called Bubba when you were in school, because he's my boss, and he sure remembers you?"

Tears welled in her eyes. "I know Bubba."

"I seem to have struck a nerve. Don't tell me you and Bubba . . . oh, m'goodness. That's it, isn't it? Now, I know why the picture on your dresser looked familiar. It's him, isn't it?"

"Yes, but please, Lexie, please don't mention that you saw it. Not to anyone, but especially not to Bubba." The tears that welled in her eyes, now made their way down her cheek.

"Oh, Jackie, I'm so sorry. I'll get another job. I won't work there if it bothers you."

"Don't be silly. You won't find a better man to work for than Bubba Knox."

"I'll explain to him tomorrow that I'm just a renter, and not your daughter."

Jackie chewed her left thumb nail. "Do you have to tell him?"

Lexie's brow raised. "You want him to think I'm your daughter? I don't understand."

"I know you don't, honey. Maybe it's wrong for me to be so prideful, but if he knows I've taken in a renter, he'll assume I'm destitute, and I don't want his pity. Besides, he'll likely assume you are—" She paused and wrung her hands together. "Lexie, there are things that happened in Virginia that I'm ashamed of. Terrible things. Hurtful things. Although I can never make up for what happened or take away the shame, I hope to eventually right some of the wrongs. I suppose it's a bit ludicrous to think such news won't eventually find its way to Mobile, and probably already has . . . but of all people, I don't want Bubba Knox feeling sorry for me."

"No problem, *Mom*." Lexie winked. "I think we favor. What do you think?"

Jackie's face lit up. "You're precious, and I can tell you, if I had a second daughter, I'd want her to be you." Her eyes glazed over. "The truth is, I have a daughter, Her name is Camille. I call her Cami, but that's another story for another time."

"I thank you for the compliment, Jackie, and I'm sorry for whatever you went through in Virginia, but I have a past, also, that I'd rather leave behind. Brother Blocker told me God has a wonderful plan for my life. It almost made me angry that he'd have the gall to say such, since he knew what I was going through. Although things are still far from perfect in my life, If there are such things as miracles, it seems the fact that I wound up here with you, in a place where I feel secure, certainly fits in the miracle category."

CHAPTER 17

Homer Maitre was busy working his Crossword puzzle in the diner, when his wife snatched it away. His brow creased. "What in tarnation did you do that for, Renie?"

"I wish you'd look at Greta, over there flirting with those truckers. Have you ever seen such in all your life?"

"Don't reckon I have. Now, give me back my paper."

"Homer, I think you ought to say something to Bubba."

"Fine. As soon as he comes back in the dining room, I'll ask him how his day's going. Now, hand me my puzzle before I forget the word I had on my mind."

"Homer Maitre, Bubba has been like a son to us, and you're saying you're gonna sit by and let him ruin his life?"

"Renie, we've prayed for years for Bubba to find a woman to love, who'd love him. I agree Greta doesn't appear to be a great fit for him, but you'll have to admit, love is strange. If she's what he wants, we should stay out of his business. He's a grown man. I'm confident he knows by now what he's looking for in a mate, and apparently, he's picked Greta. So stop meddling."

"There's a big difference in meddling and caring. I *care* what happens to him, and frankly, I'll never believe he picked her. I'm quite sure she picked him."

"Well, it worked for us." He covered his smile with his hand.

"Are you trying to say you didn't pick me, but I picked you? I happen to remember exactly what happened over half-a-century ago on a certain hayride at Lois Abernathy's."

He let out a chuckle. "Okay, okay. I'll admit, I was smitten, but you didn't have to slap me. My cheek smarted for days. I simply wanted to snuggle up to keep you warm. It was your welfare I had on my mind."

"I didn't buy that line then, and I certainly don't buy it now." She snickered. "I'm just glad you didn't give up."

"Me too. I enjoyed the next hayride a whole lot more than the first one." He raised a brow. "Ooh, doggie, you sure changed in a week's time. What a night that was."

"Shut your mouth. Nothing happened unless it was in your dreams, ol' man."

He chuckled. "Just fooling with you, darlin'. At the present, I'm dreaming how nice it'd be to finish my puzzle."

Lorene waved her hand when Greta glanced their way. "Miss, as soon as you can pull yourself away from the fellows, our coffee cups are empty, and I'll need extra cream."

Greta grabbed a coffee pot and hurried over to the Maitres' table. "Sorry, ma'am." She gestured toward the window. "It's a beautiful day, isn't it? Makes me wish I could be working outside. Are you a gardener?"

Homer looked up over the top of his spectacles and smiled, waiting for his wife's response.

Lorene's chin lifted. "No!" She glared at the waitress. "Playing in the dirt is not my favorite pastime, but if it was, I have a feeling there's plenty I could dig up around here, if so inclined."

Greta's smile appeared forced. "I'm not sure I follow you."

"Just as well. Thank you for the coffee. That'll be all."

When Greta walked away, Lorene whispered, "You see what I mean, Homer? She poured my coffee to the brim, even after I told her I take lots of cream."

"Now, sugar, are you sure you aren't trying to find something about her to dislike? Seems to me she's been very kind to us."

"Ha! She doesn't fool me. I'm telling you, Homer, that woman is a conniving ol' cuss and I won't sit idly by and let her ruin Bubba's life."

"I'm sure you won't, sugar."

Greta sneaked up behind Bubba in the kitchen, with her hands over his eyes. "Guess who?"

He reached up and rubbed his fingers over hers. "I'm guessing these soft hands belong to one of the prettiest girls in the world." He turned around to kiss her, but she turned away. "What's wrong?"

Her bottom lip protruded. "One?"

"Pardon?"

"You said *one* of the prettiest. Who else did you have in mind?"

"No one, honey. Honest." He lifted her pouty face by placing his thumb under her chin. "I guess I'm not very good when it comes to paying compliments."

Tears welled in her eyes.

He wrapped his arms around her. "Hey, I said I'm sorry. I didn't mean it the way you took it. You're very beautiful, Greta. Surely, you know that."

"It's not that, Bubba."

"Then what's wrong?"

"The elderly couple that comes in every day. The Maitres? They hate me and I can't imagine why, unless Keely turned them against me. I've tried so hard to be extra nice to them, but the more I try, the worse they treat me."

He chuckled.

"It's not funny, Bubba. The old woman is rude and hurt my feelings."

"Honey, Aunt Lorene and Uncle Homer practically raised me and they're very protective. They'll come around when they see how much you love me. All they care about is my happiness. Don't let it bother you. Aunt Lorene is rather strong-willed and outspoken, which is not always a bad thing. You never have to wonder how she feels, but when she finally comes around, you'll have no better friend. Just be patient with her. For my sake?"

"Okay, sweetheart. I'll try, but it breaks my heart that she doesn't think I'm good enough for you." She lifted to her toes. "I'll take that kiss now."

****

Trey rushed into the house, yelling "Honey, I'm home." He ran up the stairs, searching. "Keely?"

Keely stayed seated downstairs at the kitchen table. When her husband came pounding down the stairs, she waited. Though eager to see him, he had to understand how furious she was that he didn't take the Greta situation seriously. Bubba was about to make the biggest mistake of his life, and yet his best friend was doing nothing to stop it.

"Hiding from me, were you? You little tease." He waited for her to stand. "What's wrong, honey?"

"What's wrong? How could you even ask?"

"You still angry because I didn't drop everything and rush home to tell Bubba how to run his business?"

"See? You're doing it again"

"Doing what?"

"Blowing me off as if I'm a hysterical female. When I called you on the phone, I needed you to listen to me, Trey."

He reached for her hand to lift her from the chair. "Aww, honey, I've missed you. Let's don't argue. I'm sorry you feel I blew you off. You know I love you, babe."

She stood and wrapped her arms around his neck. "Apology accepted. I love you, too, and I'm glad you're home, but Trey, I'm sick over what's going on and I can't do anything to stop it."

Trey winked. "And not for a lack of trying, I'm sure."

"Well, someone needs to do something, and you may be the only one who can get through to him. It's almost as if Greta's hypnotized him. She's convinced him that I'm the enemy, trying to take over the diner. Have you ever heard anything so absurd?"

He cleared his throat and smiled. "You think maybe it might not be so much what Greta said to him, but perhaps Bubba concluded on his own, after you fired *his* help—at *his* diner—without *his* input?"

"I only did it because he has such a tender heart. I know how difficult it is for him to fire someone, and trust me, that woman needed firing."

"Seriously, honey, don't you think you should've discussed it with him first, and offered to do his dirty work. . . if it was truly what he wanted?"

She formed a pout. "Are you taking his side?"

"Keely, I'm not judging you. I'm sure you thought at the time you were doing the right thing."

"I did, and I still do. But you should've heard how harsh he talked to me, Trey. I know you can't believe it. I'm serious, I was dumbfounded. My jaw dropped, and I couldn't say a word."

He chuckled. "Well, that's a day that'll go down in the books. Couldn't say a word?"

She grinned. "Okay, but only three. I said, 'Fibromyalgia, my foot, before I stormed out.'"

Trey popped his palm to his forehead. "Oh, honey, you didn't!" He clamped his lips together, then took her hand in his, in a firm grip. "Sweetheart, fibromyalgia is very real and extremely painful, and just because it isn't evident externally doesn't mean it isn't incapacitating to the sufferer. I'm sure your insinuation that his girlfriend was a liar went over with Bubba like a lead balloon."

"Oh, puh-leez. Don't refer to that witch as his girlfriend."

"Isn't she?"

"A witch? Yes!"

"I meant isn't she his girlfriend."

"Only because she's blinded him. Trey, please go talk to him and pound some common sense in his head, before that woman convinces him to elope with her."

CHAPTER 18

River Braxton called his friend, the Reverend Blocker. "And you say you have no idea where Lexie went?"

"Not a clue. Joanie and I came back from the Conference and found a note, telling us she appreciated our hospitality and thanked us for trusting her. If only she'd trusted us enough to let us know where she was going. Joanie has been worried sick about that sweet little thing. I can see why you fell in love with her."

"Love? Did I say that?"

"Aren't you?"

"Maybe I am, Preacher. I'm having a difficult time sorting out my feelings. Doesn't matter, though, because Lexie still believes I'm getting married."

"You aren't?"

"I don't think so."

"You don't *think* so? What does Celeste think?"

"I honestly can't say. I've begun to wonder if she she's more in love with the idea of planning a big wedding than she is in being married to me. She's a great girl, and we've been friends forever, but maybe we both had the idea we were doing what was expected of us. Since ninth grade, we've been like Siamese twins. Neither of us have dated anyone else. I never thought outside the Celeste box, until the stress of planning a wedding began to change her. We never argued about little things until planning this stupid wedding. Frankly, I'm wondering if getting married might wreck a great friendship, and I'd hate to lose my best friend. I'm so confused. Preacher, is it possible to be in love with two women at the same time?"

****

Trey walked into Bubba's Diner and took a seat near the window. A waitress called from across the room. "You here for lunch? I'll grab you a menu."

"I'd like lunch but won't need a menu. It's Thursday, right? That would be Pork Chops today. I'll take turnip greens, candied yams and crispy cornbread." She walked over to his table, and though he'd never met Greta or Lexie, Keely had described them well. "You're Lexie?"

She nodded. "That's right. Have we met?"

"No. I'm Trey . . ."

She gushed, "Keely's husband?"

"Yes,, but don't believe all those nasty things my wife said about me."

"Ha! I'm sure you know better. I must admit, I've been eager to meet the Perfect Man."

"Well, trust me, I'm far from perfect, but I probably come a bit closer while I'm out of her sight than I do when she's having to deal with me daily."

"Your wife is really sweet."

"Yes, she is. I'm a blessed man ."

"Dessert comes with lunch . . . but I suppose you know that already. Coconut or chocolate meringue pie?"

"Tough choice, but bring me the coconut, and while you're in the kitchen, please let Bubba know I'm out here and would like to chat with him when he has a few minutes to spare."

Bubba walked out shortly, with Trey's lunch.

Trey drew back and grunted. "Ugh. The other waitress was cuter than you."

Bubba didn't appear amused. He sat the food on the table. "I've been waiting for you, Trey. I don't know how much Keely told you, but . . ."

"I figure she told me everything, Bubba."

"Then I don't suppose there's anything else to be said. Enjoy your lunch. I need to get back to the kitchen."

Trey's eyes squinted. "Really? Look around, Bubba. What's the hurry?"

"Maybe I'm not up to being chewed out, and I'm sure that's why Keely sent you here."

"Sit down, man. I'm not here to chew you out. I'm here because you're my best friend. Whatever transpired between you and Keely is not the problem, but rather the result of a problem. I want to help you dig down and let's destroy the root."

"I guess you think it's Greta."

"Could be. Could go deeper than Greta. I only know that whatever it is, it's eating away at you. I've known you for years, and I've never seen you like this."

"Trey, I love Keely, but she had no right . . ."

"Bubba, I'm not here to defend anyone's rights. Not hers. Not yours. I'm here because I feel you're both under attack by the enemy, and until you and Keely stop blaming one another, and see what's really going on here, I'm afraid things will snowball into something you'll both regret for a long time. Maybe even the remainder of your life, and it's senseless."

He simply nodded.

"Does that mean you're in agreement?"

"Yeah. I do feel I'm under attack. I'm having trouble sleeping at night, I can't eat, I know what I want to do, but when it comes down to doing it, I can't bring myself to it."

"Bubba, where do you send me when I begin to stress?"

"To Ephesians Six Chapter?"

"Exactly! The armor fits you too, you know.

A slight smile crossed his lips. "How did you get so smart?"

"I had a good teacher."

"Trey, no one hates conflict more than I do, yet I've never had as much conflict in my life as I've had since Greta came into the picture—but it's not fair to blame her."

"So, you're still set on marrying her?"

"I am, and there's nothing you can say to make me change my mind, so please don't go there. She's more than I deserve. The customers are crazy about her. In fact, *everyone* seems to love her except the two people who mean the world to me—Aunt Lorene and Keely. They act as if Greta's a monster, out to ruin my life. Naturally, their actions make me defensive, and actually draws me closer to Greta, which is not a bad thing—but the rift with Keely is killing me. I wish she could see Greta the way I do. You know I couldn't love Keely more, if she were my own daughter."

"I do." He took a sip of cold coffee. "And she knows it, too, Bubba."

"Are you sure? The words that spewed from my mouth the other night made me sick. I tossed and turned in bed all night, reliving every stinking moment. I hated myself for what I said to her. I know she can never forgive me, and I don't expect her to."

"You aren't serious. We're talking about the same girl who was kidnapped by a homeless man when she was only four, then jerked around all her life, often hungry with no place to lay her head. The man physically and verbally abused her . . . yet when they sent him to prison, what did she do?"

Bubba choked up. Wiping his eyes, he said, "She forgave him."

"Exactly. And you'd sit here and tell me you're afraid she can't forgive you for a few angry words, spoken out of a heavy heart? Not our girl, Bubba. All it's gonna take is for one of you to step up and decide you'll be the first one to utter the two hardest words in the English language."

Bubba raised a brow. "I'm sorry?"

"That's the two. Now, you can wait for Keely to say it, or she can wait for you, but you both know you'll be miserable until there's forgiveness."

When Greta walked in the front door, Trey stood. Bubba reached out for a handshake, but Trey grabbed him in a bear hug. "I'll be praying for you, friend. I love you."

"I love you, too, Trey. Thanks for coming. I needed to hear what you had to say. I think I know where the root lies, but I'm afraid it's like dollar weed. Ever tried to get rid of it? You can dig and dig and think you've got it all, but it never goes away. Ever. It comes up somewhere else, and before you realize what's happening, it's taken over."

Greta strolled over to where they stood, tossed her head back with her lips puckered. "Miss me, sweetheart?"

Bubba's face lit up like a red Christmas light, as he bent down and pecked her on the lips. "Uh . . . Greta, I don't believe you've met Trey."

Her brow creased. "You aren't . . ."

"Keely's husband? The one and only." He clasped her hand between his two palms.

She dropped her head and gazed at the floor "I suppose your wife told you about our little run-in. I'm so embarrassed. Bubba is crazy about her, so I know she must be a wonderful person. I hope she'll tell me what I've done to cause her to resent me, so I can apologize."

"Give her time, Greta. I'm sure it'll all come out in the wash, whatever that means."

Greta said, "I hope I'm not running you off, Trey."

"Not at all. I was leaving."

"Well, it was a pleasure meeting you. I know Bubba thinks the world of you, and I hope one day Keely and I can develop a friendship, such as the one you two have. I'd really like that."

Bubba put his arm around her tiny waist and drew her close. "Didn't I tell you she was a gem, Trey?"

Bubba went into the kitchen and began cutting up chicken. He recalled his last words to Trey. It was true—Greta was a gem—everything a man could want. Wasn't she?

Everything except. . . she wasn't Jackie.

CHAPTER 19

Lexie ambled into the kitchen Wednesday afternoon, as Bubba slid three meringue pies from the oven. "More pies? You must be expecting a crowd tonight. Something special going on?"

"There's a College and Careers class at the church on the corner, and normally fifteen to twenty young people walk here after the evening service."

"In that case, we'll need to let them know we're out of the Roast Beef."

"They aren't coming for dinner. They come for dessert and coffee."

"Then I'll put on a fresh pot."

"That won't be necessary. One of the more charismatic guys in the group, entertains the crew by pretending to be a barista. He not only brews the coffee on Wednesday nights, he serves it also. You'll need to take their orders for chocolate, coconut or pecan pie."

"You made pecan pies?"

"Yep! It's Jamal's favorite."

"Jamal? Is he someone special?"

"All the kids are special, but he's the barista I told you about. Something disturbing has been going on with that boy, lately. I haven't been successful in getting him to talk about it, so I thought I'd try going through his stomach. If pecan pie can't get him to loosen up, he may be hopeless."

"No one is hopeless, Bubba."

"Hey, I was joking, but Jamal has always been the life of the party, intent on making people have a good time. Now, he attempts to go through the motions, but it's fake. His eyes reveal his pain. I thought he might open up to Keely last week, but it didn't happen."

"You have a very caring heart, Bubba. It's almost seven now. Is there anything I need to do to get ready for them?"

"Nope. Other than making sure I have enough pies baked, they're no trouble. I do have to run them out, sometimes."

"Rowdy, are they?"

"Not rowdy, unless you call laughter rowdy. I simply meant they'd stay here all night if I didn't remind them I need to close and get some sleep."

Lexie glanced out the window. "I see a large group walking this way. Must be them."

Bubba glanced at his watch. "Right on time."

He stood in the doorway and introduced them to Lexie, as they entered. Jamal, who normally led the way, lumbered in, several paces behind the group. "Jamal, I'd like to introduce my new waitress. Lexie . . . Jamal."

Jamal hardly looked her way. He gave a slight nod. "Glad to make your acquaintance, ma'am." And with that, he headed toward the coffee pot.

Lexie followed. "I'll be happy to make the coffee, Jamal."

He picked up the empty pot and handed to her. "Thanks. I'd appreciate it."

The chatter in the room ceased. A girl they called Dani said, "Am I hearing things? Jamal offered to let someone take over his barista position? Are you sick, Jamal?"

One of the guys hollered. "He's sick, alright. We've been here two minutes already and he hasn't asked the cute new waitress out. Make your moves, man, so we'll know you're okay."

"Shut up, Brian." Jamal slid down in his chair, his brows meeting in the middle.

Brian's eyes widened. "Hey, I was joking. Didn't mean to offend you."

"Not offended. It's just . . . Aww, who cares? Forget it."

Lexie went around the table taking orders for pie. Chocolate appeared to be the favored flavor. Standing behind Jamal, she said, "What will it be? Chocolate, Coconut or Pecan?"

"Nothing, thank you. I'm not hungry." He glanced around the table and grunted. "What's everyone staring at?"

"We're staring, Jamal, because you're acting peculiar. I was worried when you chose not to make the coffee, but I've never known you to turn down Pecan Pie."

"I've always been strange, Cheri. Surely, it's no surprise to you. Anyone can tell you. Jamal's a clown. Jamal's a nut. Jamal's crazy. I've heard it all my life. Acting peculiar is what I do best."

The room grew quiet.

Bubba stepped up to the table. "Sorry to cut the night short, but I'd like to get out of here as quickly as possible."

Chloe said, "Sure, Bubba. The chocolate pie is scrumptious."

Someone else said, "It couldn't hold a candle to the coconut."

"Glad you all enjoyed." He walked behind Jamal's chair. "Jamal, I made the Pecan Pie especially for you. Since you weren't hungry tonight, come on back to the kitchen when the place clears out and I'll wrap it up for you. It'll still be good tomorrow."

"You don't have to do that. I'm sure you can sell it."

"You're right. I could, except this one belongs to you. Wouldn't feel right selling your pie."

"Thanks, Bubba."

After the crowd left, Jamal helped Lexie clear the table. They carried the dishes to the kitchen, just as Bubba sat the wrapped pie on the counter top. He said, "If you two don't mind loading the dishwasher, and wiping the counter tops, I could get out of here much quicker."

Jamal said, "Not a problem. I'll be happy to help."

"Thanks. I need to check out the supplies in the stock room. Shouldn't take me long."

When Bubba walked out, Lexie said, "I've never lived in one place long enough to bond with friends. Jamal, do you realize how blessed you guys are to have one another? It's evident these people really love you."

"Tolerate me may be a better description."

"No. They sensed something was wrong, and I thought it cool how they wanted to help. However, I get it that it's sometimes easier to talk to a stranger, than to bear our souls to those who know us best."

"Is that something you learned in Psychology classes, or are you speaking from experience?"

"Are you always snarky, or just with strangers?"

"Sorry. I suppose it did come out sounding snarky. I seem to have a habit lately of always saying the wrong thing, or even the right thing the wrong way."

"To answer your question, I didn't go to college, so I've never taken Psychology. I speak from experience. There's no one in this world I love as much as I love my daddy, but we're estranged because I can't discuss the problem I have with him. I wish I could."

"Which one of you broke the bond?"

"I suppose that would be me. But I was deeply hurt."

"Was the pain worth being forever separated? I have a feeling the answer is no. So why not give him a call, and instead of bringing up the problem that separated you, take baby steps. Keep it light. Tell him about your day. Ask about his."

Lexie's lip curled upward. "Is that something you learned in Psychology classes, or are you speaking from experience?"

A heart-melting smile stretched across beautiful white teeth that sparkled like jewels against his handsome tan face. Until he smiled, she'd paid little attention to his good looks.

He said, "Parental love is an experience I'm not familiar with, and I didn't take Psychology."

"Could've fooled me."

"My ol' man skipped shortly after I was born, but I think if I had a dad, I'd do anything to keep the communication going. When I was little, I'd lay in bed at the orphanage and make up long conversations between me and my imaginary parents."

Lexie's heart pounded. She had a sudden peculiar longing to feel those muscular arms holding her close. Was she nuts? There was no denying the chemistry was there, but she was in love with River Braxton, and he loved her, too. As soon as River ended it with Celeste—and she had no doubt that he would—he'd come looking for her.

He said, "You clammed up. Did I say something wrong?"

"No, I was thinking about that little boy who was so desperate for a mom and dad that he made them up."

His jaw jutted forward, and his voice changed. "I've never told that to anyone. Not sure why I told you, but I've made it okay so far, so don't pity me."

"It's not pity, but admiration I have for you, Jamal. I need a friend, and I'm flattered that you trusted me enough to tell me something about yourself that no one else knows."

"Seriously?"

"Of course, I'm serious."

Bubba came out of the kitchen with the pie. "Here ya' go. Maybe you can enjoy it tomorrow."

Jamal chuckled. "Thanks, Bubba, but this pie won't last until tomorrow. Suddenly, I'm hungry. I plan to cut it as soon as I get home."

He started out the door, then turned around and said, "Uh . . . Lexie, I think I know what you'll say, but I'll ask anyway. This is a big pie for one person. Would you be interested in sharing it with me?"

Lexie glanced at Bubba. His smile was the approval she needed. "Pecan Pie is my favorite, but since I was told this one had your name on it, I dared not ask for a slice. I live around the corner. Close enough to walk, although I do have my car here. Why don't you follow me?"

"You live in the apartments by the church?"

"No, I live in a house on Bay Street."

"Alone, or do you have a roommate?"

Bubba said, "Am I gonna have to shove you two out? Lexie and her mother live in the old Adkison house, Jamal. It's her grandparents' home place."

****

Jackie ran to the front door as soon as she heard the car drive up. "Lexie, is that you?"

"It's me." Before Lexie could stick her key in the door, Jackie jerked it open. "I hope your day was . . ." She grabbed Lexie by the arm and pulled. "Get in the house, quick. A strange car is pulling up in the driveway. Someone must've followed you home."

"It's okay. He's a friend. I'm sorry, Jackie, I suppose I should've asked permission first, before inviting him over."

"Oh, honey, that's a relief. Please don't ever feel you need permission to invite friends over. I want you to think of this as your home for as long as you live here." Jackie stood in the door to invite him in.

Jamal extended his hand. "Now, I know where your daughter got her stunning looks. The name's Jamal, ma'am."

"Nice to meet you, Jamal. I'm Jackie."

"Hope you don't mind me dropping in at such a late hour . . . Jackie. I come with a peace offering. You like Pecan Pie?"

"It looks yummy, but I dare not eat anything this late, or I wouldn't sleep a wink. Lexie, darling, get a couple of desert plates from the cabinet above the sink. You'll find the knives in the drawer by the dishwasher." As if an afterthought, she added. "We haven't been here long, Jamal. We're still learning where things belong. If you kids will excuse me, it's past my bedtime."

Lexie said, "Goodnight, Jackie. And thanks."

Jamal whispered, "You call your mom Jackie?"

"It's a lovely name, don't you think? She's a jewel. Now, let's dig into this pie."

CHAPTER 20

Greta traipsed into the diner, all smiles, thirty minutes before her ten o'clock shift.

Lexie let out a heavy breath. "What a wonderful surprise. You're here early."

"Are you trying to be smart?"

"Goodness, no. I apologize, if it sounded that way. I just meant it's been a crazy morning and I can use the help. I trust your lumbago is better?"

Greta made no attempt to hide her irritation. "Fibromyalgia! *Not* lumbago."

"Sorry."

"No problem, but just so you know, lumbago can be cured. There is no cure for what ails me. Would you mind wiping the table by the window? I would, but I need to see Bubba."

"Sure, as soon as I wait on the gentleman at the back table."

"Sweetheart, wipe the table, so the next customers will have a clean place to sit, and then you can take care of the customer in the back."

"Yes ma'am." Lexie wiped the table and rushed over to take the man's order. "Sorry to have kept you waiting." Her eyes squinted. "Hey, aren't you Johnny? I met you at Jackie's."

"I remember. Lexie, isn't it?"

"Correct."

"Well, this is interesting."

"Pardon?"

"You're living with Jackie and working for Bubba. Interesting, indeed."

"So you know Bubba?"

"Yep."

She put her pencil to the pad. "What can I get you?"

"Bring me a hamburger, all the way. I'm glad Jackie isn't alone, during this grieving period. So, Lexie, are you originally from Mobile?"

She swallowed hard, and carefully constructed her answer, hoping to conceal Jackie's privacy. If Jackie didn't want people knowing she needed money, it was her business. "Uh, yes. My grandparents were from Mobile." She mulled her answer in her head. He did say *originally,* didn't he?

His eyes lit up. "Were they, now?"

"Yes. We recently moved in the house on Bay Street."

"*We*? I know *Jackie* recently moved back, but where did you come from?"

Hoping Bubba wouldn't walk out while they were having this

conversation, she had no recourse but to admit the truth. "I grew up with my father, and just recently came to Mobile."

"Really! Is your father from Mobile?"

"You're a very curious guy, aren't you? What's with all the questions?"

"Just my way of getting to know you better. How old are you, Lexie?"

She glanced toward the kitchen door. "Twenty-two last August."

He laughed out loud. "Well, blow me down. Who woulda thought it?"

"I hear that a lot. People always tell me I look younger. Excuse me, I have things to do. I'm sure Bubba would like to see you, but if he doesn't come out, it'll be because he's swamped. We've been unusually busy this morning."

"I won't hold my breath waiting for him."

Lexie smiled, though his last comment sounded a bit abrupt. "I'll let him know you asked about him."

"Did I?"

Now, she was sure it wasn't her imagination. Who was this man, and what was it about him that caused the air to turn frigid whenever he entered a room?

Lexie smiled when she drove up to the house that night and saw the living room light on. She was glad Jackie hadn't gone to bed. "I tried to get around his questions, Jackie. He was relentless.

I finally had to admit the truth—that I grew up with my father."

"That's okay, honey. I'm sorry to have put you in an awkward position. Johnny's my brother-in-law, so he knows you aren't my daughter."

"I'm glad you aren't upset. I was afraid Bubba would walk out and hear the conversation. But I think Johnny assumes we're related."

"Why would you think so?"

"I told him my grandparents are from Mobile."

"Are they?"

"Yes, but I've never met them. I doubt they're still living. Daddy said my grandparents were good people, but when my mother died, they blamed him for her death."

"That's a shame."

"Yes, it is. I wish I could've known them, but Daddy took me and left Mobile, for fear they could take me away from him. Apparently, they had money and he didn't. I was only a couple of years old when it happened."

"Who was your mother, Lexie? I grew up here. Maybe I knew her?"

"Honey."

"That was her name?"

"Probably not. I'm sure Daddy must've told me her name in the past, but he always referred to her as Honey. She and Daddy were musicians, known as Honey and the Bee. He played guitar and my mother wrote the lyrics and sang. I have a couple of their

CD's. I think they were pretty good, but maybe I'm prejudiced."

"So how did your mom die?"

"Murdered."

"Oh, honey, that's horrible. I'm so sorry."

"Daddy has never stopped looking for the killer, even though my step-mother goes ballistic if he mentions anything about it around her."

"I gather you aren't too fond of your step-mother."

"You're right. And for good reason. The woman made my life a nightmare. I'll never understand the hold she has on my daddy."

CHAPTER 21

The week drug by, with Lexie counting every hour, eagerly awaiting Wednesday night. What was it about Jamal that made her feel as if a jackhammer was implanted where her heart should be? Her breath caught in her throat at the mere mention of his name.

Sure, he was handsome, but so was River. Lexie knew practically nothing about Jamal, yet she couldn't get him out of her thoughts. Was she really so shallow, or was Jamal right? Was it pity she felt? Such a sad story of a lonely little kid, dreaming up an imaginary family. But was it any more depressing than her own young life? Though she'd never doubted her father's love, her step-mother made both their lives miserable. She had no choice growing up, but why did her daddy continue to stay?

At ten after seven, Lexie watched out the window for the young people from the College and Career Class to come through the door. Her heart sank when the last of the group walked in, and Jamal was nowhere to be seen.

She made a fresh pot of coffee, and listened for someone to

mention his absence, yet his name never came up. The mood was noticeably different tonight than last Wednesday. Somber. The majority of the conversation centered on a robbery that had taken place at the church the night before. Someone apparently had stolen a couple of computers and raided the food pantry. Who would rob a church?

The group didn't linger as long as last week, and after everyone left, Lexie helped Bubba clean up. "I happened to notice Jamal didn't come tonight."

Bubba smiled. "It's hard not to notice when Jamal isn't in the room. Until a few weeks ago, he was always the life of the party—the class clown—but I've felt it's a cover up for something deep within."

"Is there anyone he's close to? Girlfriend, maybe?"

"Jamal? No. He jokes with all the girls and puts on an act of being a real Romeo, but he won't let anyone get too close to him. I won't deny I'm worried about that boy. For him to miss church on Wednesday night, further proves there's reason to worry."

"Any idea what it could be?"

"No, and we'll probably never know. It's a shame. How can you help someone if they won't confide in you?"

****

Friday morning, the breakfast crowd had cleared out of the diner, except for the elderly couple that Bubba referred to as Uncle Homer and Aunt Lorene, although he explained they were no relation.

Lexie walked up to their table with the coffee pot. "Could I offer you a refill?"

The woman pushed her cup to the edge of the table. "Why, thank you, sweetheart. I know I've had plenty, but it's especially good on this chilly morning. You're a pretty little thing. I declare, you look familiar. Where did you work before coming to work for Bubba?"

"I . : . I worked in Wetumpka."

"I believe that's in North Alabama, am I right?"

The man laid his pencil down. "No sugar, it's more Central. Near Montgomery."

Lexie nodded.

He said, "I believe there's a women's prison there. Is that right?"

She swallowed hard. "Yessir."

The woman said, "What did you do there, dear? Did you wait tables?"

"Yes ma'am. You're right. I did wait on tables." Lexie smiled, thinking of the many times she waited for a table when the only seats available were with unsavory characters.

The woman cocked her head sideways and with squinted eyes, she said, "Well, I've never been to Wetumpka, so that's not where I've seen you. Where did you live before then, sugar?"

"Oh, I lived in so many towns, it's hard to remember them all."

"Well, I Suwannee, I know you from somewhere. You don't

remember seeing me somewhere besides here, I don't suppose?"

"No ma'am."

"Homer, doesn't she look familiar to you?"

His attention was glued to the Crossword Puzzle. "Can't say that she does."

"Homer Maitre, you haven't even looked at her."

"Aww, Renie, I had the word on the tip of my tongue, and now it's gone. What were you saying?"

"I knew you weren't listening. I said doesn't this sweet child look familiar?"

He chuckled as he wrote an answer in the squares. "You've said that so many years, you're still doing it, even after you decided that we found her." He laid his pencil down and glanced up at Lexie. His jaw dropped. "Well, I be dog, I see what you mean."

His wife frowned. "Are you humoring me, or do you really think what I'm thinking?"

Lexie said, "Have y'all ever been to Lake Wales, Florida? We lived there longer than anywhere."

"No. Can't say that we have."

The man said, "Yes, we have, Renie. Don't you remember that's where we stopped for lunch, the last time we went to Ocala on our way to Silver Springs?"

"Well, of course. That must be where we saw you."

"Yes ma'am. You could be right."

"Well, I'm glad I figured it out. Things like that can drive me batty."

The old man chuckled. "You're glad *you* figured it out?"

CHAPTER 22

Who'd be calling at two o'clock in the morning? Bubba rolled over in bed, grabbed his cell phone, and grunted, seeing the familiar number on the screen. "Greta? What's up?"

"Oh, Bubba, I'm . . ." Sobs drowned out the remainder of the sentence.

"I can't understand you, Greta. Slow down and tell me what's going on."

"I'm in the hospital."

He muffled a yawn. "The hospital? Oh, no, I'm sorry, hon. Fibromyalgia flaring up again?"

"That's only a part of it. I didn't want to worry you, but I thought you should know."

"You did the right thing by calling, Greta, I'll pray for the pain to ease, so you can get a good night's rest. I'm sure you're exhausted."

"When I need prayer, I'll call a church hot-line, Bubba. I called because I need you here with me."

He glanced at his watch, lying on the bedside table. "Sure, honey. Sorry if I sounded callous. I'll be there in the morning as soon as the breakfast crowd leaves."

"That's not acceptable, Bubba Knox. I need you *now.*"

Bubba rubbed his eyes. "Honey, you know I would if it was absolutely necessary, but there's nothing I can do for you. Try to get a little shut-eye, and I promise to be at the hospital in the morning by nine-thirty."

She screamed, "I'm dying, Bubba. I wanted to keep it from you, but I can't handle this by myself. I need you with me, darling. It frightens me to think I might die without you by my side."

He could hear her sobbing. *Dying?* He sat upright in the bed and tried to gather his thoughts. "Honey, this is such a shock. I don't know what to say."

"I don't want you to say anything. I want you here by my side, holding my hand. I'm scared, Bubba. I'm so scared."

He jumped up and grabbed his pants from off the valet. "I'm pulling on my pants, now. I'll be there in fifteen minutes, if not sooner." There were so many questions he wanted to ask, but they'd have to wait until he could talk to her face-to-face.

He pulled up to the emergency door at the hospital and ran inside, still wearing his pajama top. "I'm here to see Greta Pugh."

The nurse at the desk peered over the top of her glasses. "I'm sorry, and who are you?"

"Bubba Knox."

"No, I mean how are you related to the patient?"

"She's my . . . my . . . she's a friend." He couldn't bring himself to say fiancé.

"Sir, do you realize what time it is? Visiting hours ended almost six hours ago."

"I know, but she's awake. She called less than fifteen minutes ago, pleading with me to come. She'll be expecting me."

"I'm sorry. We have rules, and we don't make exceptions for friends."

Bubba nodded. "I understand, but could you please go let her know I came and I'll be back later?"

She glanced at the nurse sitting beside her, who nodded. "We can do that. It's time to check her vitals, anyway."

"Thanks." He turned to walk away, then swung back around. "She's very upset, so if you could give her something . . ."

She and the other nurse exchanged confused glances. "Frankly, sir, I don't think that'll help her situation."

His heart sank. So, it was true. Knowing Greta tended to exaggerate at times, Bubba had wanted to believe this was one of those times.

Back home, Bubba tossed and turned in bed for the next couple of hours. How could he sleep? A few days earlier, after much prayer, Bubba had concluded Trey was right—to go through with the wedding would be a huge mistake. He'd been waiting for the right words to say to her, at the right time. Now there were no right words. No right time. He would've felt like such a heel if he'd left her to face death all alone. His gut tied in knots.

****

Bubba opened the diner at five o'clock, but everything he attempted turned into a disaster. First, he put water in the coffee pot, but forgot to put in the coffee. He took a carton of eighteen eggs out of the refrigerator and dropped it on the floor, splattering eggs everywhere. In the length of time it took to clean up the mess, the grits burned.

Lexie came in at six o'clock. "What happened here?"

"I had a little accident." He feigned a smile. "Actually, I had a series of little accidents."

"How can I help?"

"Is anyone out front?"

"Two men just walked in."

Bubba chewed on his bottom lip. It was time to swallow his pride and eat crow. He jerked his cell phone from his pocket and dialed Keely's number.

"Bubba, what's wrong?"

"Everything." His voice cracked. "I have no right to ask, I know, but I need you, Keely. Can you help me at the diner for a few hours, today? I'll explain the situation when you get here."

"Of course. When do you need me?"

"Thirty minutes ago?"

"Gotcha. I'll leave right away. I've been up and dressed for over an hour, wondering what to do with my time today. I'm miserable here by myself when Trey's out of town."

Keely ran into the diner. "Hi, Lexie, Bubba called, and it sounded urgent. Do you know what's going on?"

Lexie shrugged. "Beats me, but something has him in a dither."

Keely grabbed an apron and headed into the kitchen. "Okay, Bubba, I'm here. What's wrong."

"Greta's in the hospital, and I need to be with her. Lexie can handle the dining room, but bless her heart, she can't boil water, and that's not an exaggeration. Would you mind cooking until I can get back?"

"Not a problem. Lexie must've made the grits. I smelled them when I opened the door."

He shook his head. "I can't blame Lexie, I burned them all by myself."

"No problem. I'll clean up and make another pot. What's wrong with Greta?"

"I can't talk about it. I've gotta go."

"Sure, Bubba. You do what you need to do. Lexie and I can handle this."

"Thanks, Pretty Girl. By the way, I've missed you."

Her eyes welled with tears. "I've missed you, too, Bubba. Now, go and don't worry about a thing."

By nine-fifteen, the diner was empty, except for the Maitres.

Lexie and Keely sat down for a short cup of coffee, before preparing for the lunch crowd.

Lexie leaned across the table and whispered. "What do you know about the elderly couple sitting in the corner?"

"Maw-maw and Paw-paw Maitre?"

Lexie's eyes widened. "They're your grandparents?"

"No, but they like to pretend they are, and I go along with it. I think we all know I'm not who they want me to be."

"Bubba calls them Aunt and Uncle, but they aren't related to him either, are they?"

"No, but they practically raised him."

"They're sweet. Mrs. Maitre is convinced we've met somewhere before, but I think I would've remembered them."

"Poor Maw-maw." Keely sighed. "I didn't realize she was still doing it. It's a long story. They're a little eccentric, but both are real sweethearts. You'll learn to love them in no time."

Keely, picked up her coffee cup and stood. "Bummer. Looks like our break just ended. Here comes a customer."

Lexie turned her head. "Oh. It's Johnny."

"Johnny? You know the jerk?"

Lexie giggled. "Jerk? What's wrong with him?"

"He's extremely arrogant. He's the only person I know that Bubba Knox doesn't get along with. If you're around him for long, you'll understand why."

"He came over to the house the other night to visit Jackie, and he's been in here a couple of times, but I he's always been nice around me."

"Jackie? You know Jackie?"

"Uh . . . yeah, I live with her."

"Really? How did that happen?"

"I don't mean to sound mysterious, Keely, and I'm sure it'll all come out soon. But for the time being, please forgive me if I don't answer that question."

CHAPTER 23

Bubba jerked off his baseball cap and rushed up to the nurses' desk, panting. "I'm here to see Greta Pugh. I think she's in ICU?"

The nurse rolled her eyes, then let out a long sigh. "Mrs. Pugh is in room 212."

Bubba shuffled on his feet. "*Miss.*"

"Yes, is there something else?"

"No, I was saying she's *Miss* Pugh. Not Mrs." Bubba normally would've let it slide, but the nurse's unprofessional attitude made him feel the urge to correct her.

She looked down, shuffled a few papers, then looked up, and in a condescending voice, said, "My bad." She glanced at the nurse sitting beside her and winked. "Let me warn you, sir, your lady friend—*Miss* Pugh—is in a foul mood this morning. Instead of finding fault with everyone at this hospital, she should be on her knees thanking the Lord. She could've died last night."

Bubba's pulse raced. Of course, she'd be in a foul mood. Who wouldn't with Atilla the Hun for a nurse. He gently pushed the door to Room 212 open. "Greta? Sweetheart? You awake?"

Her eyes were red from crying. "Awake? I haven't slept a wink since being brought here. Please, Bubba, lean down and hold me tightly. Where have you been?"

"I came last night. Didn't the nurse tell you?"

"She said you came and left."

"It wasn't my choice, hon, but it was two o'clock in the morning. Visiting hours were over and they wouldn't let me go in."

She turned her back to him and sobbed. "I was so frightened. I needed you and you weren't here for me."

"Please, honey, don't cry. You don't understand. I tried, honest."

"You're right. I don't understand. If you were dying, no one could keep me away from you. Rules or no rules, I'd be there for you."

He rolled his cap in his hands. "Sorry, Greta. I don't know what else to say."

"You can tell me you love me. You never say it, Bubba. Sometimes, I wonder if you really do."

He stroked her hair away from her face. "Aww, honey, we're getting married, aren't we?"

"Are we? Sometimes I get the feeling you're trying to find a way out."

"You're upset with me, and I understand. I'm sorry I couldn't be with you sooner, but I'm here now."

She reached up and wrapped her arms around his neck. "I suppose I panicked, at the fear of being alone if anything should happen."

"Does that mean I'm forgiven?"

"You know I can't stay angry with you, Bubba Knox." She slid up in bed. "Sweetheart, could you place the pillows under my head? I know you've been worried about me, so while my pain is minimal, I'd like to sit up. I have something to tell you that will lift your spirits."

Bubba, fluffed the pillows and his pulse raced when she spread her long, shiny black hair across stark white pillow cases. She looked like a Princess. His gaze took in her flawless olive complexion, paused on beautiful brown eyes, and then lingered on thick luscious pink lips. How could he *not* be in love with such a beautiful creature? The bigger question was how could such a gorgeous female be in love with him. He pushed a lock of hair from her forehead. "Comfortable?"

"Yes, thank you. Bubba, I have a wonderful surprise planned for you, but last night, I was frightened that I might not live until morning to tell you about it."

Moisture filled his eyes. "But you did, and I'm here, now. So, what's this great surprise?"

"Remember when you told me you've always wanted to go to Alaska?"

"Yep, but I've also always wanted a Lamborghini. It's good

179

our wants don't hurt us."

"Well, honey, I can't promise you a Lamborghini, but if I can hold on until April, you'll have your Alaska wish."

He reared his head back and laughed out loud. "You're joking, I know, because I couldn't have won the lottery without a ticket, and Publishing Clearing House doesn't know where I live."

"I knew you'd be surprised. We have two tickets for a Honeymoon cruise. It took all my emergency fund to pay for them, but there's nothing I wouldn't do for you, sweetheart. I want to be your dream come true."

His expression changed. "What are you talking about, Greta? Honeymoon cruise?"

"Yes, darling. I've also booked the ball room at the Moring Mansion for our wedding, April 15th. There should still be plenty of azaleas and dogwood in bloom. It'll be such a gorgeous time for a wedding, don't you think?"

Bubba raked his hand across his mouth. "April 15th?"

Her lip trembled, and her voice cracked. "Oh, darling, I know what you're thinking. I wish I could move it up, too, but let's not concentrate on the negative. I'm trying to be brave, and I want you to, also. I plan to follow all the doctor's orders for the next seven weeks and two days, until we set sail." She jerked a tissue from the box beside her bed and blotted the corners of her eyes. "You are happy, aren't you, darling?"

He stood up and shifted on his feet. His throat felt dry. *Married?* Hearing the date set made it suddenly seem real. It turned from a faraway thought tossed about in his head to a point of no return. *April 15th?* He couldn't breathe.

Greta's lips formed a pout. "I must say, I expected a little more excitement than what you've shown. This is what you want, isn't it?"

He ran his hand over the back of his neck. "I'm sorry, hon, but it's hard to muster up enthusiasm, when I haven't had time to absorb the news of your—"

"Death, Bubba. You can say it. I've come to grips with my fate. But I plan to live for the moment and relish every single day I have left with you."

"Illness was the word I was searching for, Greta. Have the doctors indicated how long you'll be hospitalized?"

"Didn't the nurse tell you? I'll be discharged this morning, sweetheart."

"Discharged? Are you serious? Why?"

"I can see you're upset, but there's nothing more they can do for me, Bubba. I've accepted it. Please promise me you'll try to accept it also. I can get through this as long as I have you by my side."

A nurse walked in with a wheelchair and a form for Greta to sign.

Bubba helped her into the car. Pulling out of the parking lot, he said, "Greta, I hesitate to ask, but I'm concerned. You haven't shared the diagnosis. Maybe there's something that can be done at another hospital. We can get a second opinion."

She snubbed and wiped her eyes. "Don't ask me to talk about it, Bubba. I can't. I refuse to be morbid."

"If that's how you feel, I'll respect your wishes." He glanced at his watch. "After I get you home, I'll help you settle in, then I need to run to the diner and make sure everything's under control. I'll only be a phone call away, if you should need me."

Her eyes widened. "You can't be serious."

"What do you mean?"

"Please, Bubba. Please don't drop me off like a sack of flour. I'm frightened at being alone."

He chewed the inside of his cheek. "I'm sorry, honey. I should've thought. I'll make the necessary arrangements to make sure you are never alone."

"Thank you, Bubba. You're the best."

"I'll call your doctor as soon as I get you in bed and ask him to recommend a caregiver to come stay with you. I believe there are agencies that do this sort of thing."

Her lip trembled. "A *caregiver*? Seriously? You think I want a stranger holding my hand, if it happens again?" She sobbed in between breaths. "Don't you understand? It's you I need, Bubba. Not some cold-hearted caregiver."

"Okay, okay. Calm down, honey. I'm sure it's not good for you to get upset in your condition. We'll figure out something." He drove to her house and helped her inside.

Her voice weakened to a whisper. "I'm feeling faint, darling. Would you pull the covers back, and help me in bed?"

"Sure." His throat ached. How many women could face death so bravely? Had a hard life made Greta strong? His emotions scrambled for clarity. Something inside him made an abrupt change when he learned he was about to lose her. Was it pity—or had he fallen in love with her? He gnawed on his fist when his thoughts turned to Jackie. Jackie was a young man's fantasy, and he was no longer a young man. It was time to live in the here and now. He sat by Greta's bed, and in a matter of minutes, she was sound asleep. After staying awake all night, she'd likely sleep for hours.

Bubba left a note on the bedside table in the event she happened to awake before he got back. *Gone to check on the diner. Will be back shortly.* He slipped off his loafers and tiptoed out.

****

Just as Bubba hoped, everything was under control. Keely and Lexie appeared to be enjoying one another's company, and hearing their laughter was a welcomed sound. He walked in the kitchen, and took the lid off the turnip greens, checked the fried chicken, gravy, creamed potatoes and corn bread. He had to admit he couldn't have done better. He smiled. "I suppose you two set out to prove I'm not needed around here."

Keely giggled. "We've had a couple of near disasters, but the customers are awesome. Not a single gripe all morning."

Lexie said, "Best not to look in the oven."

Bubba's lip curled. He walked over, opened the oven door and laughed. "What happened?"

"The meringue flopped. We don't know what we did wrong. It's getting late and we don't have time to try it again."

Bubba laughed. "I'm sure you didn't beat it long enough."

"We beat it and beat it. It wouldn't froth up like it does with you."

"Then likely you dropped a little yolk into your egg whites. It won't take us long, working together. I'll make the crust, and Keely, you stir up the ingredients for the chocolate pie. Lexie, you watch the front, and I'll make the meringue."

He spread the fluffy white meringue atop four pies, when his cell phone rang. He pulled it from his pocket and groaned, seeing Greta's name appear on the screen. "But Greta . . . but . . . Greta, I thought . . . Calm down, honey. Please don't cry. Since you said you were awake all night last night, I thought you'd sleep for several hours. I needed to check on the girls. I didn't intend to stay, but they had an emergency."

"Girls? What girls?"

He stalled.

"Bubba, please tell me you haven't hired a new waitress." She snubbed. "As your accountant, I can tell you that now is not the time to be hiring extra help."

"Greta, I need for you to let me worry about the diner. You don't need the added stress."

"Bubba. Is it true? Did you hire a new girl?"

He bit his lip and glanced at Keely and Lexie, both obviously eaves dropping.

"No, Greta."

"But you used the plural."

His pulse raced. He hated what she was going through, but was that any reason to allow her to turn him in to a henpecked milksop? He inhaled, causing his broad chest to protrude. He glanced at the two eavesdroppers, then covered his mouth and whispered into the phone, "Greta, I couldn't leave Lexie to handle the diner alone. She can't cook, and Keely can."

Her voice cracked. "Keely?"

"Yes. I needed her, Greta, so I could be with you, and she was gracious enough to put our differences aside and come. I know how you feel, but I have a diner to run." He was ashamed of his curt answer, but he felt as if he'd fallen into a giant pool of swirling water, being tossed around, flailing out of control. He supposed the fact he'd been single all his life, making his own decisions, left him unwilling to accept someone else making decisions for him. Would things be different, once they tied the knot? He knew the answer. Greta's strong will could be both an asset and a liability. But the knot wasn't tied. Not yet. Not until April 15th. Scarlet O'Hara in Gone With the Wind had the perfect solution. Why worry today when you could put it off until tomorrow.

Greta's voice softened. "Don't be angry with me, darling. I'm just suggesting you should've discussed it with me first."

"And what would you have told me to do, Greta?" He hoped his tone didn't reflect his frustration.

"Well, you'll never know, since you didn't bother to share it with me, but let's don't waste precious time arguing, sweetheart. Just come home when you can."

"*Home*? You make it sound as if we're living together, Greta. If someone should hear you say that, they're likely to misunderstand."

"Who cares? I love the sound of it, darling, don't you? Oh, how I wish April would hurry and get here, but I suppose it's wrong to wish my life away. I've already looked at quite a few houses and can't wait to show them to you. Maybe this weekend?"

"We'll talk about it later, Greta. The lunch crowd is beginning to come in, but Keely and Lexie seem to be handling things, so I'll be there in a few minutes."

He hung up the phone and caught Keely staring. "What?"

"My question is not what, but why, Bubba?"

"I don't know what you mean?"

"Why are you letting that woman run all over you?"

"Is that what I'm doing?"

"I think you can answer that better than I. What do you think?"

He nodded. "I suppose you're right, but you don't understand. She's dying, Keely."

Her face paled. "Dying? Are you sure?"

"I'm sure."

Keely's eyes squinted into tiny slits. "Wait. Is that what she told you, or do you know it for a fact? I'm sorry, Bubba, but I

186

don't trust that woman."

"Greta told me, but the nurse confirmed it when I was at the hospital."

Keely cringed. "Yikes. I'm sorry, I didn't know."

"It was a shock to me also. I need to get back over there. Think you girls can handle things here?"

"Sure, Bubba. Do what you need to do."

"Thanks." He knew exactly what he needed to do, although Greta would pitch a fit. He had to make her understand he had a business to run and couldn't possibly walk off and leave it. Bubba looked up the number of Greta's doctor.

"Dr. Harmon is in surgery, sir. This is his nurse. Can I help you?"

"I hope so. A patient, Greta Pugh was released from the hospital earlier today."

"Oh, I'm quite familiar with Miss Pugh. I was the nurse on duty when you came for her this morning."

"Well, you probably aren't aware, but Greta lives alone. I'm calling to see if the doctor will approve a home health nurse to stay with her."

"Sir, I can tell you now, she doesn't qualify."

"You know that without consulting the doctor?"

"I do. I'll try to say this as gentle as I know how. Home Health nurses aren't assigned to coddle unstable individuals."

Bubba felt his blood boil. He refused to respond, afraid of what he might say.

"If your Miss Pugh gets ready to pull another stunt like last night, she'll find a way to do it, with or without the pills, even if you hire someone to watch her 24/7. She may not be so smart next time."

"Excuse me? You sound as if you're implying Greta tried to commit suicide."

"Well, I apologize for implying something that would be far from the truth."

Bubba cringed. How could a head nurse be so incompetent? "I'm talking about the lady in Room 212 who was discharged earlier today."

"I'm quite aware which room she was in." The brashness in her voice suddenly softened. "Sir, I sense your heart is in the right place and that you have no idea what transpired last night. Please allow me to set your mind at ease. Miss Pugh had no intention of committing suicide."

"Then why did you—"

"Hold on, I haven't finished. I'm saying she knew what she was doing. She knew exactly how many pills to take to win sympathy, and she wasted no time calling 911. Likely, she held pills in one hand and the phone in the other."

"That can't be. She called me shortly after she was brought in, and she was in tremendous pain. When I asked the nurse on duty to give her something, she said there was nothing that could help her. And then, if I'm not mistaken, it was *you*, who told me quite plainly that Greta was dying."

"I beg your pardon, I never said she was dying. I said she *could've* died. It's a stupid stunt for someone to pull who has no desire to make it permanent. The Rescue Squad was there within minutes, but anything could've happened to cause a delay. Her plot could've easily backfired. I suppose you know this isn't the first time she's tried this trick."

Bubba's heart beat against his chest. "Thank you, ma'am. I had no idea."

"I'm sorry for being blunt, but I felt obligated to explain why your lady friend doesn't qualify for Home Health."

"I understand." He scratched his head. "Well, actually, there's a lot I don't seem to understand, but I will soon."

Bubba used the key Greta had given him and tiptoed back to her bedroom. "Greta? You awake?"

"Oh, honey, I've been so bored. I thought you'd never get here. Please don't leave me again. I have too much time to think about my condition, when I'm alone."

He drew a deep breath. "What *is* your condition, Greta?"

"I told you earlier, Bubba. I can't talk about it. Please don't ask."

"Then maybe I should tell *you*."

"What d'ya mean, darling?"

"Since you overdosed and have had your stomach pumped, the way I see it, you no longer have a *condition*."

"Who told you such nonsense?"

"Greta, stop it. I know the truth. The only nonsense is what

189

you've led me to believe. You must think I'm a real idiot, and personally I don't think it'd be far from the truth."

She turned on the waterworks. "Bubba, it's not like you think. Honest, you have it all wrong."

"I'm sure you don't know what I think, Greta, because if you did, you wouldn't continue to lie. I know what you did. I just can't understand why you did it."

Tears rolled down her face like a gusher. "Okay, I admit it. It was an overdose. And I did it because I was depressed. I thought I was losing you, Bubba. I wouldn't want to live without you. I couldn't. I'd make sure to do it right, the next time." She dried her face with the corner of the bedsheet.

"Greta, that's not fair. Promise me you'll never do anything that stupid again. I was worried sick about you."

She peeked out from behind the sheet. "Were you, darling? That's all I needed to hear. I promise to trust you from now on."

"Have I ever given you reason not to trust me?"

"Bubba, I was terrified you'd leave me for *her*."

"Her? What are you talking about, Greta?"

"You hear a lot when waiting tables. They say you were in love with a girl in high school, got her pregnant and she left town to have the baby. While she was in Virginia, they say she met and fell in love with a boy whose family once lived here, and that he adopted your baby girl."

Bubba bit his lip. "*My* baby girl?" He stared into space.

"They say her husband recently died, and now she's moved

back with your daughter, so she can be near you."

"This gets crazier by the minute. Is there more?"

"Only that you're still in love with her." She whined. "Please tell me they're wrong, sweetheart. Don't you see? That's why I did what I did. I'd rather die than to live without you."

Bubba had trouble catching his breath. After several seconds of silence, he said, "Greta, did you count how many times you used the phrase, 'they said?' I don't know who you've been listening to, but '*they*' are peddling nonsense."

Greta's squeal indicated her delight. She slung her legs off the bed, jumped up, ran over to Bubba's chair and plopped down in his lap with her arms wrapped around his neck. "That's all I wanted to hear, my darling." She showered his face with rapid kisses. "How could I have doubted you?"

"Now, that we both know you're fine, I'm going to the diner to make sure the girls don't need me."

Her lips formed a pout. "Bubba, Lexie is as sweet as they come, but for whatever reason, Keely hates me, and you know it's the truth. She's out to turn you against me."

His jaw jutted forward. "Greta, Keely is my niece and she'll work there, whenever she chooses, and if you can't take it, maybe you should be the one to leave." Greta's quivering lip indicated his sharp words cut to the bone.

Her voice trembled. "Sure. Whatever you say, hon."

"Aww, Greta, I've hurt your feelings, and I apologize." What was wrong with him? Why did he keep hurting those closest to him? First Keely, then Trey, now Greta. He thought of the Apostle Paul and suddenly could relate. The things he wanted to do, he didn't, and those things he didn't want to do, he managed somehow to do. He'd never had this problem before. Before what? He only asked himself once, for he knew the answer. *Before Greta.*

"You're forgiven, darling. Does that mean you'll tell her not to come back?"

Bubba bit his tongue and shook his head. "No, Greta. You and Keely need to put your differences aside, since you'll likely be working closely together at times. I've stayed longer than I intended. It's time for me to go."

Bubba drove to Municipal Park and sat in the car, allowing Greta's words to soak in. So, tongues were wagging, spreading lies. Not that he cared for himself—he'd long ago learned to deal with the false accusations—but it wasn't fair to Jackie to be treated like a trollop, when she'd done nothing wrong.

He thought of her beautiful daughter, Lexie. Surely, she'd be crushed if she were to get wind of the gossip. Instead of a solution, his thoughts quickly turned to vain imaginations. What would his life have been like, if Lexie really was his daughter? His throat tightened as he imagined the three of them living together as a family.

A song came over the radio, which reminded him his situation wasn't unique, although it didn't make the pain any less raw. He drove away, and on the way to the diner, found himself singing, "If you can't be with the one you love, love the one you're with."

He gripped the steering wheel until his knuckles turned white.

CHAPTER 24

Lexie tried to remember a time in her life when she was this happy. She knew the answer. *Never.* She loved her job. She loved her boss. She loved Jackie. She loved River.

Her throat tightened. *River?* Was it love? Really? Or was it an infatuation with a Chaplain who befriended her and showed compassion when she was at her lowest ebb and desperate for someone to care?

Ridiculous. Of course, she loved him. She recalled saying goodbye at the Tutwiler gate, and the longing in her heart to feel his arms closing around her. He felt it, too. Not that he said so with his lips, but his eyes confirmed it. If that wasn't love, she didn't know what it could be.

For the first time in a long time, life was good. She could hardly wait to get to the diner every morning. The breakfast crowd was the best. Most were elderly, and her favorites were the Maitres. Uncle Homer and Aunt Lorene. They appeared pleased that she referred to them with the same affectionate terms as

Bubba.

Uncle Homer finished his Crossword Puzzle, and they'd said their goodbyes, when he stood and knocked over Aunt Lorene's cane. Aunt Lorene, still seated, said, "I can reach it from here, Homer." Lexie screamed when Aunt Lorene leaned forward, causing her chair to fall. The elderly lady hit the floor with a thud.

Bubba ran out of the kitchen. "Stand back everyone. Aunt Lorene, don't try to get up. I'll call the Rescue Squad and they'll take you to the hospital. And Uncle Homer, you need to sit back down. You don't look so good."

"I don't feel good, son. It's all my fault. If I hadn't knocked over her cane, this would never have happened."

Aunt Lorene said, "Nonsense, Homer. I should've let you pick it up, but I had to be hard-headed and insist I could reach it. I leaned over too far."

"Where do you hurt, Renie?"

She rubbed her wrist. "I tried to catch myself with my hand, and I'm afraid my wrist may be broken."

Her husband's voice trembled. "Where else do you hurt?"

"Sugar, to tell the truth, I'm so shook up, I can't tell which part of me hurts the worst. I hit on the side of my hip, but then my leg aches all the way down to my toes."

Within ten minutes the EMT guys rushed into the diner and had Aunt Lorene on a stretcher and were shoving her into the vehicle.

Bubba said, "Come on, Uncle Homer, you can ride with me

and we'll follow them." He turned to Lexie. "I hate to leave you by yourself."

"No. Go. I'll be fine."

"Thanks. There are plenty of cooked grits on the stove, ham and bacon fried, and biscuits in the warmer. Uh . . . can you cook eggs?"

She snickered. "I can boil them."

He winked. "Folks around here are super. They'll understand when you tell them what happened. Most who are here for breakfast know the Maitres."

Lexie's heart sank, hearing the siren whisking Aunt Lorene away.

Bubba called Greta when he reached the hospital. "Greta, can you cook?"

She giggled like a school girl. "Of course, darling. I'm a great cook. Is that one of your requirements for a wife?"

He ignored the question. "I need you to get to the diner as soon as possible to help Lexie with breakfast and finish up lunch. I have cabbage and yams cooking, but I need you to fry up the pork chops and make the cornbread."

He heard a loud groan. "Greta, I need you. You don't have to come back tonight, but Lexie can't cook, and I can't leave here."

"Can't leave? Where are you?"

"At the hospital. Aunt Lorene took a bad tumble this morning at the diner, and she's in surgery."

"Oh, m'goodness. You don't think they'll sue, do you? Have you contacted a lawyer? You need to get ahead of them on this, sweetheart."

"For crying out loud, Greta, we're talking about Uncle Homer and Aunt Lorene. You haven't even asked what type surgery she's having. Or don't you care?"

"What kind of question is that? Of course, I care. But I care more about you, sweetheart. I know how much the diner means to you. It'd break my heart to have some high and mighty lawyer steal it from you. What about Keely? You've said she's a great cook."

Bubba bit the inside of his cheek. Now that it was coming down to Greta having to cook, she was willing for Keely to work? "As a matter of fact, Greta, Keely's out of town." Why waste time talking? "Can you do this for me, or not?"

"Well, I suppose so, since it's an emergency, but cooking in a hot, greasy diner is not my thing."

"I know, Greta. We'll find your thing later. Right now, I need help."

"Bubba, are you being sarcastic?"

"Yeah, I guess I was. I need to get off the phone and check on Uncle Homer. He's holding up as well as to be expected. Thanks for asking."

"Bubba, what's happened to you lately? You're being cruel. I was just about to ask about the old fellow. I'm glad he's doing well."

She was right. He *was* doing it again. "Sorry, Greta. Not trying to make excuses, but I'm under a lot of stress. These two people mean the world to me, and I'm really worried about Aunt Lorene."

"Of course, you are, and I understand, Bubba, but it hurts when you talk mean to me."

"I know, and there's no justification for it. I apologize. As soon as I hear from the doctor, I'll let you know."

"Please try not to worry. I'm sure the old woman will fair fine. She's a crusty ol' soul. Come back as soon you know something."

"I promise. And thanks for taking care of lunch."

"Of course. I'm sorry I was slow to agree when you asked me, but I didn't want to tell you how bad I was hurting. If it hadn't been for the horrific pain, I would never have hesitated."

"Feeling better, now?"

"It doesn't matter. We do what we must do. Right? I'll be in no shape to close tonight since I'll need to go to bed as soon as lunch is over. It'll wear me out to stand in front of a hot stove for hours. Don't bother making the night deposit. Just bag up the money and receipts and lock them in the safe. I'll take care of it tomorrow."

"No problem, and thanks again for pitching in."

CHAPTER 25

Bubba paced back and forth in the surgical waiting room, anxiously awaiting the doctor's call. He raced to the phone when it rang. After a brief conversation, he hung up, walked over and knelt beside Uncle Homer, who sat with his head lowered in prayer.

Bubba nudged him. "Uncle Homer, the doctor just called, and they've put a pin in Aunt Lorene's hip, and a cast on her arm."

"Can I see her?"

"Not yet, but she's gonna be fine. However, there's something else we need to take care of. I talked to your cardiologist earlier and he'd like to see you in his office at four o'clock."

Uncle Homer choked up. "Not today. I know you're concerned about me, Bubba, but I'll be fine. It's Renie I'm worried about."

"I understand. But she's getting great care. She's going to need you in good health, so promise me you'll go and let the doc check you out."

"I appreciate your concern, son, but Renie will be in a room by four, and you know I can't leave her."

"Uncle Homer, the doctor's office is on third floor here in the hospital, and you *can* do this—not for me, but for Aunt Lorene. She needs you to stick around to go with her to breakfast every morning, more than she needs you holding her hand for a few minutes in a hospital room. You have good friends here with you, so you won't be alone, and I really need to get back to the diner. I can't leave, though, until you promise you'll go. Four o'clock."

He nodded slowly. "Okay, son. I'll be there. I promise."

****

Bubba got to the diner at one-thirty and rushed into the kitchen. "Thanks, Greta. Looks like everything is running smoothly. I know you don't enjoy cooking, but I really appreciate your helping out."

"Well, I think this little episode, helps us to see we should hire another waitress. Let's try to find someone who not only waits tables but can pitch in and cook when needed. We'll need someone in April, for sure, while we're on our cruise."

His teeth ground together. "Greta, I thought you were against hiring extra help?"

"I was, darling, but I see now, you were right, and I was wrong. I'll put an ad in the paper tomorrow."

"No, Greta. I'll take care of it."

With her arms crossed over her chest, she said, "Bubba Knox, you are such a stubborn man. When will you realize we're a team, and you need to allow me to share in the responsibilities? You had no problem telling me to come cook, and I came, didn't I? I wish you'd learn to trust me with decision making. After all, I've handled a trucking business. Running a diner is nothing compared to what I've done in the past."

Why bother with an answer? It would likely come out wrong, anyway.

"Bubba, are you listening to a word I'm saying?"

"I hear you, Greta."

Lexie pushed the kitchen door open. "I need two hamburgers, one all the way, the other without onions, and a plate lunch."

Bubba gave a quick salute. "Got it."

Lexie grabbed a couple of tea glasses and headed back to the dining room.

Greta stood on her tiptoes, and kissed Bubba on the cheek. "Hon, I wouldn't leave you, but to tell the truth, I'm worn to a frazzle. Heat takes a lot out of me. For some reason, my fibromyalgia is always worse after I stand over a hot stove for any length of time. But don't you worry about me, ya hear? I'll go home, crash in bed and stay there until morning."

"Yeah, go rest. I can handle it from here."

She tilted her head back and closed her eyes, waiting for a kiss.

Bubba turned the sizzling burgers. He didn't feel very romantic, but didn't she deserve a little affection for all the pain she'd endured for his sake? He kissed her and held her in his arms. Now, he didn't want to let go. It felt good. Maybe married life was just what he needed to prevent him from turning into a contrary old codger, and lately it seemed to be the track he was on. Maybe Greta wasn't the one he loved, but he couldn't deny she was a good woman—a little temperamental—but a good woman. More than he deserved. He pecked her on the nose and loosened his grip.

"Bubba Knox, you're the best. What a lucky girl I am to have found you. I'd love to stay, and I would if not for the pain."

"It's not necessary. Lexie and I have this, so get outta here. Thanks for coming, Greta. You were a big help."

"I'm glad. I love you, sweetheart." She waited. When he didn't respond, she said, "Remember to put the money and the receipts in the bank bag and lock them in the safe. I'll take care of the deposit tomorrow night."

Bubba nodded, then rang the bell to let Lexie know her order was ready.

She walked in and glanced around. "Where's Greta?"

"She left out the back door."

"Is she coming back."

"Nope. I'm staying. Think you might help me close?"

Lexie picked up the tray. "Not a problem."

"Sure you don't mind?"

"Of course not. In fact, I wanted to talk to you about the possibility of closing on Wednesday nights. Only if Greta agrees, of course."

"Why Wednesday?"

"I need to get this out to the table first. Be right back."

When she returned, she said, "Bubba, if you or Greta have a problem with my idea, please don't mind telling me. It's just a suggestion, and it's okay if you say no, but I enjoyed being around the church singles last week, and just thought . . ."

He smiled. "Do you mean you enjoyed the Church Singles, or is there a particular 'Church Single,' who caught your eye?"

She chewed on her lower lip. "I have no idea what you're talking about."

"Just picking at you, Lex. Not a problem with me, and Greta won't mind. The less she has to work, the better she likes it."

Lexie tried to cover her smile. "Thanks, Bubba. You're the best."

At the end of the night, Bubba said, "Lexie, would you mind totaling the receipts, then take the money from the register and make sure it balances?"

"I don't mind, but Greta instructed me to put the money in the sack along with the receipts and let her take care of it tomorrow."

"I heard her, but you need to learn to do this."

"Thanks, Bubba."

"For what?"

"For trusting me."

"You've given me no reason not to."

Bubba finished cleaning up in the kitchen, then walked out to the dining room. "What's wrong, Lexie?"

"Not sure. I have all the tickets, but the money doesn't add up."

"Too much or too short?"

"Short."

"How much?"

"A lot. One-hundred ten dollars and twenty-five cents."

He shrugged. "Don't worry about it. I'm ready to get home and I'm sure you are, too. Just make a note. We'll let Greta find it tomorrow. If it was only a few dollars, we could assume it's a mathematical error, but an error that large sounds more like Greta might've paid a vender and got busy cooking lunch and forgot to put the receipt in the box."

"I don't remember seeing a vender come in, but maybe you're right, because I've added it three times and it comes up the same every time."

"Venders sometimes come through the back door. I'm sure Greta can find the problem, so put it in the safe and we'll let her figure it out tomorrow. I need to get out of here and head back to the hospital."

"Have you heard any more, since you left?"

"Yeah. I called Uncle Henry and he's upset because the doctor told him to find a caregiver to help with Aunt Lorene. Of course, he's stubborn as an ox, and doesn't want to admit he needs help, but I'll start looking for someone tomorrow."

"Oh, that breaks my heart. He's such a precious soul. I wish there were two of me. I'd help him for free."

"You've got a big heart, kid." Bubba locked up the money and turned out the lights. "Let's get outta here."

CHAPTER 26

Lexie trudged in the house with a heavy heart.

Jackie laid her book down and looked up from her chair in the living room. "What's wrong, honey? You look as if you've lost your best friend."

She feigned a smile. "That would be you, Jackie, and you're still here."

"Sweetheart, God was so good to send you to me. He knew what I needed. You're more than my best friend. What's going on?"

Lexie told her about Aunt Lorene, and how Bubba was worried about Uncle Homer, and the problem with locating a caregiver.

Jackie didn't bat an eye, as she listened to every detail. Then, she said, "I can do it."

"What?"

"Be her caregiver."

"Oh, Jackie. You would be perfect. But are you sure?"

"I need a job, Lexie, and I have no qualifications. This, I could do." A knot formed in her stomach. "Just one problem, I didn't consider."

"What?"

"Bubba. He'd be over there a lot."

"Yes, but that shouldn't keep you from doing what you know you need to do." She chewed her lip. "Sorry. Who am I to tell you what you need to do?"

"But you're right. There's no reason why I should keep trying to avoid Bubba. Tomorrow, tell him not to look further. I'll do it."

Lexie giggled. "But you have no idea how much it pays. Are you sure?"

"I'm sure."

"Then you come in the diner tomorrow and tell him yourself. The sooner you face your fears, whatever they are, the sooner you can get over them. Come around ten. That's after breakfast, but before the lunch crowd comes in."

Jackie laughed. "Yes ma'am. You're getting a mite bossy, aren't you?"

"Maybe. But you remember I told you about Pastor Blocker telling me that God has a wonderful plan for my life, and how I found it hard to believe, but discovered he was right?"

"I remember."

"Well, I think God's working something good out in your life, also."

"Honey, I don't doubt God loves me, but there are often lasting consequences to the bad decisions we make in life. I thought marrying the father of my baby would be for her good. I was wrong, and I'll live with the consequences forever."

"Your life isn't over, Jackie. You're a beautiful woman and have lots of years ahead of you, so don't sell yourself short."

"You remind me of Cami. She would've said it the same way you did. I wish you two couldn've met."

"You've never told me what happened. Not that I'm pressing you, but whenever you get ready to share it, I'd love to know more about her."

"Thank you, honey. She's a year younger than you. Her hair was the brightest red when she was born and stayed that way until she was eight or nine, when it began to turn a dark auburn. She has the most beautiful skin, and those eyes . . . oh, m'goodness, they're the brightest blue and twinkle like stars." Her eyes welled with tears.

"Jackie, you speak of her in the present tense. Is she . . . is she alive?"

Jackie's lip quivered. "I don't know, but I want to believe she is. I want to believe it with all my heart, yet I know I'm probably in denial. It's easier than admitting I'll never see her again."

"Can you tell me what happened?"

"Thank you for your interest, sweetheart. I've kept quiet so long, but I'd love to talk about her. Jacob reprimanded me any time I brought up her name. He was a hard-hearted man, and never showed me or Cami any affection. I never understood why he was so cold toward us, until the night he died." She covered her face with her hands. "I didn't mean to get into the negative. I want to forget the bad times and concentrate on the good times we had. She was my heart."

"How did it happen, Jackie? I mean, was she sick? An accident?"

"That's the thing. I don't know. I'm afraid I'll never know. She disappeared."

Lexie reached for her hand. "I'm sorry. I'm so sorry. Kidnapped?"

"That's what I believed. The police tried to convince me she ran away, but I know it's not true. Why would she run away? She and I were very close, and she lacked for nothing. We lived in a mansion, she drove a new convertible, had credit cards to all her favorite stores. Yet, it was all left behind. Even her car. Tell me, does that make sense to you?"

"Jackie, did you ever consider it might not have been material things she wanted?"

"I hear what you're saying, but if I made it sound as if that's all she had, it wasn't my intention. She was dearly loved, not only by me, but by everyone who met her. She had that winning personality that drew people to her. She was a freshman at Virginia Tech when she disappeared. She was elected Freshman Beauty and was on the dance team. I'm telling you, Lexie, she had everything going for her, and it doesn't make sense that she'd run away."

Jackie glanced at the clock on the mantle. "Goodness, I didn't realize it was so late. Sleep well, sweetheart. I'll see you in the morning."

Lexie's tone softened. "Ten o'clock, right?"

Jackie sucked in a lungful of air and let it out slowly. "I'll be there."

CHAPTER 27

Jackie tossed and turned all night. *I can do this. I can. I can.* She continued to repeat if until the sun shone through the shutters.

She crawled out of bed and pulled out her yellow wool skirt and matching sweater. She knew exactly what she'd wear, since she'd had all night to think about it. Bubba's favorite color was yellow. Her pulse raced. Was she insane? She had no idea what his favorite color might be. She was thinking of a high school kid, who said over twenty years ago that she looked beautiful in yellow. Since that day, it had been her favorite color.

Dressed by seven o'clock, she tried to read as she waited for time to go. After reading the same page several times, she threw the book aside. How could she concentrate? What would she say to Bubba? *Hello, Bubba. How are you?* Or *Hi, Bubba, Good to see you?* She shook her head and tried again. This time, out loud. "Bubba, I was sorry to hear about Mr. and Mrs. Maitre. Lexie tells me they're looking for a caregiver.*"* That was it. Sounded casual enough, and to the point. When the hands on the clock finally reached nine-forty, she grabbed her purse and walked out the door.

****

Jackie walked in the diner with her heart beating so fast, she was afraid she'd faint. Lexie ran up and gave her a hug. "He's in the kitchen. I'll go get him."

She whispered. "Shouldn't we wait until he comes out?"

"Why? He's not busy. I just checked when I saw your car pull up. I'll go get him."

Before Jackie could object further, she saw Lexie's back as she ran into the kitchen.

Bubba walked out, drying his hands on a cloth. He gave a slight nod of his head. "Mornin', Jackie. Lexie says you have something to talk over?" He licked his dry lips. She'd always been a beauty, but never had he seen her looking so breath-taking. The sun coming through the plate glass window caused her hair to shimmer as if her head had been sprinkled with hundreds of tiny diamonds. She smiled, and his heart raced so fast it hurt.

"Hi, Bubba. You're looking good." Her face lit up like a red neon light, as if her own words caught her by surprise.

"Thanks." *Stupid. Stupid. Stupid. Why didn't I come back with a funny response? Something like . . .* He sighed. *Like what?* It was if every thought had been deleted from his mind. Wiped clean. Nothing there. Their gaze locked. He pressed his lips together. "You look good, too, Jackie." Yikes. What must she think of such a lame remark. He wanted to pound his head against a brick wall. *'Too?* You look good, *too?* Sounded as if he agreed he looked good. "I didn't mean *too.* I just meant . . ."

Her smile melted his insides. "I know what you meant, Bubba. I'm nervous, too." Her eyes twinkled. "And for the record, I meant to say *too.*"

His tight muscles relaxed. "Really?"

She nodded. "Really."

He sat two cups of coffee on the table. "Coffee?"

"I'd love that, but I didn't come for coffee. I came to talk to you about something. If it's a bad time, I can come back later."

"Not a bad time at all. What's on your mind?"

"Lexie told me you're looking for a caregiver for Mrs. Maitre."

He nodded. "That's right. Do you have someone in mind?"

She wrung her hands together. "What about me?"

"You?"

Her brow creased. "Do you have a problem with me taking care of her?"

"Of course not. It's just . . ." He stroked his chin. "I don't know."

"I really would like to do this, Bubba. What are your concerns? Maybe if you tell me, we can figure what we can do to make it work."

"Jackie, Aunt Lorene will need someone strong enough to help her in and out of the wheelchair. Help her dress."

213

"And you're saying I can't do that?"

"Have you ever had nursing experience?"

"No, but from what I understand, she doesn't need a nurse. She needs a caregiver. I'm stronger than I look, Bubba. My daughter and I belonged to a gym in Virginia. I'd have no problem lifting her."

"You seem determined."

"I am. I need something to do, Bubba, and this is something I could do and feel good about. Please?"

He chewed the inside of his cheek. "There's a problem you aren't aware of, and I don't know any way to avoid telling you. Aunt Lorene has held a senseless grudge against you, for over twenty-years, and I'm afraid it's not lessened one iota in all this time. As much as I'd like for you to be her caregiver, she won't approve."

"A grudge? You must be wrong, Bubba. She hardly knew me. What could she possibly have against me?" She covered her eyes with her hand. "Oh. I get it. Because she heard I left town because I was pregnant. Right?"

He couldn't look her in the eyes. With his head lowered, he nodded. "Jackie, when you left so suddenly, talk got out that I got you pregnant."

Jackie's mouth flew open. "You? Oh, no, Bubba. I had no idea. I am so sorry. I never should've left. If I could do it over, I wouldn't leave."

He wanted to say, "If I had it to do over, I'd go get you," but he didn't, because there were no do-overs. "Now, you know why I said you wouldn't want this job."

"But you're wrong, Bubba. I do want it. More than ever now. I want her to know me and to know the truth."

"If you really think you're game, but I'm warning you, she's tough as nails, and doesn't give in very easily."

"Please, give me a chance?"

"I'm afraid I don't get the last word, but I'll talk to both Uncle Homer and Aunt Lorene and get back with you. She won't need anyone until after she gets out of rehab."

"Thank you. That's all I ask." She picked up her cup and sipped the coffee.

He stood. "Coffee's cold by now. I'll get you a fresh cup."

"Don't bother. I've done what I came to do."

"Fine. I'll let you know their answer as soon as I have an opportunity to discuss it with them."

He watched as she walked out the door. Out of his life, just as she did twenty-three years, two weeks and four days ago.

CHAPTER 28

Greta sashayed into the diner at five o'clock Wednesday afternoon and announced, "Time for you to go home, Lexie."

"Home?"

Greta waved her hand, as if to shoo her out the door. "Yes, or wherever you go when your shift is over. No need to keep hanging around here, now that I'm here."

"I don't understand. I thought Bubba told you."

She lifted a shoulder in a shrug. "Oh, you mean about you wanting to close on Wednesdays?"

Lexie nodded.

"He told me you suggested it, but frankly, I don't think it's a wise idea. Have a good night. I'll see you tomorrow."

"But Bubba said . . ."

Greta plunked her hands on her hips. "I said good night, Lexie. It's time for you to go, sweetie."

"Is it because I couldn't get the books to balance? That's it, isn't it?"

"I didn't plan to bring it up, but now that you have, you'll recall I specifically told you to leave everything in the safe and I'd take care of it today. I hope I can find the error, for your sake, Lexie."

"For my sake? What do you mean? You don't think—"

"I'm not accusing you of anything, yet. I haven't had a chance to look for the error, but I will. It's time for you to go. See you tomorrow."

Bubba walked into the dining room, just as Lexie walked out. "Greta, you weren't scheduled to come in. Where's Lexie going?"

"I'm feeling better than I've felt all week, so I decided to come on to work. I told Lexie she could leave."

He rushed out the door. "Lexie! Where are you going?"

She turned. "Greta told me to leave."

"Who's your boss, Lexie?"

"You are, Bubba?"

"Who told you to close on Wednesday nights?"

She smiled, though her eyes glistened with tears. "You did."

"Exactly. Come inside. Greta will be taking the night off."

Lexie couldn't hear the conversation between Bubba and Greta, but it was like watching a silent movie. Greta's expression, and the way she slung a pointed finger in Bubba's face, left no mistaking that she was not happy with his decision.

From five o'clock until church let out at seven seemed like an eternity. Then, the door opened, and though he was in the middle of the crowd, Jamal was the first face she saw. Their gaze locked. She smiled. He didn't. Lexie's legs buckled.

She headed for the coffee pot, but he stopped her. "Excuse me, Lexie, but I'll make the coffee."

Her lips trembled. "Sure, Jamal. I'm sorry."

"No need for apologies." He took the top from the cannister and scooped coffee into the coffee maker.

Lexie couldn't get into the kitchen fast enough.

Bubba looked up from slicing pies. "Hey, what's wrong."

"Nothing."

"Something's wrong. Those are definitely tears I see."

"I'll be fine."

"Is it Jamal?"

She lowered her head. "Yeah, but I'm okay now."

"Lexie, I don't know what he said or did, but don't take it personally. There's something eating away at that boy, and I've been unable to find out what it is. I was glad when you said you wanted to close on Wednesdays, because I had hopes you could reach him."

She shook her head. "You can forget that idea. He made it obvious he wants nothing to do with me." She threw up her hands. "I don't get it, Bubba. He went over to the house two weeks ago, and we laughed and talked, and I thought . . .I really thought he was interested in me. How crazy is that?"

"Not crazy at all."

"Yes, it was. He probably acts like that with all the girls.

When he didn't show up last Wednesday, I should've known he was avoiding me. Then, tonight, he couldn't have made it any clearer if he'd written it in giant letters across his chest, saying, 'BUG OFF, LEXIE.'"

Lexie let out a long sigh, picked up a tray of pies and headed back into the dining hall. "Who wants coconut?" she asked, plastering a fake smile on her face.

When she placed a slice of pie at Jamal's place, he looked up and whispered. "Can I talk to you after everyone leaves?"

Her pulse raced. "Sure. I'll need to stay and help Bubba clean up, but it won't take long."

"Good."

Lexie glanced at her watch every ten minutes, wishing nine-thirty would come.

Everyone left, but Jamal, who lingered just outside the front door.

Bubba looked outside the plate glass window, then said, "Get outta here, Lexie."

"But I need to help you."

"Hey, I've done this for years. I can handle it. I see someone pacing back and forth in front of the diner, and I have a feeling he's not waiting for me."

"Thanks, Bubba," She reached up, hugged him, then hurried out the door.

CHAPTER 29

Jamal followed Lexie to the house on Bay Street. Jackie rose from her chair and laid down her book when they walked in. "Hey Jamal. Good to see you, again."

"Thanks Jackie. I hope you don't mind me dropping in this late."

"Not at all. You kids visit as long as you like. I almost went to sleep reading, so I think I'll call it a night."

After she left the room, Lexie said, "I thought you were mad at me."

"Why would I be mad at you?"

"You acted distant when you walked in. the diner tonight. Jamal, I haven't known you long enough to read your moods, but Bubba seems to think something's troubling you. He says you haven't been yourself lately. Is it something you can share with me?"

He pressed his lips together and stared into space.

Lexie waited.

His chest heaved out when he sucked in. "I'm stupid."

"Why would you say such a thing?"

"Because it's true. I'm stupid, Lexie. I'm twenty-seven years old. Older than any of the kids in the Singles and Career Class."

"So? They enjoy having you around, Jamal. I see how they interact with you."

"That's because they don't know the real me. It's all an act. Inside, I'm a scared little boy."

"What are you afraid of?"

"Winding up like my father. He was an alcoholic. Couldn't keep a job and wound up pan-handling in Pensacola. The state took me away when I was three. Does that shock you?"

"Should it?"

"No. But you're different. I think it would shock most of the girls in the group, who came from solid Christian homes with two loving parents. It's all gonna end soon, though."

"What's gonna end?"

"Me, being a part of the group."

"You're leaving?"

"Yep. Lexie, the truth is, I'm failing History. I can't afford to fail another subject. I might as well drop out now."

"Can I help?"

"You're sweet, but unless you know a quick way to grow brain cells, the answer is no. Like I said, I'm stupid."

"That's not true. Do you not like History? Because I love it.

Maybe I could study with you and together we'll make it fun."

"Sounds good, but I've struggled with this problem for years. I've tried to hide it, but I thought if I could just get a degree, I could land a good job. I don't want to be my daddy."

"And you don't have to be."

"Don't I? What if it's genetic? I always believed he couldn't hold a job because he drank. Maybe he drank because he couldn't hold a job."

"I don't believe it, Jamal. Are your books in your car?"

He nodded.

"Go get them."

"It's no use, Lexie. I'd be embarrassed."

"Why?"

"The truth is, I can't read."

"Then we'll work on reading."

"You don't understand. I. Can't. Read."

Lexie insisted he get his history book. "Turn to a chapter and read."

"I can't."

"We'll do it together."

He glared at her. "Why do you care if I fail?"

"Because I care about you."

He opened the book, attempted the first paragraph, then slammed the book shut. "I know you mean well, Lexie, but trust me, I'm wasting your time. You see how I stumbled over it, and you want to know the truth? I have no clue what I read. It could've been written in Latin. I'm hopeless."

"Not true, Jamal. So, you didn't learn to read in those first informative school years and I suppose no one took the time to notice. But you're very intelligent, and you can learn. I know you can."

"Lexie, I appreciate your willingness to help, but trust me, I've tried for years. I've spent hours forcing myself to read passages, but I always wind up with a terrific headache and the words all run together. Why keep putting myself through this? I'm done."

"No, Jamal. Please, don't. I know you can get past this. Don't give up."

"Why? What's the use? My next-door neighbor's kid is in third grade, and I'm serious when I say he reads books that I can't. I've always heard stupid can't be fixed. I didn't go to church last week, because my peers keep getting younger and younger, as more and more graduate, and move on to great jobs, while I keep struggling to finish. It's humiliating when they make jokes about me being a lifetime student. I only went to the Singles Group tonight, because I wanted to see you to thank you for your kindness, two weeks ago."

"Kindness? I don't understand."

"You invited me into your home when I was at my lowest ebb and made me comfortable in my own skin. I didn't feel the need to clown around and be someone else with you. It was a good feeling." He stood, tucked his book under his arm, and stretched out his hand for a handshake. "I hope I haven't embarrassed you."

Lexie ignored the outstretched hand and threw her arms around his neck. "Embarrassed me? Are you kidding? I'm the one who should be thanking you. I needed a friend, and I couldn't have found a better one."

"Even if he can't read?"

She pushed back, looked him in the eyes and winked. "Reading is overrated."

He smiled. "Tell that to my Professors."

"Don't give up. You've gone too far to quit now. Promise me you won't quit."

"I know you mean well, Lexie, but it's no use."

"I don't know what the problem is, Jamal, but as long as you have a problem, it will be my problem. Don't you dare drop out of the Singles Group. Honestly, I think they'd stop coming to the diner after church if you quit. It's your quick wit, and fun, lovable ways that keeps it lively. There was no laughter last week, and everyone left early. Can I tell you why? Because they missed you. They love you, Jamal."

CHAPTER 30

Thursday morning, Bubba determined to be firm. He braced for what was sure to come.

"Have you lost your mind, Bubba Knox?" Aunt Lorene screamed from her hospital bed. "It's out of the question. I won't hear of it."

Uncle Homer patted her arm. "Now, sugar, calm down. The doctor insists we get someone to help you get around until you're on your feet again."

"Why do I need someone to help me get around? That's what that confounded wheelchair is for. If they were doing their job here, I'd be walking by now."

Bubba said, "Aunt Lorene, you've had excellent care from the first day we brought you here. And if you continue to get good care, maybe you will be on your feet real soon."

"Homer is all the help I need. I don't want someone hanging around me all day long, treating me like an invalid—and especially that woman."

Bubba swallowed hard. "Aunt Lorene, you don't even know her."

"I know all I want to know about her. I know she came close to ruining your life. In fact, in a way, she did ruin it."

Homer said, "That's enough, sugar."

"I'll tell you when it's enough, Homer Maitre. I'll not stop protesting until you and Bubba both promise me you won't send Jackie Gorham over to my house. I can't stand to call her name, much less think of her putting her hands on me."

Homer glanced at Bubba. "Renie, the truth is, we've looked for someone else. Bubba has. I have. The nurses have. No one seems to be available."

Bubba sucked in a deep breath. "Aunt Lorene, I don't know why you say she ruined my life. I think I've had a pretty good life. I own the diner, where I get to do all the things I enjoy—visit with friends, meet new people, and cook. What's so bad about that?"

"Well, if not for that woman turning you sour on love, I'm sure you'd be married to a good woman and have a houseful of children. Instead, you pined your life away."

Bubba felt heat rising from his neck to the top of his head. His eyes burned. "Aunt Lorene, you can make up your mind to like the idea, because Jackie *will* be at your house when we get you home. And I don't want to hear of you doing or saying anything rude to her. Are we clear?"

Aunt Lorene's jaw dropped. "Well, I never!"

The corner of his lip held a gentle curl. "You may be doing a lot of things in the future that you *never*, so get used to it."

Uncle Homer put his hand over his lips to hide his smile. He looked at his wife's scrunched up face. Then slowly, the muscles relaxed. "I can see I'm not gonna win this war. Fine. She can come, but I'll tell you two right now, I'm not gonna like it."

Bubba said, "Y'all excuse me. I'll be right back." He walked down the hall and made a phone call. "Jackie, can you meet us at the Maitres' house in fifteen minutes?"

"No problem. I'm ready. So, Mrs. Maitre agreed?"

"She did, but under protest, so you might want to wear a suit of armor. Aunt Lorene was ornery before the fall. She's downright impossible now. Are you sure you're up to this?"

"Don't worry about me, Bubba. We'll do fine. Thanks for getting me the job."

He walked back to the room, just as the nurse walked in with the discharge papers. Bubba said, "You stay put, Aunt Lorene until the nurse helps you into the wheelchair."

Jackie was at the Maitre's house, waiting on the porch steps when Bubba drove up.

Lorene gave a loud huff. "Apparently, she couldn't wait to get here, but she doesn't fool me. She'd as soon put a spoonful of arsenic in my food. It's you, she's hoping to see, Bubba. I Suwannee, if that woman—"

"Aunt Lorene, if you care anything about me at all, you'll be civil to her. I assure you, she isn't interested in me and I'm not at all . . ." He stopped. "This is ridiculous. I don't know why I'm being defensive. The feelings Jackie and I shared in high school ended long ago. We've both moved on, and for you to keep harping on the past, makes it uncomfortable for both of us."

He walked around to the passenger side of the car and opened her door. She sat, unmoving.

"I can't help it, Bubba. I don't trust the woman, and to think she's going to be in my house, telling me when to get up, when to lie down, when to go to the bathroom makes me ill."

Bubba said, "Fine." He slammed her door, walked around the car, got in, and cranked it.

She said, "Where are we going?"

"To the nursing home, where you'll have caregivers who won't give a plug nickel about how you feel about something that happened over twenty years ago. They'll feed you, bathe you and push you in the hall to sit until time to be pushed into the dining hall. You should love it there." He put the car in reverse, backed out, then spun off.

"Stop this car this instant."

"Can't. We're going to Bay Minette. There's no rooms available in the nursing homes in Mobile."

"I'm perfectly capable of staying home. Take me back this instant. Homer, tell him!"

Homer spoke up from the back seat. "I don't see that you've given him a choice, Renie. Seems to me he's already checked into all your options, and he's offered you Jackie at home, or a stranger at the nursing home. It's a decision I can't make for you, hon."

"Okay, okay. She can stay. Turn around and take me home. Please?"

Bubba pulled into the nearest driveway and turned the car around.

Jackie was still sitting on the steps when they pulled up. Aunt Lorene said, "I suppose she knew we'd be back. She's still here."

Bubba didn't respond. He took her wheelchair from the trunk, then pushed it around to help her in it.

"Now, how do you propose to get a wheelchair up those three steps? I think if you help me, Bubba, I can manage to walk."

"Don't worry about how I'll do it, you sit there and watch."

He glanced up and acknowledged Jackie's presence with a nod, then pulled a wide board from under the steps, made a temporary ramp and pushed Aunt Lorene into the house. "I'll have someone over in the morning to build a permanent ramp at the back door."

"No need in going to that trouble, son. I don't plan on being in this chair much longer."

"I understand, but I've been meaning to have a ramp built for some time, now. You and Uncle Homer need to avoid steps wherever you can, even if you aren't using a wheelchair."

CHAPTER 31

After Bubba left, Jackie repeated the words she'd said to herself, only last night. *I can do this, I can do this, I can do this.* Being hated wouldn't be a new experience for her. She'd lived a lifetime with a man who despised her. How much worse could it be?

She knelt beside Mrs. Maitre's wheelchair. "Can I get you anything?"

The old woman didn't bother to look at her. "I want to get in my bed, but Homer can help me, thank you."

Homer shook his head. "You need to let her help you, sugar. That's what she's here for."

"Well, what's wrong with you, ol' man?"

Jackie spoke up. "Mrs. Maitre, he's right. It's my job to help you. The doctor has given your husband explicit instructions not to attempt holding on to you, or helping you in bed, in the car, or in the shower. You wouldn't want him to fall, too." Jackie pushed Mrs. Maitre's chair up to the bed. "Which side do you prefer?"

Her husband said, "She sleeps on the left side."

Jackie pulled the covers back, then lifted the patient to the bed, although the old lady made no effort to make the transition easier.

From her cocky expression it was evident Mrs. Maitre felt confident she'd won the first round. "Not as easy as you thought, is it?"

"No trouble at all. We'll do just fine. I've put a bell beside your bed. Ring it when you need to get up." Jackie walked out of the room, but heard the old woman say, "Homer, I had to give in to keep Bubba from doing something crazy. The only reason he was being so hard-headed was because he wanted that woman here where he could see her. Law, I don't know how he could stand her after the way she did him. Watch what I say. He'll be over here every night."

"Sugar, that won't be unusual, now will it? He dropped by about every night when she wasn't here."

"I wish he could get her out of his system. Fooling him once was one thing, but I thought he had better sense than to let her fool him twice."

Jackie's throat ached. *If only she knew the truth.*

****

That evening at nine-thirty, after a long and tiring day, Jackie pulled the potty chair to the edge of the bed where the elderly couple lay sleeping. She switched out the lights and tiptoed out.

Seeing a light on in her house when she drove down Bay Street, brought a sense of comfort. "Thank you, Lord, for Lexie. I know you brought her here for me."

Lexie threw open the door. "How did it go?"

Jackie rolled her eyes. "Well, she didn't dip me in tar and feather me, but only because she couldn't get out of the chair to do it."

"That bad, huh?"

Jackie groaned. "Worse."

"So, do you plan to quit?"

"Quit? That word's not in my vocabulary. No, I'll be back tomorrow for some of the same, but she hates me."

"Oh, Jackie, maybe it's your imagination. I can't imagine anyone hating you, and especially not sweet Aunt Lorene."

Jackie chuckled. "We must be talking about a woman with a dual personality. You get the good one, I get the evil one."

"Then tell Bubba you can't do it. There are other jobs. You can find one, I'm sure."

"Trust me, I considered it several times during the day. But the pay is better than any job I'll find with no qualifications. Besides, Bubba needs me."

"Jackie, you still love him. Why don't you tell him?"

"You're a romantic, Lexie. Things are more complicated than you could possibly understand."

"I'm sure you're exhausted, but I couldn't wait for you to get in, to talk to you about Jamal. I wanted to talk last night, but you were asleep when he left. Do you mind staying up a few minutes longer?"

"I couldn't go to sleep now, if I wanted to. I need to unwind. Give me time to take a hot bath and get on pajamas, and you can talk all night. I'd love it."

"Thanks."

Jackie came out wearing cute pajamas, and her hair tied up in a towel, looking much younger than her forty-two years. "Okay, kid. What's going on with that good-looking Jamal?"

Lexie giggled. "He is cute, isn't he?"

"He's a hunk." She chuckled, and pulled her feet under her, while sitting on the sofa. "So tell me all about him."

"I found out why he's been so down."

"Oh?"

"Yes! When he wasn't at church last week, everyone said it was unusual and all agreed he hadn't been himself lately—then they began to talk about a church robbery . . . Jackie, I'm ashamed to admit it, but the thought crossed my mind—"

She smiled. "That it was Jamal?"

Lexie swallowed. "Yes, and now I feel awful."

"Honey, you'd only been around him one time, when he came to the house the week before. You didn't know him. In fact, even though he came over again last night, you still don't know him. Not really. It pays to go slow in making new relationships, especially with all the mind-altering drugs that are out there. Drugs can cause good people to do bad things."

Lexie laughed. "I may not know who robbed the church, but I

know who didn't. It wasn't Jamal. I'm sure of it. I'm also sure he's not on drugs, because I now know what's been troubling him."

"Sweetheart, all I'm saying is be careful. You've just met this young man."

"He's embarrassed, Jackie. He feels everyone keeps graduating but him, and yet he's older than any of the others. I want to help him, but how? What can I do?"

"Well, I'm sorry he's having a difficult time getting his degree, but knowing the problem relieves my mind. Is it a time issue? Perhaps his part-time job keeps him from spending enough time in the books." Jackie's heart ached, looking across at this beautiful young girl, who sought her advice. How grateful she was for the opportunity, but how desperately she wished she could be having such a conversation with Cami. *Oh, Lord, where is my baby?*

Lexie said, "No, his job isn't the problem. Jackie, he can't read."

Jackie swallowed hard and gathered her thoughts. "He can't what?"

"Read. Jamal can't read. That's why he's become withdrawn. Said he felt stupid and was certain everyone in the group looked at him as being dumb, which is far from the truth. But he clowned around to feel accepted. He has an amazing wit, and I don't think it was hard for him to be the life of the party, until he got his last test back."

"How did that change things?"

"He said he'd never missed a class, he knew the material, and had studied all night the night before the test, but he failed. It devastated him to think he might fail the semester. He felt it was hopeless to continue."

Jackie's eyes squinted. "Honey, do you think he could be dyslexic?"

Lexie bit her lip. "No way. He's super intelligent. He has an amazing vocabulary and is a great conversationalist. I don't get it, unless it's a mental block that happens at test time."

"Honey, people who are dyslexic are often brilliant. They do well on oral tests, but will often flunk a written test, even when they're familiar with the material."

"Seriously? I thought it was people who were . . . you know . . . slow learners. I'd love it if it turned out that this really is his problem, but it seems too much to hope for."

Jackie chuckled. "Perhaps I've not explained it well. Even though many dyslexic people are brilliant, I didn't mean to imply it's something to be desired."

"I understand, but there's more to it than I've told you. If being a slow reader was his only problem, I wouldn't be so concerned. Truth is, I've been afraid to admit my fears."

"What is it you're afraid of?"

She closed her eyes and mumbled. "He may have a brain tumor."

"Oh, sweetheart, are you serious? I'm so sorry. What are his symptoms?"

"He gets headaches when he tries to read. He said the words jump around and he often reads the same passage several times trying to make sense of it. Doesn't that sound like a tumor to you?"

Jackie smiled. "No, Lexie. It sounds exactly like dyslexia. Cami had those same symptoms, and she was smart as a whip." Jackie's throat ached, realizing she spoke of her daughter in the past tense. Something she'd made a point of not doing, but it had become harder after so long a time.

"Oh, Jackie, do you mean it? You really think that could be the problem?"

"From what you've told me, he fits the profile."

"I wish I had his number. I'd call him now and tell him."

CHAPTER 32

Friday morning, Jackie was at the Maitre's at the crack of dawn. The scowl on the elderly woman's face confirmed this would not be a good day.

"I wondered if you'd quit, already?"

Jackie feigned a smile. "Not a chance."

"Well, Homer and I like to be at the diner when Bubba opens up. It's five-fifteen, already, and I don't see how I can possibly get myself ready by six o'clock."

"You probably can't, but I can." True to her word, Jackie had the old lady dressed and out the front door at five minutes past six.

"I knew I'd be late."

Homer said, "But Renie, she did real good. You look mighty spiffy for someone who's been married to me for over sixty years."

She looked over her shoulder as Jackie rolled her out the door. "Did you hear that? Over sixty years. I'll bet he has no idea how many years it's been."

Jackie breathed a soft sigh, comforted that someone besides

her was sharing the heat.

He didn't seem to mind, since he leaned over and kissed his wife of sixty-some-odd-years. "I may not know the exact number without stopping to count on my fingers, but I wouldn't swap a single minute of being married to the love of my life."

The love of his life? What would it be like to be married to the love of your life for over sixty years? Jackie could only imagine.

After parking at the diner, Jackie pulled the wheelchair from the car, helped Mrs. Maitre in it, then turned to Mr. Maitre. "Watch out for the curb."

The old woman quipped. "We've been coming here sometimes twice a day for over twenty years. We're well aware of the curb."

"Yes ma'am. Sorry."

Homer said, "Mama's not normally this hard to get along with. It's only because she doesn't feel well."

"Don't make excuses for me, Homer Maitre. I feel just fine." When Jackie pushed her to the right side of the room, Mrs. Maitre said, "Land sakes, where are you shoving me, girl?" She pointed. "That's our table, over yonder by the window."

"Yes ma'am. Sorry."

Homer smiled. "Seems you're having to use that line a lot, young lady."

"I don't mind, sir. I aim to please, so it's important that I know your likes and dislikes. It'll take a while to become accustomed to one another, but I'm sure we'll soon be great friends."

Mrs. Maitre's mouth turned down at the corners but when Lexie rushed over with open arms, the frown was quickly replaced with a smile.

"Three of my favorite people," Lexie squealed. "You look terrific, Aunt Lorene. I can tell Jackie's doing a great job, taking care of you."

"I think she put too much rouge on my cheeks."

"Not at all. Your makeup looks perfect." She glanced toward Jackie and winked. "So, Jackie, I know what these other two want for breakfast, but what can I get you?"

"I'm not very hungry. Just take care of them."

Bubba walked over to the table. "Nonsense. You need to eat. What if I fix you one of my famous omelets?"

Jackie's lips quivered when she tried to smile. "Thanks, Bubba. An omelet does sound good."

"What would you like on it?"

She laughed. This time, it wasn't forced. "Whatever goes on Bubba's Famous Omelet?"

His tone dropped, as their gaze locked. "I like my omelet all the way—loaded with everything I can find in the kitchen."

"Sounds good." When his expression abruptly changed, Jackie turned and looked behind her. Darts shot from the glaring eyes of a woman Jackie immediately recognized from Lexie's description, to be Greta Pugh.

Jackie cleared her throat, then turned back to address Bubba. "Thank you. Coffee and an omelet."

He said, "Will that be all?"

Greta stomped over and draped her arm around Bubba's waist and grinned. "You can bet your bottom dollar that'll be all. You hear a lot of talk working in a diner, so don't think I don't know who you are and what you're here for, girlie."

Jackie's brow shot up. "I beg your pardon?"

"You're here to stalk the prey, but you're on the wrong Safari, sista. This big ol' lion is already captured. Tell her Bubba." Greta chuckled, as if entertained by her own words.

Bubba pulled her hands from around his waist. "Greta, I know you're joking, but it isn't amusing."

She cackled. "Who's joking? I'm a lioness, hear me roar." She reared her head back and let out a loud, obnoxious imitation of a growl, causing heads in the diner to turn. Her lip turned up in a snarl, as she glared at Jackie. "Find another prey to snare, pussy cat, or get out of the jungle, because this trophy's mine, all mine."

Jackie dropped her head. There were no words.

Bubba turned and clomped into the kitchen, with Greta on his heels.

Mrs. Maitre cupped her hand over her mouth and pretended to whisper, though her voice could be heard across the room. "I'd like to give that woman a piece of my mind."

With tongue in cheek, her husband said, "Sugar, are you sure you have enough left to share? Seems to me you've been giving away pieces of your mind ever since the accident. Where's my sweet Renie?"

Jackie clenched her eyes shut and waited for another outburst, this time aimed at Mr. Maitre.

The old woman said, "Homer, I'll admit I haven't been the easiest to get along with lately, but I'm going through an adjustment, and it's been very difficult for me."

Tears welled in Jackie's eyes. "It's me. I'd so hoped this arrangement would work, but Greta's not the only one who wants me to leave town, is she?"

Homer slammed his fist on the table. "This has gone far enough. Tell her Lorene. Tell her everything you want her to know and get it out in the open. Now! No more nasty innuendos and accusations. Go ahead. Have your say, then move on, because Jackie isn't going anywhere."

"Homer Maitre, don't you raise your voice at me."

"I should've raised my voice on this subject long ago. You need Jackie, Lorene, but you aren't the only one who needs her. I need her, too, so I'm saying she stays and you need to thank the Good Lord she's here for us."

"Homer, what's got into you?"

"I'm tired of all this nit-picking, Lorene. I'm giving you a chance to air all your grievances and let Jackie hear what you have to say. Then, we're gonna close that history book of Bubba's love life and let Jackie do her job in a peaceful environment."

"I must say, I'm baffled why you'd take her side over mine."

"Let's evaluate the two sides, Lorene. Seems to me she's here to make our lives easier. That's her side. You seem intent on making hers miserable. That's your side. So, if it comes to choosing sides, I reckon you're right, because I'm all for making our lives easier."

Jackie sucked in a heavy breath. "Thank you, Mr. Maitre, but your wife can't help how she feels toward me. If my feelings were the only ones to be considered, I'd stay, because I can take the vocal attacks. However, it's obvious my presence is causing friction between the two of you, and for that, I'm truly sorry."

Mr. Maitre said, "Please, don't make any rash—"

Bubba walked out of the kitchen with the breakfast tray, while Lexie watched from behind the counter. He said, "Jackie . . ." He shuffled on his feet, then stared out the window. "Uh, I just want to say . . . well, I feel I need . . ." He blew out a faint whistle. "I'm trying to say Greta might've been out of line, but I don't think she meant it the way it came out. I think it was her odd way of trying to make a joke."

Mrs. Maitre said, "Shug, I think we all know better than that. When are you gonna see that woman the way everyone else sees her?"

"Aunt Lorene, Greta sometimes speaks out of turn, but don't we all? I'm marrying her, so I hope you'll learn to accept her."

She threw her hand over her heart. "Mercy! If that's meant to be a joke, you're worse than she is, Bubba. Marry her? You can't possibly be serious."

Her husband laid his hand on her arm. "Mama, admit it. In

242

your mind, there's never been a woman good enough for Bubba. If he can be happy with that woman, it's his choice, not ours."

Jackie cut a few bites of her omelet, then pushed it around on her plate several times with her fork before bringing it to her mouth. The lump in her throat made it difficult to swallow.

It wasn't as if she'd held any expectations of ever being with Bubba, but to think he'd waited this long to marry, and was about to wind up with such a vengeful, vindictive woman, tore her heart out. At least that's one thing for which she and Mrs. Maitre could agree. She gently laid her napkin over the portion of the uneaten omelet on her plate.

Lexie walked over to the table and picked up the dirty plates. When the napkin fell off, she said, "You didn't like your omelet? Would you like me to ask Bubba to fix you something else?"

Jackie fought back the tears. "No. Please, don't. It was delicious, I wasn't as hungry as I thought. It was plenty."

Mrs. Maitre said, "What she really means is she's as upset as I am that Bubba Knox is about to make the biggest mistake of his lifetime."

Lexie nodded. "Yeah, I'm pretty upset about it myself. They just had a knock-down, drag-out verbal fight in the kitchen when she accused him of being in love with someone else. But the craziest was when he yelled and told her to go ahead and set a date. Men!"

Mrs. Maitre said, "That woman is holding something over his

head, and nobody can make me believe differently."

Jackie's voice cracked. "Are we ready to go?"

Mr. Maitre nodded. "Yes, thank you. I'll go open the trunk for you, so you can put the chair in the back."

Jackie pushed her arms under Mrs. Maitre's and lifted her into the chair.

The old woman muffled a couple of words that sounded an awful lot like "thank you."

Could it be the cold, cold heart was beginning to thaw?

CHAPTER 33

Johnny Gorham walked into the diner Saturday morning, holding a newspaper. "'Morning, Bubba, where's that cute little waitress of yours?"

"Lexie doesn't come in for another thirty-minutes. What can I get for you?"

"Oh, it's too early to eat. I'll just take a cup of coffee and eat a little later."

When Bubba brought his coffee to the table, Johnny said, "I see in the paper congratulations are in order. I'll have to say, you sure pulled one over on me, but I'd be lying if I didn't say I'm not genuinely pleased."

"What do you mean?"

"You and Greta. To be truthful, I thought you'd be my competition—not that I didn't plan to give you a run for your money. After hearing the gossip running rampant in this town—the announcement in the paper this morning was quite a shocker."

Bubba's breath caught in his throat. "You're talking in riddles.

What announcement?"

Johnny's smile couldn't have been bigger if he'd won a lottery. "You haven't seen it? Here's the picture, and the write-up. Congratulations. I hope you two will have a long and happy life together. I'm happy for you, and I mean that with all my heart."

Bubba's eyes barely scanned the picture, and headline, when his jaw flexed. "Excuse me, Johnny." He trudged into the kitchen and pulled out his phone. He slammed it back into his pocket when it went to voicemail. He should've known she wouldn't be up until mid-morning. He had to get hold of himself. Didn't Greta tell him she had set a date? Why was he shocked she'd put it in the paper? Isn't that what engaged couples did?

Johnny's gloating made Bubba's heart sink like lead. *He won't stop until he gets her. Oh, Jackie, how I love you, sweetheart. How I wish—*

****

When Lexie got off work at five o'clock, Jamal was waiting outside the diner. "Thank you for coming, Jamal."

"Are you serious? I've been counting the hours since you called me at lunch,"

"Why don't we ride over to the park? I have something to tell you."

His expression suddenly changed. "Whatever."

Lexie attempted small talk, but Jamal drew deeper into a shell. His unexplained moodiness caused her to question if this was a good time to bring up the subject. He parked the car, went around and opened her door. "What's wrong, Jamal?"

"What do you mean?"

"You were in a great mood when you got to the diner. Why the sudden long face?"

"Maybe it's because I feel we're wasting each other's time."

Her throat ached. "I see. I'm sorry I called. If you'll take me back to the diner, I'll get my car, and I won't be guilty of wasting any more of your time."

"Fine, because I already know what you were gonna say."

"You have no idea, but since I don't want to waste your time, there's no need to discuss it, is there?"

"Reckon not. I can tell you word for word. Trust me, I've heard it before. It goes like this: 'You're a super guy, Jamal, and I love you like a brother, but . . . blah, blah, blah —' Lexie, the truth is, I have more 'sisters' than Solomon had wives. There. I hope I've made it easier for you."

Her jaw dropped. "Oh m'goodness! Is that why you think I called you?"

"Isn't it? To blow me off?"

"No. Jamal, I wanted to tell you that I know what's wrong with you."

He pursed his lips. "Somehow, I think being your brother trumps seeing your eagerness to share my faults with me, but regardless of what you *think* you know, five dollars says I know more of my short-comings than you do."

"Jamal would you stop it! I didn't call and ask you to meet

me, to blow you off. Don't you get it? I *love* you." Her mouth flew open and she popped her hand over her lips. "I'm so sorry. I didn't mean to say that."

"Don't worry, I didn't take you seriously."

"No. You don't understand. I meant it. I just didn't *know* I meant it until it came from my lips." A tiny snicker turned into full-blown laughter. "I'm sorry, Jamal. I laugh when I'm nervous, and I'm shaking like a leaf on the inside. I can't believe I blurted it out. I'm sorry if I shocked you, but it couldn't have been a bigger shock to you than it was to me."

"I don't get it. You aren't saying—"

Her lips quivered. "Yes, I am."

"You're saying you're . . . you're in *love* with me?"

She nodded. "Yes, but I know this wasn't what you were prepared to hear, any more than I was prepared to say it. The reason I asked you to meet me here was because I wanted to ask you if you've ever considered you might be dyslexic?"

"No. Why?"

"Have you heard of it?"

"Sure, but I've also heard of typhoid fever, yet I've never had reason to suspect I might have it."

"Jamal, I want you to study the symptoms. I believe with all my heart, you have dyslexia, and that's the reason reading is difficult for you."

A slight grin caused his lips to separate. "So, are you saying I can be fixed?"

She laughed. "Maybe not fixed, but by understanding the problem, I believe we can work at making your life easier."

"Lexie, I'm trying to take in what you're saying, but to tell the truth, I haven't gotten past the part where you said you love me. Or did I only hear what I wanted to hear?"

Their gaze locked. She licked her dry lips. "Do I need to say it again?"

He didn't wait for an answer. He pulled her close, and gently touched his lips to hers. "I've never kissed an angel before. I love you, Lexie Garrison. I love you, I love you, I love you, and I've never said that to any other girl." He caressed her face with his eyes. "Not to a single one of my many sisters."

They walked around the lake, hand-in-hand.

****

Jackie walked in her house at nine-fifteen, kicked off her shoes and fell across the sofa. Never had she been as tired in her life. What she'd give for a cup of hot tea, but she was too exhausted to get up and make it. When the doorbell rang, she assumed Lexie had forgotten her key. "Coming, sweetheart." She trudged to the door and opening it. "Johnny. What's wrong?"

"Wrong? Nothing's wrong. Sorry to come so late, but I've been waiting for you to get home. How's your job going?"

"Fine."

"Well, aren't you going to invite me in?"

"Oh, Johnny, I'm sorry, but I'm bushed. Would you mind coming back later?"

"I won't stay long. I promise. Please?"

She let out a long, drawn out sigh, stepped aside, and walked back to the sofa. "Have a seat."

When he sat beside her instead of choosing the chair, she wanted to object, but hoped he'd keep his word and wouldn't stay long. "So, to what do I owe this visit?"

"You owe nothing sweetheart. I'm the one in debt to you. I guess you've heard the news."

"I have no idea what you're referring to. Johnny. I don't wish to be rude, but honestly, I just want to put on my pajamas and crawl in bed. I'd offer you a cup of tea, but I'm too tired to make it."

"I'll be happy to help you make both those desires a reality. I'll go put the tea on while you go slip into those pj's."

"Thanks, but I'll wait until you leave."

"What if I give you a massage to relax those tired muscles?"

"No thank you."

He pulled a folded paper from his inside coat pocket. "Have you seen this morning's paper?"

She nodded. "No. Why?"

"I think you may be interested in learning that a mutual friend of ours is about to tie the knot."

"If you're talking about Bubba, it's old news, so if that's all you came for, you can leave."

Johnny laid the paper on the table beside the sofa and stood. "I'm sorry you're tired. Go to bed, beautiful and get some rest.

Don't bother to get up. I'll see myself out."

When the door closed, she reached over and picked up the newspaper article. She ran to the bedroom, fell across the bed and cried herself to sleep.

CHAPTER 34

Lexie hurried home, eager to tell Jackie about the conversation she had with Jamal, and how she made a fool of herself when the unexpected words blurted from her lips.

She hadn't stopped laughing since she left him. He was funny, handsome, smart . . . and he was in love with her. She relived the kiss over and over in her mind. So sweet, so gentle, so heart-stopping. Never had she been kissed with such tenderness.

Disappointed that Jackie had not waited up, she went in the kitchen and made a cup of hot chocolate. How could she sleep with so much whirling in her head? Lexie picked up a newspaper from off the floor, and Greta's pictured caught her eye.

Was that why Jackie went to bed early? She's still in love with Bubba! Lexie threw the paper down and mumbled. "And he's in love with her. So why is he marrying someone he doesn't love?"

****

Lexie arrived at work shortly after Bubba opened. Someone had to save him from himself. Whatever reason he had for proceeding with this foolish little scheme needed to come to an end, and soon.

He was sitting at the table, reading the Sports page, when she burst in. "Bubba, you can't do it. You can't."

"I have no idea what you're talking about, sweetheart. Can't do what?"

"Marry that woman."

His smile turned upside down. "That's no concern of yours, Lexie."

"I'm making it my concern. I care about you and I care about Jackie—and I refuse to sit by and watch you ruin two lives."

"How did Jackie get in this conversation? She means nothing to me."

"You can lie to yourself, but you aren't fooling me. You're in love with her, and she's in love with you, so why are you pretending to be in love with Greta Pugh?"

"Hon, stay out of this. Forgive me for being blunt, but frankly, it's none of your business who I'm in love with. Maybe you haven't seen the paper. The date is set, so there's no need to discuss it further."

"Bubba, tell me why? Why would you do this? I've watched you around Greta. I know you don't love her. And as for her—she doesn't even know how to love. When I first met her, I thought she was nice. I was wrong. She's a heartless fraud."

"Lexie, you're young. There are things you don't understand."

The front door opened, and Johnny Gorham walked in.

Bubba whispered, "Take his order but don't let him wangle

you into a conversation."

Lexie bit the inside of her cheek. What was Bubba afraid of? Maybe talking to Johnny was exactly what she needed to do. He knew both Jackie and Bubba. Knew them back when . . . back in high school, when they first fell in love. Maybe he could help before it was too late. Was that what Bubba was afraid of? That Johnny would confirm what she already knew?

She took his order, then glanced over her shoulder and whispered. "Mr. Gorham, there's something I'd like to discuss with you, but I'd rather not have anyone know."

His face lit up. "Sure, kid. What's on your mind?"

"Not here. I get off at five. Would it be possible for you to meet me at my house about five-thirty?"

"Sure. Could you give me a hint what this is about?"

"Jackie."

He nodded. "My favorite subject. I'll see you at five-thirty."

****

Bubba couldn't get Lexie's words out of his head. *You're in love with her and she's in love with you.* Was it possible? Why didn't he ask Lexie to explain? His heart raced. Did Jackie say it? How else could Lexie know? Did she understand the circumstances surrounding her birth? So many questions, so few answers.

****

Johnny was waiting on the steps when Lexie arrived. "Thanks for coming, Mr. Gorham. You're early."

"Better early than late. Didn't want to keep you waiting."

"Thanks. Mind if we stay on the porch?"

He chuckled. "Has my reputation preceded me?"

"No, I apologize if it sounded offensive, but I've discovered gossip travels faster than truth, so for your own protection—" She giggled.

He smiled. "I understand. I gather from what you've just said, that you're aware of the nasty gossip making the rounds, and I'm sorry, kid. Though sad to say, the children do suffer for the sins of the fathers, and it's a crying shame, especially when they're as sweet as you."

Lexie nodded, though she had no idea what he was talking about. "Mr. Gorham, I wanted to talk to you—in confidence, of course—because I figure you know Bubba and Jackie better than most people, since you grew up with them. I know they were in love in high school, so there are things I'd like you to help me understand."

"I'll help clear things up for you as best I can, Lexie, but there are some things I didn't know until I came back here for my brother's funeral. Feel free to ask me anything, and I assure you our conversation will be in the strictest of confidences."

"I'm not sure how to ask this—"

"Let me make it easier for you. You wonder why Jackie didn't marry Bubba when you were conceived, if they were so in love? Am I right?"

Lexie almost stopped him but decided to wait and see where this was going. *Did he say when I was conceived?* She could understand why Bubba might be fooled into thinking Jackie was her mother, since he'd never met her daughter. . . but Johnny Gorham was Jackie's brother-in-law. He knew she wasn't his niece, so what gave him the cockeyed notion that Jackie had given birth to two daughters? Weird.

He locked his hands around his knees and reared back. "I promised to be honest with you, and now that you're grown, I think you deserve to know the truth."

"Thank you." This certainly didn't appear to be headed in the direction she expected when she invited him over.

"To tell the truth, I didn't learn until recently that the summer Jackie left town, after her Junior year, it was because she was pregnant. Since she didn't bring you back with her, as far as I know, it was the best-kept secret this town has ever had. I'm sure Bubba was privy, but it certainly never made the gossip circuit . . . not until someone from their past recently let the cat out of the bag."

Didn't bring me back? A part of her wanted to blurt out that it was all a lie, and the other part wanted to keep quiet and hear every piece of gossip making the rounds so she could tell Jackie, allowing her to put a stop to the crazy rumors.

"Lexie, if it sounds as if your mother was promiscuous, it's not true, honey. She loved your father with all her heart, and she made one mistake. Only one." He rubbed his hand across his face.

"I'm sorry. I didn't mean to imply you were a mistake . . . I think you know what I meant. But then, when my brother, Jacob . . . uh, had his way with Jackie the following year, she came up pregnant, this time with my niece, Cami." He lowered his head. "Jacob always was a rounder. Couldn't stay away from pretty girls, but trust me, your sweet mother wasn't responsible for what took place. Your grandparents threatened to bring rape charges against Jacob if he didn't agree to marry Jackie. My parents only agreed because Daddy was up for re-election and couldn't stand a scandal." Johnny stopped and stared at Lexie. "Are you alright?"

"Sure. I'm fine. Why wouldn't I be?"

"I can understand if you're upset that your father plans to marry Greta instead of your mother. It's only natural. I'm sure you love them both, but as sweet as young love is, our wants change as we get older."

Lexie nodded. She was catching on. "So, were you in love with . . . with Jackie?"

His face lit up like a full moon. "You can't imagine how much I loved her. Would it shock you if I told you I still love her?"

"So, you're saying *your* wants didn't change?"

"No. If anything they've grown deeper."

"Does she love you?"

"Let me put it like this. I wouldn't be hanging around if I didn't honestly feel I have a chance to give her the kind of love she's always wanted."

"You don't have to worry about me standing in your way."

"I was hoping you'd say that. Now, may I ask you a personal question?"

"Not promising an answer, but you're welcome to ask."

"I suppose you were curious and searched for your parents after you were grown?"

"I'd rather not go into detail about my personal life, but I can tell you my father has always known where I was, from the moment I was born. My mother has not. I appreciate your coming over, but it's getting dark, and I should go inside. Thanks for coming, Johnny. It's been very enlightening."

CHAPTER 35

When Jackie's car lights lit up the driveway, Lexie ran to meet her and practically pulled her inside the house. "I could hardly wait for you to get here. Kick off your shoes and get comfortable, *Mom*, while I get your hot tea ready. I've got so much to tell you."

"Mom?" Jackie giggled. "What's going on? I don't think I've seen you this excited over anything."

"It's all good. Hold on. I'll be right back." Minutes later, Lexie walked back in the room with the tea.

Jackie took a sip. "Perfect. You know just how I like it. Lexie, I'm so sorry your mother didn't live to see what a sweet daughter she had. My heart swelled when you called me Mom. I've learned to love you so much, it sometimes feels like you are my 'other' daughter."

"Thanks. That means a lot. I wish my daddy would've waited and married someone sweet as you. I could easily think of you as my mother."

"So what happened today that has you so excited?"

"I opened my mouth at work and blurted out something to Bubba, but he looked shocked, so I decided to check it out."

"Oh? I can't imagine what you could've said to shock Bubba Knox." She laughed. "So, what did you say?"

"I'm furious that he's determined to marry that dreadful woman, when I know he doesn't love her."

"Now, honey, love is strange. We can't possibly know how he feels."

"Then you may not approve of what I said to him."

"Try me."

"I told him I know he doesn't love Greta, and that I know for a fact that he loves you and you love him."

Jackie's eyes rounded. "Lexie, you didn't."

"I did."

"Oh, honey, what would make you say such a thing?"

"Because I believed it to be true. But seeing the shock on his face, I wondered if I could be wrong. So, I decided to find out."

"I'm afraid to ask."

"I talked to Johnny Gorham."

"Johnny? How did he get into the conversation?"

"He's known you both for many years. I wanted him to either convince me I was on the wrong track or tell me that I wasn't, because if I was right and you and Bubba love one another, I knew we had to stop a wedding."

Jackie's smile appeared forced. "And I suppose you know less now than when you asked, because Johnny Gorham doesn't know me as well as you might think, and I'm quite sure he can't speak for Bubba, either. I know you mean well, you little romantic, but please, Lexie—let it go."

"I did find out something that's left me wondering if it's true or not."

"I'm afraid to ask."

"Seems there's juicy gossip going around that you left town the summer after your Junior year."

"Whew! You scared me for a minute there. That's not gossip, Lexie. It's true. I spent the summer as a nanny for a couple in Florida. I loved it at first." She chuckled at the memory. "But, oh my goodness, I got so homesick before the three months was over. I couldn't wait for school to begin again."

"Are you ready for the best part? This is really funny."

Her throat tightened. "Go ahead."

"People are saying I'm Bubba's child, born the summer you left for Florida, and that you gave birth to Jacob's baby the following year when you left for Virginia. Then others are insisting there was only one pregnancy and it seems there's confusion over whether the father of the baby girl is Bubba's or Jacob's."

"Bubba's? That's absurd. Coming back here has resurrected all the old ghosts and obviously invented a few more, but I hope you never feel the need to defend me, Lexie. I've done nothing that needs defending."

"I believe you, but isn't it a hoot the way gossip gets twisted?"

Jackie shook her head. "No, no, honey. It's not a hoot, as you call it. It's vicious how folks gossip, but I suppose Johnny set you straight, because he's one of the few who know the truth."

"You'd think, wouldn't you? But obviously, he heard the gossip when he got back here, and bought into it, because he kept referring to Bubba as my father and you as my mother."

"What?" She shook her head. "You must've misunderstood. Johnny *knows* better."

"No, I promise you, he doesn't. It was sweet the way he wanted to console me, saying that despite getting pregnant twice, my mother—that would be you—was a sweet, innocent young girl, and not the promiscuous teen a few people were portraying. He encouraged me not to pay attention to the nasty gossip."

"Unbelievable! Lexie, honey, I know you couldn't tell him why I left that summer, since you didn't know, but why didn't you tell him you aren't my daughter?"

"I apologize, Jackie, but when I moved in, you said you wanted Bubba to continue thinking I was your daughter, so I assumed you wanted everyone to think so, but I didn't lie. He's the one who heard the gossip and swallowed it hook, line and sinker, as they say."

"I can't believe he's serious. He knows I didn't bring a baby back with me when I returned from Florida. I was back in school at the beginning of the school year."

"He assumes you put me up for adoption."

"Ridiculous. Did he say that?"

"Well, he asked if I came to Mobile, to find my birth parents, and I told him my daddy had always known where I was. . . .and that's the truth."

"Oh, honey, it may be the truth, but you knew . . . you knew from what he'd already said, he assumed you were referring to Bubba."

Lexie chewed her left thumbnail and grimaced. "I see I've upset you, so I'm not sure if I should tell the rest."

Jackie closed her eyes and swallowed hard. "There's more?"

"He asked if I'd have objections to him marrying my mother."

Jackie rolled her eyes. "You've gotta be kidding. Like that would ever happen." She buried her face in her hands. "Oh, Lexie, I don't even care anymore that people talk behind my back, but this is so unfair to Bubba. He's done nothing wrong. I've got to stop this ridiculous rumor from spreading further."

"Jackie, I'm sorry I had no idea you'd be so upset. Honestly, I thought you'd laugh, it's so ridiculous. I'll tell Johnny the truth."

"Honey, I'm not upset with you. I'm not even angry at Johnny. I'm angry at myself for having so much pride. I fed this rumor when I asked you to allow Bubba to continue believing a lie."

"I don't know what you mean."

"The day you told me Bubba assumed you were my daughter, I was glad because I didn't want him to think I was needy and had to rent a room to make ends meet. That was pride, and the Bible tells us that pride leads to a fall." Jackie's lip trembled. "Oh, the webs we weave . . . "

Lexie finished it for her. "When we deceive?"

"Exactly."

"Jackie? You wanna know something?"

"What's on your mind, sweetheart."

"I loved being your daughter—even if it was only for one afternoon."

CHAPTER 36

Lexie tossed and turned all night, unable to sleep. Too much on her mind. Bubba was about to ruin his life, and no one could talk sense into him.

Lexie was fond of Mrs. Maitre, but it bothered her that the elderly lady was making Jackie's life miserable. Lexie couldn't understand why Jackie needed money. From what she'd been told, her late husband was a very wealthy man. Nothing made sense, but Jackie hadn't pried into Lexie's affairs, and it was none of her business why Jackie was in a financial bind. Still, she wondered.

Then there was Jamal. She smiled at the very thought of him. Was it fair to get his hopes up, without knowing for sure she could help him? She bit her lip, suppressing a giggle, when she recalled his shocked look when she blurted out that she loved him. Random thoughts continued to fill her head, when the phone rang. Her first impulse was to let it ring. Who'd be calling her at eleven o'clock at night? She rolled over, picked up her cell phone and saw River Braxton's name on the screen. "River? Hi . . . I'm good . . .

What's wrong?"

"I'm not there with you, Lexie. That's what's wrong."

She giggled. "Seriously, what's going on."

"I called to tell you it's been called off."

"What?"

"The wedding, of course. I told Celeste about my feelings for you, and frankly I don't think it fazed her. If you want to know what I think, I think she was more in love with the thought of planning the event, than she was in making a lifetime commitment."

"When did this happen?"

"Tonight. I couldn't wait to get home to call you. I should've done it long ago."

Lexie hesitated. "I see."

"Is something wrong, honey?"

"No. Nothing's wrong. I'm surprised to hear from you, that's all."

"Lexie, I wish I could've come tonight, I didn't know how to find you. I wanted to see the look on your face when I told you the news, but. What's your address, babe?"

"Uh . . . 104 Bay Street."

"What time do you get off work?"

"Normally, I get off at five, but tomorrow I won't get off until nine. I work late on Wednesdays."

"Bummer. Well, I'll try to be there Thursday, and we'll go out for dinner. How does that sound?"

"Nice."

"Lexie, are you certain nothing's wrong? You sound peculiar."

"I'm fine. I'll see you Thursday, River. Thanks for calling."

"I'll be counting the hours."

"Yeah . . . me too."

When she hung up, her heart beat so fast, she could hardly breathe. She'd waited so long for River. Why now?

Wednesday night, the church crowd cleared out, all except for Jamal.

"Lexie, I could hardly wait for tonight to come, so I could thank you."

"For what?"

"I've spent hours researching dyslexia, and I believe you're right. I have all the classic symptoms. All my life, I've dreamed of becoming an engineer, but I was on the verge of giving up, thinking I was too stupid to pursue a degree. Lexie, there's no doubt in my mind that God heard my tears and sent you to me to give me hope. You're a very special person."

"If I helped, I'm glad, Jamal, but Jackie is the one who deserves the credit."

"You can't imagine how happy this has made me, to find the truth. Did you know that many dyslexic people become engineers? It's true. If they could overcome the obstacles, so can I, now that I have you by my side, helping me along the way." When she didn't respond, he said, "Can we begin tonight? I want to tell you what I've learned about coping with dyslexia and get your input."

"I'd like that." Lexie gathered the day's receipts at the register. "But first, I need to close out and take the deposit to the bank for Bubba. It won't take long."

Jamal was waiting in his car in front of Jackie's house when Lexie drove up. He jumped out to open her car door. "Lexie, you can't imagine how long this day has seemed. You're all I've thought about all day. I've never felt this way about any girl."

Lexie bit her lip. What had she done? Had she allowed Jamal to fall in love with her, only to find out she was in love with another man? How could she tell him?

He reached for her hand. Tucked under his left arm was a thick book. They walked in the house and Lexie offered him a seat on the sofa, then reached for the book. "A textbook?"

"You might call it that, since it's a subject I'm studying. It's called *The Dyslexia Cure*."

Her brow lifted. "There's a cure?"

He lifted a shoulder in a shrug. "Not really, but it tells ways to overcome obstacles, and if I can learn to do the things it talks about in this book, it'll feel like a cure. Lexie, I've been given a new lease on life, and I owe it all to you." He slid over next to her, draped his arm around her shoulder and pulled her close. When he leaned in to kiss her, she pushed against his chest and turned her head away. *I can't do this. I'm so confused.* "Please . . . not now,

Jamal."

The crushed look on his face made her want to take her words back, and hold him in her arms, but she couldn't. It would be so wrong. River had broken his engagement—for her—and he'd be coming tomorrow. It's what she'd been dreaming of—hoping for—waiting on. Wasn't it? Her lip quivered. "I'm sorry, Jamal."

"Don't apologize. I understand."

"Do you?"

"Of course. You felt sorry for me, and I jumped to conclusions." He glanced at his watch. "Hey, it's getting late. I should go." He stood and extended his hand. "Take care, Lexie."

"Jamal, you don't understand. I didn't know . . ."

"Actually, I think tonight I understood for the first time." He walked out the door and Lexie went to bed, then cried for hours before falling asleep.

Thursday morning when Lexie got to work there were two police cars in front of the diner. She walked inside. "What's going on."

A policeman said, "Are you Lexie Garrison?"

"Yes."

"You're under arrest."

"What?!"

Bubba walked in the door and hung his head, seeing the police put handcuffs on Lexie.

"What's going on, Bubba?"

Greta said, "You know perfectly well what's going on, you little thief?"

"No. No, there's been a mistake."

Greta said, "You'd better believe there's been a mistake. How long did you think you could get by with it?"

Lexie screamed, "Bubba, help me. Please help me. I have no idea what she's talking about."

The policeman said, "You'd better come with us, miss."

When Lexie arrived at the station, her parole officer was there. He said, "Lexie, I didn't want to believe it, when they called me."

"You'd be right not to believe it, Mason. They haven't even told me what it is I am supposed to have stolen, but it doesn't matter. I'm not guilty."

"Lexie, I believed you last time when you said the same thing. But twice? I deal with crooks every day, and you'd think I'd know when I've been had, but you're good. You're really good. You fooled me."

The next hour was a blank. Nothing anyone said or did mattered. Maybe they told her what she'd supposedly taken, maybe they didn't. She wasn't sure. Her fate was set and there was nothing she could do to change it. Why try? She was still on probation, and with this accusation she'd be sent right back to Tutwiler. When given the opportunity to make one phone call, she stalled. No need to call a lawyer. She had no way to pay one, and she was too humiliated to call Jackie. Who else would care? Not Bubba. He apparently was in on this horrible fiasco. Not Jamal.

He'd never want to see her again. River. She'd call River. Maybe he could help find out what was going on. He was her only hope. She got a recording.

Lexie could only guess she must've fainted after dialing River's number, because she woke up in a jail cell. If only she could've left a message for River. *He's coming today. Bubba will tell him I'm here, and he'll know I've been framed. He'll know what to do.*

After spending a week in jail, waiting to be transferred back to Tutwiler, Lexie lost all hope. River never came. *He believes them.* Even if he didn't, what difference would it make? They could never be together. Jackie came every day and cried the whole time. Lexie supposed this was what it was like to have a mother—someone to truly love you and believe in you. It broke her heart to see Jackie so distraught.

Jackie said, "Lexie, I know you didn't take that money. I only wish I could prove it."

"Jackie, coming here, pulls you down and makes you feel worse. Forget about me."

"Honey, you're asking me to do the impossible. No way will I ever forget about you." The jailer walked up. "Time's up."

Jackie threw Lexie a kiss. "I'll be back. Don't give up, honey. Please, don't give up."

Lexie feigned a smile and nodded, though she considered no hope to be less painful than false hope. Why get her hopes up, only to painfully crash? This time, they'd probably lock her up and throw away the key. So, what? She didn't care. She didn't care about anything anymore. Nothing good ever happened to her, unless it was to set her up for a harder fall.

The following Thursday, the jailer told her she had a visitor. "River!" Her throat tightened when Jamal walked around the corner. She bawled. "I'm so sorry, Jamal. I suppose you're here to tell me what a disappointment I am. You have no reason to believe me, but I'm not guilty of what I've been accused of."

"You? A disappointment? Never. And for the record, I don't believe a word of any of this. They say you've been stealing money from the diner, but I know it's not true, and I intend to prove it, Lexie. We're gonna get to the truth. I would've come sooner, but I only found out last night when we went to the diner after church, so I had to wait until morning to come."

"You . . . you really believe me?"

"Of course, I believe you. You're no thief. I plan to hire a lawyer."

She shook her head. "I appreciate your concern, Jamal, but you can't do that. I know you don't have the money for a lawyer, and neither do I. It wouldn't do any good, anyway. My goose is cooked. I'll be heading back to Tutwiler." She swallowed hard. "I suppose I've shocked you, since you didn't know I was in prison before I came here."

"Lexie, I don't know about your past, and I don't care. You came to me when I was ready to give up, and you gave me hope. I want to return the favor. We'll get to the truth."

"Don't you want to know why I was in prison?"

"No. I'm only interested in the Lexie I got to know after you came to Mobile. The Lexie I fell in love with."

"Oh, Jamal —"

He held up his palm. "Don't! I'm sorry. I shouldn't have said that. You don't owe me an explanation. Love isn't always reciprocal. I get it."

Jamal went to the diner and sat down at a table with Bubba. "Bubba, do you really think she did it?"

"You saying you don't?"

"I'm positive she didn't do it. What did she say when you told her the money was missing?"

Bubba sucked in a heavy breath. "That's the thing. I didn't have a chance to talk to her about it."

"I don't get it. Why would you call the police and have her arrested without at least giving her an opportunity to confess or deny?"

"Jamal, it happened so fast. I never had the opportunity to discuss it with her."

"What do you mean? You had her arrested. You obviously talked to the police."

"That's not how it was."

Jamal ran his hands through his hair and groaned. "Then, please, Bubba, help me understand."

"Greta came in early last Thursday morning. She was here

when I arrived, and she was very distraught. She said she'd suspected for some time that Lexie had been fooling with the books but hadn't wanted to say anything until she could prove it. She insisted that's why Lexie asked to close every Wednesday. Greta showed me the discrepancies. I didn't want to believe it, but it certainly appeared a large amount of money was missing. Over three-thousand dollars, and it suspiciously began about the time Lexie was hired."

"So, without talking to Lexie, you called the cops?"

"No. I wouldn't have had her arrested. I thought you knew me better than that. I would've talked to Lexie and given her an opportunity to explain. But after Greta showed me the books, I had to go to the warehouse, and when I got back, Greta had already called the police. Lexie and the police were here when I drove up. They were putting cuffs on her when I walked in."

"Bubba, I'm sorry, but I find it hard to understand how they could've arrested her without the owner of the diner making a charge. Didn't the police ask for a statement? Did you honestly think she was guilty?"

"I didn't want to, Jamal. But no one else had access to the books, except Greta, of course, and why would Greta bring it to my attention if she was the one stealing the money?"

His teeth meshed together. "Because she's shrewd and knows something you don't?"

Bubba rubbed his hand across his chin. "That might've crossed my mind, if not for one thing."

"And what was that?"

"I learned something that I'm sure you don't know."

"There's nothing that can ever make me believe Lexie would steal from you or anyone else."

"The police told me Lexie had recently been in prison for the same offense. Seems she stole a car, got caught and served two years at Tutwiler, yet never mentioned it. I'm sure you're as surprised by that as I was when I first heard. I can't tell you how it messed up my head. My sweet little Lexie in prison? It was too much for me to comprehend. I still find it hard to believe."

"Have you been to see her?"

Bubba shook his head.

"Why not?"

"What can I say?"

"Maybe you could tell her you're sorry you let her down." And with that, Jamal pushed back from the table and stormed out of the diner.

CHAPTER 37

Jamal skipped classes Friday and spent the day on his computer. After doing a search on Greta Pugh, he found an inactive account on social media. It listed her place of employment as Best Trucking Company, Nashville, Tennessee.

He recalled Lexie once telling him that Greta owned a trucking company before working for Bubba. He dialed the number, hoping to speak to an employee who could give him information on why Greta would sell the business to become a waitress at a diner.

Though he expected the number to be disconnected, he was shocked when a man answered the phone. "Best Trucking."

"Sir, my name is Jamal Jamison and I'm looking for someone who might know a woman named Greta Pugh."

"Oh yeah? Well, I'm looking for her, too. I'm Kyser Best, Jamal, and I'm very much interested in talking to you about Greta. To make sure we're talking about the same woman, what does your Greta look like and if you don't mind saying, why are you looking for her?"

"She's not my Greta, and I'm not looking for her, sir. I know where she is. I'd like a little background info. The Greta Pugh I'm inquiring about is five feet seven or eight, black hair, dark eyes. She owned a trucking company before moving to Mobile."

"Owned a trucking company, did she? Best Trucking, right?"

"Yes sir." Jamal scratched his head. "I assumed 'Best' was an adjective touting the trucking company as being the finest, but that's *your* name, isn't it?"

His laughter had a strange ring to it. "Bingo! And that's my Greta. We're related, or didn't you know?"

"No sir. I'm afraid I didn't."

"Yep, and I can't tell you how grateful I am you contacted me. I lost touch with dear ol' Greta some months ago. I believe you said you're here seeking information. How can I help you?"

Jamal hesitated. He'd never get the answers he needed from a relative. "Uh . . . You've confirmed that prior to moving to Mobile, her previous employment was with Best Trucking Company. I suppose that's all I need from you, sir. Thank you for your time."

"Wait! Mobile, you say? So that's where she lives now?"

"Yessir. She's a waitress at Bubba's Diner on Highway 90."

"Well, well, it'll be a treat to see dear ol' Greta again. Don't let her know you've contacted me. I'd like to surprise her. I don't suppose you'd happen to know what hours she works?"

"Not sure what time she goes in, but I know she works most nights until nine o'clock."

"Helps close, does she?" His raucous laughter caused Jamal to push the phone away from his ear. "Let me guess, Jamal. She's not only a waitress, but the bookkeeper, as well?"

"Yes sir. How did you know?"

"Not hard to guess. Greta's always been good with numbers. I'll lock up and leave here in five minutes. I'd like to be there before she gets off work. I think she'll be surprised to see me."

Jamal hung up. Where did he go from here? Somehow, he had to prove if anyone messed with the books, it was Greta and not Lexie. But who would listen to him? Lexie was as good as tried, convicted, and on her way to prison and there was no one standing in the gap for her. *Don't give up, Lex. I don't know how or when, but I'll prove your innocence, if it means quitting school to do it.* He pulled his phone back out and called Keely.

"Oh, no! Jamal, I had no idea. That's awful. When did this happen?"

"A week ago. I'm surprised you didn't know."

"Trey and I went to the mountains for a much-needed time together, and just got in last night. Jamal, this doesn't ring true. If there's money missing, I can guarantee Greta Pugh is behind it. I've never trusted that woman, and for the life of me, can't understand how Bubba could be so blind."

"I've always heard love is blind, but apparently in Bubba's case, it's blind, deaf and severely crippling, mentally. He's no help. Keely, but if we don't do something to prove otherwise, Lexie is going to prison for a crime she didn't commit."

"I'm in. I'll volunteer to help Bubba, and maybe it'll give me a chance to do a little investigative work. Bubba will need a waitress, so I'm sure he'll be glad for me to help. I just need to find a way to get by Greta."

Keely hung up and related the horrid story to Trey.

"Honey, I wish you'd stay out of it. I know you don't want to believe Lexie could be guilty, but the fact that Jamal says she recently served two years for the same offense should tell us something."

"Trey, it tells me nothing."

"Keely, admit it . . . you've never liked Greta from the first day you met her, so naturally, you'd rather believe she's the guilty party. I think we should sit back and let the courts do their job."

CHAPTER 38

Jackie tried for weeks to win Mrs. Maitre's approval, and found it disheartening that it was their mutual animosity for someone that made it happen.

Though Jackie attempted to hide her dislike for Greta, the elderly woman was very perceptive. Nothing got past her. The working conditions were much more enjoyable since they'd found something on which they could both agree—Greta Pugh was wrong for Bubba.

Jackie pushed Mrs. Maitre's chair over to her favorite table at the diner, at five minutes past six. Keely sprinted across the room with outstretched arms. "Good morning, Maw-Maw and Paw-Paw, if you start coming any earlier, you'll need a key to unlock the joint." She leaned over and gave them both a hug. "And good morning to you, Jackie. So glad Maw-Maw has such a great nurse."

Mrs. Maitre stuck her tongue in her cheek, then with a grin, muttered, "We're slowly getting accustomed to one another." She snickered. "Bonding, I think they call it."

Jackie pursed her lips. "I think we can both agree it's been a slow bond, but we're definitely making progress." She glanced at the menu board, and said, "I think I'll take oatmeal this morning."

"With cinnamon toast?"

"That'll be great. It's good of you to help Bubba out until this mess with Lexie is settled, Keely."

Mrs. Maitre nodded in agreement. "So sad about Lexie being thrown in that old jail when she's innocent. Stealing from Bubba? I don't believe a word of it." Cupping her hand over her mouth, she said, "She's Jackie's daughter, you know."

Jackie sucked in a heavy breath. "No, she isn't. That's a misunderstanding, and one for which I must take the blame, since I perpetuated the false impression. Lexie isn't my daughter—but I wish she was."

Mrs. Maitre's brow shot up. "Oh, m'goodness, are you serious? Goodness knows, there's enough rumors going around. I certainly didn't mean to be spreading more, but I heard—"

Mr. Maitre laid his hand on his wife's. "Sugar, Jackie says you heard wrong, so why don't we let it go at that?"

Keely winked at Paw-Paw, then left to turn in Jackie's order.

Jackie said, "I can't blame anyone but myself for the rumors. It all started a few days after my husband's funeral, when I moved to town and needed to come up with a way to make enough money to live on."

Seeing the stunned look on Mrs. Maitre's face, she said, "I'm sure that's not what you heard, either, but I'd rather not explain that part of the story at this time."

Mrs. Maitre reached over and laid her hand on Jackie's shoulder. "Bless your heart, honey, I had no idea. Heavens, I thought—"

Jackie nodded. "You thought what everyone else thought, but it wasn't true. I was broke, so I put a Room for Rent sign in my yard, and Lexie, a beautiful young stranger, stopped the very next day, and rented the room. She'd just begun work at the diner, and when she told me Bubba assumed she was my daughter because of her address on the application, I was relieved, since I didn't want him to know I was destitute and needed a renter. The last thing I wanted was pity. So, I encouraged Lexie to let it go. What would it hurt, right? I assumed it would end there, but soon the rumors escalated and everyone had the idea she was my daughter." She feigned a smile. "I understand the cog in the wheel came when none of the gossips could agree on the identity of her father. I'm told some said she was Bubba's, born my Junior year in high school, while others said she was Jacob's, born in Virginia, my Senior year."

Mrs. Maitre said, "Well, I declare, how folks can get things so twisted is beyond me. Where do her parents live? Do they know what's happened to her?"

"Hers is a sad story, Aunt Lorene."

Mrs. Maitre hid her smile behind her hand, hearing Jackie refer to her with the affectionate term.

Jackie mumbled a quick apology. "I'm sorry . . . uh, Mrs. Maitre. I suppose hearing Bubba . . . " She hid her face. "I'm so embarrassed."

"Fiddlesticks. I like 'Aunt Lorene' much better than 'Mrs. Maitre.' Sounds less like a stick-in-the mud, which apparently, I've been. But finish, sweetheart. I want to know all about her."

"I suppose Lexie's heartbreaking past was one thing that endeared her to me. She never lied. I knew from the get-go she'd just been released from prison."

"For crying out loud, I can't imagine what landed her there. Must've been in the wrong company, is all I can figure."

"In a way, you'd be right, since she lived with her father and stepmother, and it was her stepmother who had her arrested on a false charge. And now, I'm afraid Lexie's being railroaded again. That precious child is not guilty of stealing anything. I'd stake my life on it."

Mr. Maitre said, "Well, what can we do to help?"

"Only the truth can set her free, and I have no idea how to go about proving her innocence."

"Homer, call Donnie and tell him Lexie needs a good lawyer."

Jackie shook her head slowly. "That's very kind of you, Aunt Lorene, but she can't afford an attorney, and as much as I wish I could help, neither can I."

"Oh, sugar, Donnie, has been our lawyer for decades. We'll do the hiring. I'm not gonna sit by and let Greta Pugh do this to her. I'll guarantee you that wicked woman is behind this whole mess, and if Donnie can't help, no one can."

Keely walked over with their breakfast platters.

Mrs. Maitre said, "Keely, would you ask Bubba to step out here when he gets a minute?"

Bubba's Adam's apple bobbed when he walked out and caught a glimpse of Jackie. What would it have been like to have been married to this beautiful woman, the way they planned when they were much younger? He had to let those thoughts go. In a matter of weeks, he'd be married to Greta Pugh and on his way to Alaska, cooped up in a tiny cabin with a woman he not only didn't love. He didn't even like her. He shuddered. Promise or no promise, he couldn't do this. He *wouldn't* do this.

Just before sundown, a big, burly man with a beard walked into the diner. Keely shivered, observing the peculiar way his eyes searched the place. "Can I help you, sir?"

"Maybe. Does Greta Best . . . uh, I mean Greta Pugh, work here?"

"She does, but she isn't here yet."

"What time do you expect her?"

"Have a seat. I'll go get the owner and maybe he can tell you."

"I'd appreciate that young lady."

Bubba came from the kitchen, wiping his hands on a dish towel. "I hear you're looking for Greta?"

"Yep."

"Would you mind telling me why?"

"Don't mind at all. She stole my truck and almost cleaned me out."

"And who are you?"

"Greta's husband. I'm Kyser Best."

"Her what?"

"Her husband."

"Maybe we aren't talking about the same woman. Didn't you say your last name is Best?"

"That's right. Pugh is Greta's maiden name." He laughed out loud. "Greta is anything but a maiden. She's a cold-hearted thief."

"Mind if I asked what she stole from you?"

"Besides my heart?" He let out a rueful-sounding chuckle. "It happened two years ago, during that awful flu season. I had several sick truckers, so I was making a delivery and while I was on the road, she sold one of my brand-new trucks and practically emptied our joint account."

Bubba glanced over at Keely, who stood with her hands cupped over her mouth.

The man said, "Call me stupid, but when we married, Greta convinced me it would be in the interest of the company, financially, to put the trucks in her name. She was so sweet, sugar dripped from her lips, so I trusted her, but I suppose you know what I mean. She kept the books, and I assumed she knew what she was doing. Turns out, she knew exactly what she was doing."

Bubba said, "Could I get you a cup of coffee?"

"Thanks. I could use a cup."

He nodded to Keely, who came over and sat two cups of steaming hot coffee on the table. She walked behind the counter, eager to stay close enough to hear the rest of the story.

Bubba rested his elbows on the table. "How did you know where to look for her?"

"Call it Providence. A young fellow by the name of Jamal found me and told me I could locate her here, so fifteen minutes after he called, I hopped on a truck, and here I am. I was hoping she'd be here when I arrived. I can't wait to see the look on her face."

Bubba popped his hand to the side of his head. "You say your name is Best? Now, it makes sense. Greta said she owned Best Trucking Company before selling out. Naturally, I thought—"

The fellow interrupted. "That Best was an adjective?"

"Exactly. So, I suppose she sold the company out from under you?"

"Not quite. It all began the day I bought a new truck, and she insisted she go with me to pick it up. I paid cash on the spot, and yes, took the advice of my trusted bookkeeper-wife, and had her name put on the title. Fortunately, I never got around to changing the titles on the other trucks, or I'd be standing in a soup line, today." He ran his fingers through his hair. "Go ahead. Call me an idiot."

"You won't hear any name-calling from me."

"In that case, I'll tell you the rest of the story. We left there and went to the bank to have her name put on a joint checking account. I mean, she was my wife. It's what you do when you marry, right?"

Bubba blew out a heavy breath. "Don't ask me, but I find this all very enlightening. So, now that you've found her, I suppose you're here to have her arrested?"

"I wish I could, but she was shrewd. When I filed a complaint, I was told I didn't have a leg to stand on."

"Of course. I get it, now. She possessed the title to the new truck that she sold and would've had a legal right to draw money from a joint account. What a bummer. So, since you didn't come to press charges, I don't understand your purpose for being here? You want her back?"

"Surely, you jest. Jamal seems to think she may have been bilking money out of you."

"Could be." Bubba swallowed hard. *Poor Lexie.*

Mr. Best threw his arms in the air. "I don't know what I plan to do when I see her again. I know what I'd like to do." He pounded his right fist into his left palm. "I'd like to kill her."

"And where would that get you? Would it get your truck back? Your money back?"

"Maybe not, but it ain't right, man. That conniving witch has gotta pay for what she's done."

Bubba nodded. "I agree."

"I suppose I should've asked sooner, but are you in love with her?"

Bubba shook his head. "No. You can have your wife back.

287

I've heard all I want to know. Excuse me, please." He pulled his cell phone from his pocket and made a call.

CHAPTER 39

Keely called the Maitres that evening and after spilling the incredible story of Greta's past indiscretions, she said, "And get ready for this. Bubba filed charges and the police were waiting for her when she walked into the diner tonight. She's been arrested, Maw-Maw."

Lorene let out a shout. "Well, blow me down. I knew that stinking woman was no good from the get-go. It was beyond me, why Bubba couldn't see it for himself. Thanks for calling, hon. I'd like to hear more, but Donnie—he's our lawyer, don'tcha know—he's here, so I need to hang up and let him know what's going on. I'll see you in the morning, sugar. I appreciate you calling with that wonderful news."

Lorene went back in the living room. "Well, I can stop worrying about Bubba. Looks like Greta's gonna be spending time behind bars. Now, Donnie, I reckon you see I was right all along about Lexie. According to Keely, that low-down Greta framed her."

He smiled and nodded. "I'd already come to that conclusion, Mrs. Maitre. It wasn't difficult for Greta to put the monkey on Lexie's back, since Lexie was on probation for stealing. I did a background check on them both, and it left no doubt in my mind that Greta was the guilty party. I don't know how much you know about Lexie, or how she wound up in prison, but my investigation revealed a great deal. That kid has had a tough life."

Lorene said, "I don't know what she was accused of doing, but I'd trust her with my checkbook. That's how much confidence, I have in her. I heard her step-mother accused her of stealing her car, but who knows how gossip gets started."

"Well, it's true, her step-mother is the one who had her sent to prison, but I talked with Lexie at the jail and she insists her step-mother offered her the car, then called the police and had her arrested for stealing. Frankly, I believe her story."

"Poor baby. What a sad life she must have had, living in the same house with such a horrid person. I'm guessing her father isn't much of a man to allow a woman to treat his child that way."

"You don't know the half of it. She and her father had a very loving relationship, and it seems jealousy was the step-mother's motive for getting rid of her."

"Her father didn't try to help her?"

"He probably tried, but Lexie was so hurt, she wouldn't read his letters after she went to prison and refused to see him when he went to visit her."

"What about her mother?"

"Dead."

"Oh dear, poor child."

Donnie said, "Her mother was murdered when she was a toddler, and her grandparents claimed her daddy did it, and with no proof, had him arrested, simply because they didn't like him. Can you believe it?"

Lorene stiffened. "Well, I happen to know of a similar story, and the husband was indeed the murderer. No doubt about it."

"Well, I'm sure it happens, but Lexie's story differs, because her daddy went to trial and was proven innocent."

Lorene's teeth gritted. "Doesn't mean a thing. My daughter's husband had a trial, also, and if the jury had done their duty, he'd be rotting in prison today."

"Good gracious! Your daughter was murdered? I'm so sorry. How awful that must've been for you and your husband."

"Unless you've ever lost a child, you have no idea. And to know that a monster robbed your beautiful child of her life makes it unbearable." Her husband pulled a handkerchief from his pocket and handed to her. Wiping her tears, she said, "I'll never get over it if I live to be a hundred."

"Completely understandable. Are you saying you think your son-in-law was guilty, yet he was acquitted?"

She handed the handkerchief back to her husband. "I don't *think* he was guilty. I know he was. Not only that, he took our only little granddaughter and disappeared with her."

Donnie's brow furrowed. "How dreadful. Did you ever find her?"

Lorene's lip formed a tight white line.

Homer reached for his wife's hand. "Mama doesn't want to answer that, Donnie, and I can tell you why. We both fell in love with Bubba's niece, Keely, the first day she walked into the diner. We'd been looking for our Laurie for all those years, and Keely was near the same age as our granddaughter and there were so many similarities—eyes, hair, etc—and then, lo and behold, we discovered she couldn't remember her mama—well, I suppose we wanted to believe we'd found our baby."

He looked over at his wife and saw tears running down her cheek. He smiled, and pulled out the handkerchief one more time, then reached for her hand. "I think we've both known for a long time that Keely isn't our little Laurie, but we didn't want to admit it, even to ourselves."

Donnie's eyes squinted. "This is all very sad, but I pray one day it'll have a happy ending, and you'll find the real Laurie."

Lorene said, "Thank you, Donnie. I've never stopped praying, but I reckon God's ways are not always our ways. I knew Keely wasn't our grandchild, but I thought Homer believed, so for his sake, I pretended."

Homer chuckled. "Well, don't that beat all? I don't think we should let on that we know, Mama, since it could break Keely's heart to discover we're not really her Maw-Maw and Paw-Paw."

Lorene smiled. "Phooey. She knows."

"What makes you think so? She certainly doesn't act like she knows."

"No, and neither do we. I kept quiet for *your* sake, you kept quiet for *my* sake, and she kept quiet for *our* sakes."

Donnie raked his hand through his hair. "Incredible. But if she's not Laurie and yet she'd pretend to be, don't you wonder who she is?"

Lorene glanced at her husband, who gave a confirming nod. "We know exactly who she is. She's Keely Carlton Cunningham, beloved daughter of Bart and Jolie Carlton, who were gracious enough to share their beautiful daughter with us."

"I'd love to stay and let you fill in the blanks, but it's getting late and I have something important I should tend to. I'll call you folks in the morning."

Homer stood and shook his hand. "Thanks for coming, Donnie, and please, do whatever you have to do, to free that sweet little Lexie. I don't think we'll sleep a wink until she's set free."

Jamal lowered his head and wrung his hands, as he approached Lexie at the jail.

"Oh, Jamal, I'm so glad you came. Did you go to the diner with the singles group last night? I want to hear all about it."

"I didn't go."

"Why not?"

"You weren't there. Oh, Lex. I feel so helpless. I know you didn't do it." His voice cracked. "Just wish I could do something to get you out of here."

"But Jamal, haven't you heard?"

"Heard? Heard what?"

"Greta has been arrested, and I owe it all to you."

"Wait? Arrested? For real?"

"Yes! I'm surprised no one told you, since it wouldn't have happened without your intervention."

"You must've misunderstood."

"I don't think so. My attorney said it was a young man named Jamal. That would be you—"

"Your attorney?" He bit his lower lip. "State appointed, right?"

"No, an elderly couple, the Maitres, are customers at the diner, and they hired a top-notch lawyer. Can you believe someone who barely knows me would do that for me?"

"I know Mr. and Mrs. Maitre. They live very frugal lifestyles, but I understand they're loaded. He owned several large banks before he retired, but even so, it was generous of them to get you good legal counsel. But exactly what did the lawyer say that made you believe I had anything to do with having Greta arrested?"

"He said a man named Jamal told Greta's husband where to find her, and he came to Mobile and she's now been arrested."

Jamal rubbed the back of his neck. "True, I talked to a man who claimed to be a relative, but according to him, she'd done nothing illegal."

"There are still details that are unclear, but from what the attorney told me, her husband went to the diner and approached Bubba. After a lengthy discussion, Bubba called the police and had her arrested for embezzling money from the diner."

"Oh, Lexie. Does that mean . . ."

"That I go free? I'm afraid to hope, Jamal, but the lawyer seems confident he can get me out of here, thanks to you."

"If I helped, I'm thrilled. When you get out of here, do you plan to stay in town and continue to work for Bubba?"

"Of course. Why would you ask?"

"Because this will be the last time I see you. I'll be leaving Mobile."

"Why?" She popped her hand over her mouth. "Where are you going, Jamal?"

His chin quivered. "Surely, you know I've fallen in love with you, Lexie, but I've faced the truth. You're in love with someone else and it's time for me to bow out. I wish you the best, and I mean that with all my heart. Goodbye, beautiful." He turned to walk away.

"Jamal! Wait! It's true, I *am* in love. But I'm in love with you."

He turned and glared. "No. It's not true."

"Yes, yes, yes, it is. I left Tutwiler, believing I was in love with the Prison Chaplain, but I know now it was the kind of crush young girls have on their male teachers. It was an infatuation with a man who treated me kindly at a time in my life it seemed no one else cared. I wanted to believe I loved him and that he loved me, but it wasn't real. I know that now. What I feel for you is real. When you walked in tonight, my heart pounded, and my knees turned to jelly. You do that to me, Jamal. I love you with all my heart."

His Adams apple bobbed. "I don't know what to say."

"How about saying you love me, too."

Moisture filled his eyes. "I think I already have."

"If you said it every minute from now until forever, it would never be enough."

His eyes glistened. "You've made me the happiest man on earth, Lexie Garrison."

A guard walked in, escorting a smiling Donnie Voorhees. He said, "Sorry, to break up this little visit, but you'll have to continue elsewhere. Let's go, Lexie. You're outta here!"

CHAPTER 40

"Good morning, Maw-Maw . . . Paw Paw! Bubba saw you coming and has already begun your breakfast." Keely leaned down to hug the Maitres. "And a good morning to you, Jackie. Would you like your usual oatmeal, this morning?"

Maw-Maw winked at Jackie. "Go ahead. Ask her!"

Keely plunked her hands on her hips, feigning a frown. "What are you up to, Maw-Maw?"

The old woman snickered. "Jackie has something she wants to ask you."

"Go ahead. Ask away. If I don't know the answer, I'll tell you."

Maw-Maw's lip curled at the corner. "Is that a promise? You'll tell the truth, the whole truth and nothing but the truth, as they say on Perry Mason?"

"Perry *who*?"

"Never mind. Just listen carefully, then answer her question to the best of your ability."

"What are you three up to?"

Jackie said, "Keely, what's your Mother's name?"

Maw-Maw quickly added, "She means your *real* mother's name, sweetheart."

Keely's eyes squinted. "Why didn't *you* tell her, Maw-Maw?"

"I want her to hear it from you, precious. The truth."

Keely licked her lips, as her gaze traveled from Paw-Paw, to Maw-Maw and landed on Jackie. "The *truth*?"

Paw-Paw nodded. "Yes, sugar."

She hung her head and sucked in a lungful of air. "My mama's name . . . My mama's name is . . . "

"Go ahead, sweetheart. Say it."

"My mama's name is . . . " She swallowed hard. "It's Jolie."

Maw-Maw and Paw-Paw went for a high-five. Maw-Maw said, "What'd I tell you, ol' man. I knew she couldn't lie."

Keely winced. "I don't understand. Are you saying . . . "

Maw-Maw nodded. "Yes, sugar. Paw-Paw and I have known for some time now, that you aren't our granddaughter, Laurie, but that doesn't make us love you one bit less, and we still want to be your Maw-Maw and Paw-Paw. We don't believe a child can have too many grandparents."

Tears rolled down Keely's cheeks. "I agree, and I couldn't love you two more if the same blood ran through our veins."

CHAPTER 41

"Stop the squalling, darling, you're messing up your face. Besides, we have something to celebrate." Maw-Maw reached for Paw-Paw's handkerchief and dried Keely's tears.

"If you're referring to the news about Greta, I agree. I never believed Lexie was guilty."

"Of course, she wasn't guilty. Anyone who knows Lexie, knows she's not a thief. But now, that heifer, Greta . . . I've lost a lot of sleep since that woman came to town. I was afraid we were gonna have a wedding, and I don't mind telling you, I wasn't looking forward to attending."

"I understand, Maw-Maw. I'd love to stand here and talk, but Bubba will have your breakfast sitting on the kitchen counter by now. He'll wonder where I am."

She turned to see Bubba standing behind her, holding the platters. "I knew where to find you, Pretty Girl."

Aunt Lorene said, "Bubba, bless your heart, I know you're upset about Greta, but one day you'll see—"

"I see already, Aunt Lorene. Let's don't discuss it."

His gaze locked with Jackie's. "Hi, Jackie."

Her lip quivered. "'Hello, Bubba."

He shuffled from one foot to the other. "Uh . . . Aunt Lorene seems to be doing great. Thank you for taking such good care of her."

"It's my pleasure. You're looking good."

He ran his hands through his hair. "Thanks. You look great. Jackie. I just heard about your daughter, Camille, yesterday and wish to offer my belated condolences."

"I appreciate that, Bubba. How did you hear?"

"When I learned I'd mistaken Lexie for your daughter, I researched old newspapers to find out what happened to your child, because I knew you gave birth to a baby girl years ago. I'm so sorry."

"Thank you, but in truth, we may never know what really happened to my darling Cami. I know what the papers say, but I can't accept that she ran away."

"Maybe you aren't supposed to accept it. Keely can vouch that God is great at redeeming the lost." He smiled and winked. "It's one of His top attributes. He brought Keely back to us."

"Hers is an amazing story. I can only imagine the joy her mother felt, seeing her beautiful daughter after all those years."

Aunt Lorene said, "I remember the first day we came in the diner and saw . . ."

Uncle Homer gently placed his hands over her lips. "Shh!"

She smiled and nodded, knowingly. "Go ahead, Jackie. I didn't mean to butt in."

Before Jackie could respond, the front door opened, and Donnie walked in with Lexie on his arm.

Aunt Lorene turned to look, then shouted, "Glory! You did it, Donnie. You got her out of that old jail. Praise the Lord. Is she free? For good?"

Lexie ran to the table and knelt beside Aunt Lorene, sobbing uncontrollably. She took the old woman's wrinkled hand and clasped it between her own. "Yes, Maw-Maw. I'm free. For good. Thanks to you and Paw-Paw."

"Sugar, I'm so glad. And it warms my heart that you'd want to call us your Maw-Maw and Paw-Paw. You're so precious."

Lexie's brow furrowed when she glanced at Donnie.

He smiled. "No, they don't know—"

Bubba glanced from Aunt Lorene to Lexie, to Donnie. "What's going on?"

Donnie said, "After listening to Lexie's story, then hearing the Maitres tell about their missing granddaughter, I stayed up all night doing research. Lexie's birth name is—"

Lexie finished his sentence. "Laurie. I'm Laurie, Maw-Maw. Daddy changed my name."

Lorene and Homer gazed tearfully into one another's eyes. "Homer? Can it be?"

He motioned for Lexie. "Come here, sweetheart." He reached for her hand, and his voice cracked. "Yep, she's our baby, alright.

Mama, do you remember when she first learned to walk, and Laurie climbed on everything in sight? "

"How could I forget?"

"And remember the afternoon we were grilling in the backyard, and a as soon as we turned our back, she climbed up on the pile of firewood back of our house?"

"Oh, my, yes. She fell and all that firewood piled on top of her. Scared me half to death."

Paw-Paw lifted Lexie's arm and gently rubbed his finger over an old scar.

Maw-Maw said, "Poor little thing had to get stitches—" Her eyes widened, seeing the scar. She squealed, then leaned over in her chair with outstretched arms as the tears flowed down her cheeks. "Come here, baby, and give Maw-Maw a big ol' hug. We've missed you so much, sweetheart." She lifted her eyes toward heaven and sobbed. "Thank you, Lord, I'm ready to go on to Glory now, if you want to call me home. My prayers have been answered."

Lexie held tight to her grandmother. "Please don't call her home yet, Sweet Jesus. We have a lot of catching up to do. Maw-Maw, I want to thank you and Paw-Paw for hiring Donnie, even though you didn't know at the time that I was your granddaughter. That was very generous of you. I was so frightened. I thought I was on my way back to Tutwiler."

Paw-Paw said, "Sugar, it breaks my heart to know you spent two years in a stinkin' prison for something you didn't do."

"Oh, Paw-Paw, a wise old preacher, Reverend Blocker, told me the Bible says all things work together for good to those who love the Lord and are called according to His purpose. I now believe it. I can assure you, going to prison for two years wasn't something I considered to be *good,* but truly God took the situation and worked it out for my good."

"How do you figure, sweetheart?"

"If I hadn't gone to prison, I wouldn't have met the chaplain. River Braxton was Step 1 in God's plan for me."

"Pardon me, but I'm a mite confused, sugar, so help me out here. I heard you were in love with the chaplain and he deserted you when you went to jail and needed him most. Doesn't sound very Christian to me."

"Paw-Paw, River is a fine man, but he has imperfections, just like we all do. Christians aren't perfect, just forgiven. True, I was disappointed when he didn't come, but neither River nor I fully understood at the time that we weren't meant to be together. He was an instrument the Lord chose to use, to perfect God's plan for my life. You may be confused now, but I think you'll understand as you see how it all unravels. Step 2 was having my step-sister, Molly sponsor me, which took me from North Alabama to Baldwin County, near Mobile. Step 3 was when River called his friend, Reverend Blocker from Mobile and he and his lovely wife took me into their home. What an awesome God. He brought me to the precise town where I needed to be, but he wasn't through. Step 4 was when God directed my path and I wound up at Bubba's

Diner, the very spot you and Maw-Maw come to every morning. Isn't that surreal?"

"I see what you mean. It certainly seems to fit together up to that point, sugar. But why do you reckon God brought you this far, and then let Greta have you arrested for something you didn't do? Surely, God could've prevented it, so why didn't He?"

"Oh, that's the good part, Paw-Paw. God allowed Greta to carry out her devious plot, then He took it and worked it together for my good. Don't you see, Paw-Paw? In spite of her trying, Greta couldn't thwart God's plan for my life or keep your prayers from being answered. If I hadn't been arrested, you wouldn't have hired Donnie, and if not for Donnie's investigation, I would never have known you're my grandparents."

"Well, for crying out loud. Now that you put it like that, I reckon there's no other way to explain it."

"Isn't He an awesome God?"

Lorene sobbed. "I feel like I'm dreaming. There've been so many times I thought for sure, I'd found you, and yet—"

"It's true, this time, Maw-Maw. Daddy talked about my mama constantly when I was growing up, so even though I was a toddler when she died, I feel as if I knew her. He had a box full of pictures that he'd pull out and tell me how wonderful she was. My stepmother hated it."

Lorene raised a skeptical brow. "Oh, sweetheart, I'm afraid you don't know the whole story."

Homer shook his head. "Not now, Renie. If she doesn't know,

it's not our place to tell her."

Lexie's face lit up. "You mean about the murder trial? I know, Maw-Maw, but I promise you, my Daddy didn't kill my mama. I know for a fact, he loved her with all his heart. I've called him, and he wants to see you, if you'll agree to it. He says he wants the murder case reopened. The only reason he didn't do it sooner, was because he was afraid in doing so, you'd discover our whereabouts and would try to take me away from him. Will you agree to see him, Maw-Maw? Please, for my sake?"

"Yes, my darling. To be honest, I didn't really want to believe Wayne did it, but I had to have someone to blame. I'm so ashamed. I'd understand if neither of you could forgive me. I've blamed your daddy all these years for keeping us apart, when it was my own stubbornness that drove him away."

Keely walked over with the coffee pot. "Refills, anyone?"

Maw-Maw's eyes widened, when she spotted an empty chair at the table. "Now, where did Jackie go?"

Keely gestured with her head. "She's sitting across the room, talking to Johnny Gorham. I suppose Bubba was the only one who noticed when I walked over and told her Johnny wanted to talk to her."

"Oh, dear. If I'd heard, I would've stopped her. Those Gorham's are no good."

Paw-Paw said, "Now, Mama, haven't we interfered in enough lives?"

Lexie whispered, "Maybe you won't have to interfere. Bubba just walked over and sat down at their table. I'm hoping he'll do the interfering. He loves her, you know. I really wish he'd tell her, because she loves him, too."

Maw-Maw said, "Nothing would please me more than to give Bubba that bit of advice, but Homer's right. I've meddled in enough lives. Go call your daddy, sweetheart, and tell him Maw-Maw and Paw-Paw beg his forgiveness and would like for him to pack an overnight bag. It's time we had a visit from our son-in-law. We all have a lot of catching up to do."

"Yes ma'am. I'm ready to see him, too. I've missed him so much. He's no longer with my step-mother—he left after she had me arrested. He said the only reason he continued to stay with her while I was growing up was because she threatened to contact you and Paw-Paw to let you know where I was. He was afraid of losing me, but when I went to prison and refused to see him or read his letters, he felt he'd already lost me, so he was free to walk away."

****

Bubba sat at Johnny's table next to Jackie and listened to all the chit-chat he could stomach. "Johnny, I didn't come over here to get a weather report, or hear about the unusual bird migration, so get on with it."

Johnny's brow creased. "Not sure what you mean, Bubba."

"I think you do. Keely said you sent for me. Okay, I'm here. I suppose you and Jackie want to tell me you're getting married and want my blessings? Fine. I hope you live happily ever after. Now, if you'll excuse me, I have a diner to run." He shoved his chair back from the table.

Johnny's lip curled upward. "Hold on, you dumb ox."

Bubba's face burned. "I don't have to sit here and listen to insults. If you've finished your coffee, I'll show you to the door."

"Bubba Knox, are you gonna tell me you'd give up on this beautiful woman so easily?"

His jaw jutted out. "What are you getting at, Johnny? You've made it clear you've been waiting for the period of mourning to end. I assume it's ended. What do you expect me to do?"

"I want you to tell Jackie how you feel."

"Really? I don't believe you do, because if I did, I'd tell her I feel you're wrong for her."

Johnny glanced at Jackie and winked. "Is that all, you'd say?"

"Oh, trust me, there's a lot more I *could* say."

"Then tell her. Now's your chance."

Bubba glared at Jackie. "She doesn't want to hear it. She's made her choice."

"Really? You mean *me*?" Johnny threw up his hands. "Bubba Knox, don't be an idiot. I'm not in love with Jackie, and she's not in love with me. I love her like a sister, but I'm not *in* love with her. I've known since we were kids she only has eyes for you, but you've been too stubborn to tell her how you feel. I hated what Jacob did to her. I stayed in Mobile because I felt it was time for her to have a little happiness in her life. When I saw you weren't going to tell her how you felt, I thought if I could make you jealous, it might speed things along."

Bubba's eyes squinted into tiny slits. "Is this a joke?"

Jackie smiled. "I hope not. I was like you, at first, Bubba. I thought Johnny was making a play for me, and I couldn't understand it. I knew he didn't love me, so I assumed he was trying to make up for Jacob's mistakes, feeling some strange sense of duty to take care of me. I didn't want his pity. Then I caught on, and I hoped it would work and you'd fight for me." Her lips split into a craggy smile. "When you didn't, I thought the fight would be left up to me. I was afraid I'd be forced to put on my Safari hat, stalk the prey and steal the trophy back from the Lioness."

Bubba playfully buried his face in his hands. "Sheesh, don't remind me. Was that weird, or what? I've never been so humiliated as I was when Greta came out with that curious monologue. I'm not sure I'll ever want to hunt again, since I now know what the prey feels like."

Jackie's smile faded. She reached over and gently lifted his head with her thumb. "Bubba, in all seriousness, I need you to be truthful, not only to me, but to yourself. I know you had deep feelings for Greta, or you wouldn't have become engaged after staying single so long. And Greta has made her feelings toward you, quite plain. I need to know for sure if it's over between you two."

"I think I can clear it up for you, Jackie. If you have your phone, look up Amos 3:4 on the Bible app."

She pulled her phone from her purse, clicked on the app, then stared at the words. Her face scrunched into a frown.

Bubba waited.

The frown slowly faded, and a crooked little smile caused her lip to curl at one corner.

He said, "Read it out loud."

Jackie bit her trembling lip and cleared her throat. *"Will a lion roar in the forest when he hath no prey?"*

"What does that say to you, Jackie?"

Her eyes turned into tiny slits when she laughed out loud. "It says the prey got away."

"Exactly."

She jumped up from the table, stood back of his chair and threw her arms around his neck. "I love you, Bubba Knox. I always have, and I always will."

Lorene Maitre's squeal could be heard across the room. "Law, would you look at that! Bubba's kissing Jackie right in the mouth, here in front of God and everybody. Looks like we might be planning a wedding, after all."

THE END

Made in the USA
Columbia, SC
13 October 2020